dogrun

dogrun, by arthur nersesian

MTV books

pocket
books
new york   london   toronto   sydney

An *Original* Publication of MTV Books/Pocket Books

POCKET BOOKS, a division of Simon & Schuster, Inc.
1230 Avenue of the Americas, New York, NY 10020

Copyright © 2000 by Arthur Nersesian

MTV Music Television and all related titles, logos, and characters are trademarks of MTV Networks, a division of Viacom International Inc.

ISBN: 0-671-77542-1

First Pocket Books trade paperback printing October 2000

10   9   8

POCKET and colophon are registered trademarks of Simon & Schuster, Inc.

Art Direction: Deklah Polansky and Tracy Boychuk
Design: Tracy Boychuk
Photography: Warren Darius Aftahi

Printed in the U.S.A.

To Jan Jaffe Kahn
(1949–1999)

Acknowledgments

Tom Burke
Joe Druffel (In Memoriam)
Greer Kessel Hendricks
Sasha Kahn
Ronnie Kahn
Laura Kahn
Kate Lewis-Christensen
John Lewis
Suzanne O'Neill
John Talbot
Peter Traberman

You and I, we will go to Avenues A and B
and see who will die first. . . .

                    —Ossip Mandelstam

What is more annoying than coming home after a long day of temping and opening the door to find your unemployed live-in boyfriend fixed in front of the TV with the kind of permanence that compels you to believe that he has been chain-watching it all day?

Primo's muddy eyes were staring sedately at the TV set, which was blaring a mile a minute with strange sounds and snappy, zippy images. His sweet lips were casually shut. His dumb dog, Numb, had propped its narrow muzzle under Primo's small bony hand and was rocking its bell-shaped head back and forth gently. Primo, in his alpha-state, thoughtlessly pet the ever-shedding canine.

Only the dog's territorial stare flicked over to me—it was a mongrelization of every horny mutt that ever scurried through the local dogrun. I resisted the intensifying urge to be nasty. I asked Mr. Cool if he would like some vermicelli.

"Yes," he blurted. Our East Village dump—one of the many built to absorb the great flood of immigrants at the beginning of the last century—had a bathroom and kitchen separating a small living room and an even tinier bedroom. Our bed, an old twin-sized mattress, doubled as Primo's couch during his wasted hours before the tube.

In the course of the eight minutes it took to fix dinner, I told him the low-lights of my Xeroxed day. Although he seemed to be listening, I knew that he was holding me in silent contempt, watching his goddamned TV, waiting for my culinary labors.

By the time I brought over his bowl of overcooked pasta with crushed garlic, stale Parmesan cheese, and a dab of olive oil, I realized that he hadn't even said hello since I had entered. Passive-aggressively, I placed the moderately hot bowl directly on his sunken T-shirted chest.

"So, what TV shows did you watch today?" I asked, no longer able to restrain my disgust.

He obviously didn't care for my attitude and was ignoring me as a pathetic form of protest. The dog sniffed the dinner, but the bastard kept watching the tube, not even taking a bite.

"All right," I finally said, finishing my half of the low-budget meal. "I know you were looking for a job. I'm sorry." He had told me over the past few days how he had made nonstop efforts at finding a career and was going through his worst unlucky streak in thirty-odd years.

In the nonresponsive silence, I twirled some pasta and watched as he didn't so much as touch his—a final insult, as he always scarfed down whatever garbage I put before him.

"Don't take it out on me!" I shot back, offensively defensive. Still no response; his dark eyes remained fixed to some infantile commercial. They needed Visine.

Deciding to rile him, I got up and changed the channel, expecting him to start screaming. But he must have been really pissed, because he just sat there. He didn't even use the remote to flip it back.

I finished my pasta, and as I rose to go to the kitchen, I snatched his uneaten dinner off his TV-tray chest and dropped it in the sink, thinking this would break his silent treatment. But no, his Mexican standoff was still standing.

While I was in the kitchen, Numb finally rose and came over to beg off me. Finally, I cracked a smile. It was just too incredible. I began chuckling; I couldn't stay angry. All for the sake of this single dry and labored joke, Primo was exerting a Zen of self-control.

The detail that caught my attention was how dry his eyes seemed; they lost all their gloss. When I slowly put my finger on his right eye, he didn't so much as flinch. He was icy cold.

When I tugged back Primo's head to open his airways, the dog growled protectively. I tried giving him CPR, but I couldn't remember if I had to pump his chest five times for every single breath or breathe into him five times for every heart massage. I only knew that I resented having to do it.

Mr. Cool had tried to keep it from me, but I knew that he had been shooting up. No one could eat that much junk food, stay that long in front of a TV, and miraculously lose weight. Once in the course of our six-month relationship, while going through his cash-free pockets, I had discovered a Narcotics Anonymous pamphlet.

"Did you ever have a habit?" I had asked him, waving the brochure between him and the blaring, glaring nineteen-inch screen that held his attention hostage.

"Not really," he'd retorted. When the commercial came on, he lowered the volume and equivocated, "Drugs aren't a habit in the East Village—they're a tradition."

He produced a fingertip list of boring Beat scribblers—Burroughs, Hubert Huncke, Alexander Trocchi—all writers from the moronic romantic East Village who had taken drugs and allegedly had their brains enlarged.

I always had to do everything for him, and now, to avoid being single, I was breathing for him. Finally, winded, I gave up, turned off the TV, and called 911. I told the emergency operator my boyfriend was dead. She asked me the color in his face.

"Chalky blue under sixty watts," I said.

Looking at him now, I realized his complexion wasn't a result of the reflection of the black-and-white TV.

"How stiff is he?"

"Turgid." As the erection he never had.

The operator said that it sounded like he had been dead for a while.

"What's his name?" she asked.

"Primitivo Schultz," I said.

Thanking her and hanging up, I waited for the dead boyfriend ambulance. Locating a pack of American Spirit cigarettes in his pocket, I lit one.

Three other boyfriends had left me over the past six years, but Primo was the first to require a stretcher. Exhaling plumes of smoke over his remains, I eulogized silently. He wasn't a creep or a cheat. He never hit or robbed or even fought that much. On the other hand, I never felt particularly close to him; he was intimacy-impaired, challenged in the bonding department.

I opened my desk drawer and took out the Valentine's Day card he had made. Under a simple silhouette drawing, supposedly of me, he had written a poem:

IMPRESSIONS OF A WRITER

All typewriter keys jammed up into a black block of hair,
two millennia of scrolls and hieroglyphs
curl into two pouty lips.
Beautiful eyes tanned blue
by a computer monitor's monochrome hue.
keyboard-manicured fingers,
an italicized wit,
a cigarette smoke of attitude.

I should have dropped him immediately when I discovered he composed "poetry." Actually, when we first met he kept saying that he was a novelist, but when I asked what he wrote, he never elaborated. Ultimately, I had never been poeticized before, and probably stayed with him because of a schmaltzy stanza.

Even though my friend Zoë had met him first, she was able to do something I could not—resist him. He had a dark Mediterranean appeal. His short and muscular torso reminded me of a Roman centurion. He had a dry and garlicky sense of humor, a geriatric GenXer. But I always sensed that there was something more at work, an intelligence in his eyes that he wasn't sharing—a secret he wasn't divulging.

While waiting for EMS to arrive, I called Zoë, but as her out-going message unspooled, I remembered that she was on another of her endless dates. At the age of thirty-one, Zoë was panicky. She was terrified of a lonely, childless future. So she had put out an all-points bulletin. Every singles dating agency, every personals, every Internet bachelor website—all had notices posted by her. A large bosomy blonde, she had blue eyes and a blurred smiling face that hinted she had been to one too many parties. After years of girling around, she was in the bargain-basement boxes, elbowing and clawing with others of her burned-out ilk for the last of the nice Jewish husbands.

On my third cigarette, I realized the true reason I was with a corpse. He had caught me on a rebound. Simple as that. I'd been reclaimed from the dump, given eleventh-hour validation, and maybe a little something else. He was everything Gregory, boyfriend number three, was not: cool where the Gregor was hotheaded, and *caliente* where the Greg was *frio*. At that time, that was more than enough. Over the past few weeks, though, the rift between Primo and I had widened drastically.

Finally I heard the siren. Opening the window, I could see two of New York's chubbiest in their uniform blues squeezing out of their car. I wanted to holler that they needn't hurry, but I didn't and they didn't either. I could hear their walkie-talkies echoing through my narrow hallway as they came up the stairs.

"What happened?" asked the heavier cop, whose inspection of my body made me wonder if I was a suspect. I instantly wished I had worn something more revealing.

"My boyfriend died," I said.

"Did you touch anything?" the smaller, rounder cop inquired.

"I tried to revive him."

"You did the right thing, dear," said the first. I think he was trying to be polite, but only condescension was coming through.

The alpha cop, who was the weightier of the two, explained that three types of death required investigation from the medical examiner: youthful deaths, violent deaths, and accidental deaths. The insignificantly thinner cop departed. The first officer's last name was Miranda, and he asked if he could watch TV. Before I could lie and say it was broken, he plunked himself down on the couch and snatched the channel changer from Primo's cold hand. On top of everything else, I now was nervous because Primo had illegally rigged cable. Despite the wide variety of channels, the cop flipped to *Cops,* maybe hoping to learn how the job was done. Rattled, I grabbed my jacket and was about to leave.

"Whoa there." He stopped me. "I'm afraid you have to stick around, hon."

"How long?" I looked at the spot on my wrist where a watch should be.

"Till the ME gets here, dear." The dog rubbed up against the cop, and the cop rubbed the dog.

"My name is Mary," I said, transmitting my disdain for terms like "dear."

"Mary, I ain't trying to suggest something, but"—he pointed to the body as if I could forget it—"your boyfriend just died. Have a seat."

Al Camus' *The Stranger,* or more specifically the Cliff Notes for the book, states at first the stranger is emotionally disassociated from his mother's death. I wondered if I too was disassociated, but quickly realized, as I informed the doughnutarian, that I wanted to "get on with my life."

"Get on with it tomorrow," he advised, adding, "there's a pretty good show on."

Some cop who looked like Officer Miranda was arresting some guy who looked like Primo. Defiantly, I went over to my desk and took out the latest draft of my work-in-progress, entitled *The Book of Jobs.* It was a collection of stories about the people I had worked with in different chain stores ever since high school. The first franchise-themed story was just a coincidence. It was about this sad lady named Janice Fyro who I briefly worked with at a Baskin Robbins in Long Island. She had been employed there since she graduated from high school in the early seventies when the ice cream shop was still the youthful center of town. As other, newer franchises scooped up business, her place went under. Soon after it closed, she killed herself. The story was called "The Melting of an Empire." I wrote a variety of stories about the disenfranchised, but when I wrote one story called "Big Mac," about the urban survival of an inner-city McDonald's food handler, my hippie writing professor, who remembered my Baskin Robbins story, suggested I develop a thematic collection.

"But I can't stand franchises," I explained.

"Nowadays it's not enough to be a good writer," he explained sincerely. "You need a catchy idea. If an editor found a mediocre collection of stories, she'd reject it in a flash, but if they were all about mall jobs that the writer worked at, the publicity would click in—that'd sell."

Over the years of living in the city, though, first-draft writing became increasingly labored. I found it infinitely easier to rewrite. So, even though I probably had enough pages to fill three books, I still couldn't finish this one book of stories. When my writers' group disbanded a few years ago, I was the only one who decided not to look for a new one.

As I reread and marked up the same printed pages over and over, I realized I wasn't making them better, just different. I hadn't been able to dream up any new stories for a while. It was as though the strip mall of my mind was full—there was no room for any new franchises.

Soon, my thoughts magnetized toward the unrefrigerated corpse of Primitivo Schultz, still reclining on my bed. He had lived in the East Village for years. At only thirty-two, he had dabbled in the "Allied Arts"—as he called them—which included painting, music, and writing. (Though I never saw, heard, or read anything he did.) He had a mother who lived somewhere in Flatbush. That was his obit.

At ten P.M., three hours after I had discovered Primo's demise, the medical examiner finally arrived with a big black briefcase, like some commuting husband gone berserk. He snapped the case open and took out a large Polaroid camera. He was a tall ghoul in a gray flannel 1950s suit, with yellowing gelled-back hair, who looked like he'd crumble in direct sunlight.

"Does it usually take you this long?" I asked, having watched the balance of the Fox Tuesday-night lineup with Officer Miranda, who mindlessly rubbed Numb's head throughout.

"There's been a lot of strange deaths tonight," the ghoul replied mundanely. As he looked at the body, he summoned up a mental roster. "An auto-asphyxiation in Ozone Park, an accidental overdose on the Upper West Side, a probable suicide on the Grand Concourse."

He snapped some photos of the body and asked, "Was the deceased sick in any way?"

"Nope."

"On medication?"

"None that I knew of," I replied honestly. His occasional forays into drugs hardly qualified as medication.

"You didn't dress him?" he asked, a question that struck me as odd.

"Not today."

"I know this is odd, but when was the last time you had relations with the deceased?"

"Well, he wasn't deceased when we last did it," I muttered, slightly embarrassed.

"I just need to know about his physical prowess." He leaned close to me, not wanting the cop to hear.

"Let's see, not in the past month or so," I responded. I was not counting all failed efforts. He looked Primo over. I told him that when I first came home, I thought he was alive. I thought he talked to me, but it must have just been the TV.

"Do you have any idea what he died of?" I asked.

"Not yet," he replied without looking up. The ME filled out some forms and asked about next of kin. I explained that his mother lived in the Flatbush section of Brooklyn.

"We won't be able to release the body just yet, but you can make arrangements," the ME said.

"What do you mean?" I asked, nervously.

"We take the body for an autopsy, then afterward, you pick him up and handle the interment."

"Hey, I don't . . . I'm not . . ." I tried to say I wanted nothing more to do with any of this.

"So call the mother," the ME said, suggesting he had been down this road before. "I'm sure she knows what to do and would rather hear the news from someone she knows."

"I guess I can handle that," I replied, not hiding my reluctance. Then a warning light went off. "Suppose she doesn't want him?"

"Then the city will dispose of his corpse."

"Oh." A new thought bubbled up. "Is it possible that he knew he was going to die?"

"I'm sure he knew when his heart stopped," the ME said, looking at the cop. Both smiled at the shallow gallows humor.

"I mean, was he sick? Is it possible he had some terminal illness?"

"Offhand," he replied, "I'd say probably not. But I won't know till I get him on the slab. It'll all be in the death certificate."

"You couldn't call me?" I smiled, trying to play the helpless female.

"You can get the death certificate downtown. I don't make house calls."

With his big black briefcase in hand, the ME walked out,

commuting to a new death scene. Officer Miranda called EMS on my phone, then slowly rose to his feet, about to walk out the door.

"You don't want a dog, do you?" I asked him as Numb licked the cop's hands and rubbed up against his large legs.

"Sorry, but I already got one," he said as the phone rang. The machine answered. It was my old neighbor, Joey Lucas. I picked up before he could hang up.

"How you doing, hon?" Joey asked in his usual Breakfast of Champions tone.

"Primo died."

He paused reverently, perhaps twinged with guilt, as he had never cared for Primo. Then he offered, "Why don't I come over?"

"I think I should be alone. I'm still waiting for the ambulance to remove his corpse. I feel like we're on our last date."

"I'll be thinking of you," he said somberly. "Call if you need anything."

I thanked Joey and hung up.

Joey Lucas was about twenty years older than I. Like Primo, he was a romantic anomaly. Where Primo begged, pleaded, and whined his way into my heart, Joey was the only man who had ever rejected me, the only man I told to fuck off, and the only man who sent flowers with an apology begging my forgiveness for not having sex with me. How could I reject someone like that? He was also the strangest hybrid of Old World macho and cyber-age New Millennium.

About two years ago when my last boyfriend, the Gregor, first moved in with me, he got a new computer and eagerly hooked up onto the Internet. We both had our own little e-mail addresses, and for about two exciting weeks we lived little e-lives. Instead of writing at night, which I should have been doing, I got lost in the maze of stupid chat rooms and stuck in nonsensical websites. Roughly six months into my cyberlife, I received an odd e-mail from Payuptime@aol.com. Payuptime wrote, "I located your address through a search and wonder if you could be that little golden-haired Mary Bellanova I remember from so many years ago? Were you born in Hoboken? Is your mother's name Stella and your father's Rudolph? Did you live at 1025 Washington Street near the Maxwell House Coffee plant? My name is Joey Lucas, and I lived upstairs from you. Do you remember me? Ask your ma if you don't. My wife was Rosemary, and I had a girl a little younger than you, Jenny. I was wondering what became of you and your family. I am dying to hear from you and get an update. Please write and let me know if you're you. Love Joey Lucas."

What I remembered was a nice innocuous man named Joe,

who lived upstairs with his wife and baby. He seemed to know everyone who passed him, and he did a lot of public eating. His daughter was about five years younger than me, so I couldn't play with her. From time to time, he'd give me a Tootsie Roll. His sudden interest seemed odd but harmless. I jotted off a quick response telling him all was well—"We're all older and fatter. None of us have any great discoveries or inventions to our name. Mom's okay, living on Long Island. I'm in the scintillating East Village trying to make it as a writer (ha!). How're Rosemary and Jenny? Stay in touch, Luv, Mary." I sent the e-mail and forgot about it.

About two weeks later my phone rang. The machine picked it up. I heard a confident male voice speaking. "Mary dear, this is Joey. I hope my calling is okay. I looked you up in the book and figured I'd give you a ring. . . ." I picked up the phone.

"Payuptime, is this you?" I joked.

"None other," he said and laughed back. "Listen, can I wine and dine you?"

"God, I don't know." I had this healthy fear of intrusion. But the outgoing message on my machine stated that this was Gregory and Mary's number, so I felt a slight security inasmuch as it clarified that I was in a relationship.

"Listen," he said, as if reading my thoughts. "If you're busy or just don't want to get together, I certainly understand. But I swear this is nothing weird or anything. I just remember you as a little girl. I figured I'd take a leap and ask you to dinner, my treat. It would all be in public the entire time."

My growing years in Hoboken were a blur. Because they were difficult times for Ma, she rarely spoke about them. Subsequently I had developed an acute curiosity about that duration of my life, and I hoped my former neighbor could fill me in. Besides, Joey sounded so down-to-earth and we would be meeting in public. We agreed upon the Yaffa Café at eight o'clock.

Later that day I tried calling my mother, but I got a traffic jam of busy signals. Since high school, I had had trouble with Ma. It was as though the word *hello* meant *fuck you*—we would fight on contact. Our relationship was a three-legged race, and we were constantly moving out of sync. People said we were both too much alike. Perhaps. But we loved each other and were doing our best to get along.

I thought about bringing the Gregor to the dinner, but he was such an uncomfortable, ill-at-ease human, and I knew the encounter would be awkward enough, so I brought my small spray of Mace instead. At eight-fifteen that evening, I took the short flight down the steps, entered into the Yaffa, and searched from table to table. In the backyard I spotted him, an attractive older man sitting over a goblet of red wine, trying to read some in-your-face East Village newspaper in the candlelight. Joey looked a lot more handsome than I remembered, but he was vaguely familiar. He was also the only older guy dining solo.

"Joey?" I asked. He didn't respond at first. Then as if some delayed timer buzzed, he looked up startled with a big smile.

He rose to his feet, tall and slim, took my hand, and kissed it theatrically. We joked, ordered, and talked. The evening wasn't so bad. When I ordered one of the more modestly priced entrées, he insisted I have a more expensive dish. When I asked for a Coke, he upgraded it to a Chianti. We chatted about our Hoboken days. He remembered a lot more than I did and talked about what it was like being born and growing up in Sinatra's hometown. He politely inquired about my parents. I explained that my father was no longer alive and my mother had recently retired from teaching grade school. She had moved to Long Island years ago. Although I didn't detect any sexual energy, he seemed to have some deeper interest in meeting with me. Perhaps he was curious to see how people aged. I found him sincerely charming.

After dinner, we sauntered around the neighborhood. I

showed him the Calcutta-like beggars luxuriously sprawled along Avenue A, and told him how I had moved here after college a few years ago. He mentioned that he had a small yet successful collection agency; he hunted down everyone from loan-defaulted students to deadbeat dads.

"How are Rosemary and Jenny?" I changed the subject, as I was presently being pursued by my student loan officer.

"They're fine," he replied and didn't say anything else. When we crossed Fourth Street, he added, "Actually, I got divorced a few years ago, I'm single now. Jenny is grown and lives with her mother. I don't see her as much as I'd like." That remark elucidated everything. Joey missed his little girl and was looking for a surrogate.

"Life can get complicated," I said, trying to offer some relief.

"You know, that mother of yours," he said out of the blue, "she was a real looker."

"She takes after her daughter."

"I'd love to get together with her for dinner sometime," he said. "And by the way, tell her that she doesn't have to worry about my old monkey wrench. If she still has it, she can consider it a gift." He laughed.

"She borrowed a monkey wrench?"

"Actually, your father did," he replied as he walked me to my door.

"It was nice meeting you again, Joey," I said grateful that the evening had ended without incident.

"It was a true pleasure seeing you," he said, and then, to my surprise, he reached in his pocket and took out a small velvet-lined box. Inside were a beautiful pair of earrings.

"Holy cow." I couldn't believe it, particularly because my lobes weren't even pierced.

"It's just a little something. Don't worry about it meaning something or something." If he thought I was going to return them, he was mistaken. I was starved for gifts.

When I got upstairs, it was still early, so I tried my mother again. This time she answered, "Guess who I just had dinner with?"

"Brad Pitt," she replied, always aiming high.

"Better—Joey Lucas."

"Joey Lucas, the old upstairs neighbor?"

"That's right."

"Wow, how is he?"

"Fine, and he looks great."

"He was always such a nice guy. Please don't do anything awful to him," she said, suggesting I was some kind of sex-starved nitwit. Only a mother could be so effortlessly and mindlessly obnoxious. I sidestepped a fight by saying good night.

As I stared at Primo's still form, I considered calling my mother. But it was getting late and I didn't want to wake her up. Finally the ambulance came. Two burly boys put Primo's body in a large black plastic carrying case, a garbage bag for defunct humans, and toted him away. Alone, I finally felt this wave of sadness eventually interrupted by the realization that I had to use the bathroom. There I discovered, not surprisingly, that Primo had left me an unflushed memento. I contemplated calling Primo's mother, but figured she'd be asleep. Besides, it was late, I was tired, and the only thing that my temp work really required of me was coming in on time.

After a variety of cruddy jobs, I had finally got my shit together on a résumé. With my nominal typing skills and recently acquired ability not to make sarcastic remarks to a boss, I had secured a nice long permatemp gig at a corporate law firm. Recently, though, that had been scaled back to day-by-day temping.

As I brushed my teeth, I realized that I was going to need a new roommate to pay the rent, so I moved Primo's guitar case and the banana boxes that he had been living out of from his room to my already cluttered one. Then I did the dishes, undressed, and stared at the bed. Primo had been lying on it dead for the past few hours. I changed the sheets and slowly, delicately lay down on it. Eventually I drifted off to a tortured sleep that yielded a weird dream about peeling a huge avocado; both the leathery black skin and the yucky green meat came off in my hands. The entire time, I knew I was subconciously peeling Primo.

Early the next morning I bolted upright. The dog barked, and I wondered where Primo was, then remembered. I had this freaky sensation that a mouse had been crawling on me. I hadn't actually seen any rodents for a while, but every East Village apartment not constructed in the past five years harbored the possibility of mice. In order to convince me to throw out all the glue traps and poison, Primo swore that rodents were scared to come out while Numb was around. But I knew the animal was too much of a wuss to ever attack. It was about six in the morning, two hours before I intended to get up. My first thought was that I had to call Primo's mother, but I couldn't remember her first name. She was listed in Primo's phone book under *M* for "Ma."

I spent about an hour sitting at my desk, looking over the stories in *The Book of Jobs.* Over the years and after countless submissions, three of them had been published in oddly named, utterly undistributed literary magazines. During my final year of college, I entered the Portisan Writing Contest with a tale called "From Kmart to Chaos," about a "sales associate" named Kay who works and lives the Kmart lifestyle. Her home is a Martha Stewart showplace until a gas leak blows it to smithereens. Her entire family is killed, and she is left trapped in her own limbless and faceless body, clothed in Kathy Ireland separates. She spends the rest of her days lying in a hospital bed, connected to life support, contemplating chaos.

When I won the award, I decided to move to the big city and try my shaky hand at writing. But art was the first casualty in the struggle to survive in New York. In the years since I arrived here, I had been hammered down and recut, all the extraneous parts of my life melted in the great cauldron of exhaustion.

By the time I ate, washed, applied cosmetic war paint, and slipped into work clothes, I was all out of delays. It was time to notify Primo's mother. I toughened up and dialed.

As soon as I heard the hello, I introduced myself.

"Mary what?" Mrs. Schultz asked.

"Your son's girlfriend."

No response.

"You know, your son—Primo?"

"Yeah."

"I spoke to you on your birthday." Primo had drunkenly put the phone to my ear and made me say, "Hello Ma."

"Yes," she finally flickered. "You were the one with the eyes."

"Mrs. Schultz—" I began. I could vaguely hear Regis and Kathie Lee in the background.

"My name is June," she said. "My mother named me Juniper—idiot!"

"It's a nice name, June, but I have bad news for you." I waited for some indication that she was seated or braced. When I heard the volume of the TV drop, I knew she was ready.

"Your son has died." No response.

"He's at the city morgue." No response.

"The medical examiner is holding his body. He wants you to call and claim him." Still no response. "If you have a pencil, I'll give you the number."

"How'd he go?" she asked, never changing her tone.

"It wasn't painful, but they really don't know." Then, for the sake of closure, I speculated, "It might have been drug-related."

"He had a rheumatic heart," she added.

"I'm really sorry, June."

"Thank you for calling," she replied in a drone and hung up.

I was going to be late. When I opened the apartment door,

the dog dashed out. I hauled it back in and realized it had peed on the kitchen floor. I had to find the animal a new home.

While at my temp station, I couldn't help but dwell on my relationship with Primo. It had ended a lot earlier than last night. A few months ago the sex had run its course, and I knew the deadbeat had no place or money, and that he was pretending nothing was wrong with the relationship so that he could leech off of me. What was even worse was that I had let him. He owed me a month of back rent.

Around noon, I checked my messages and found two new calls, one from Zoë and the other from my old roommate in college, Emily, who informed me that in a few weeks her band would be performing at Brownies. She had come to New York with a Bonnie Raitt fixation, traded her pickup truck for an electric guitar, and decided to be a rocker. She was a bass player in an all-chicks country-western band, Crapped Out Cowgirls. Since I had dabbled with the guitar in college, when we both wound up in the city Emily riddled my machine with musical questions I couldn't answer. I would bump into her steadily about three times a month. Each time she belonged to a different band: the Fuddy Duddies, Untenable Positions, and Yo Mama. The dislocated troubadours of the East Village were like pieces of a jigsaw puzzle eternally reconfiguring themselves into ever newer bands. I dialed Zoë and asked her if she could guess what I had in common with 65 percent of New York and 40 percent of America.

"You're severely depressed?"

"Not severely. That's only six percent of America." I got all my stats from *Cosmo.*

"You're illiterate and suffer from voter apathy?"

"Yes, but I'm also single."

"Primo dumped you?" She sounded truly shocked.

"Not really." A question I had from yesterday popped into my head. "What color lipstick did you have on the other night at Void?"

"Righteous Raspberry." Who names these colors?

"Primo died," I said as I jotted the lipstick down.

She screamed so loud I almost dropped the phone. I heard her apologize to some other neurotic sitting nearby. A moment later she regained control and said, "Let's get together."

"What time?"

"Six or eight?" Those were the two commonly accepted slots of after-work meeting times. Seven was too much in the middle.

"Six," I said realizing the less time alone, the better.

We didn't need to state where; we always converged at the same place—the local cool hangout, the Cobalt Colt, where my mini-coterie of unacquainted friends amassed and stared.

chapter 3

I had met Zoë at a low-budget ashram years ago in upstate New York, where we both utterly failed at approaching nirvana but became the best of decadent Western friends. In fact, she was also with me when I met Primo at the Cobalt Colt. Zoë, the sexual beacon, was sending out all her usual amorous signals: the low-cut blouse, the push-up bra, desperately heaving breasts to contrast with the subtle, tasteful mascara. It drew Primo like the fly he was. From the pretentious way he cupped his cigarette to his ambivalent expression, I detested him on sight. He moseyed up to her with a drink and some flushable cliché like, "Haven't we met in another life?"

Zoë's mantrapping strategy was to take a guy home and sleep with him until he was so utterly exhausted he couldn't leave. But somehow they always did. My role in her mating process was to be the straight man to her signature quips and comic barbs. But with Primo, even Zoë reacted indifferently.

I suggested that we leave the place, hoping to shake the creepo. Not getting the hint, Primo asked if he could tag along. Zoë, always starved for male attention, replied, "I suppose."

In the course of that first evening, as we passed through the gauntlet of coffee shops, clubs, and after-hours bars, something strange happened. His tired delivery, his burned-out one-liners, his twisted face, all turned from plain ugly to a surreal, seen-it-all, done-it-all charming. By the end of the evening, I couldn't take my eyes off him. He made failure wonderfully stylish and reelectrified the tired, dumb, and predictable: he was the dismissed Beatle, the glue-trapped Ratpacker, the laid-off Warhol Factory worker. This man couldn't make shit stink, or a fly fly. He couldn't hold a tune, or walk a straight line. Yet despite it all, there was a distinct success to his failure.

Zoë's snappy remarks, like well-chewed pieces of Juicy Fruit, started losing their humorous flavor, while retaining their jaw-weary insults.

When she demanded, "Have you done anything at all with your life?" it signaled that she had lost all interest in him.

"Zoë." I gave her the look, which she picked up on immediately. It was the "if you're done, it's my turn" face. She restrained her confusion, yawned, and said she was tired and had to run. I wished her good night, and had him by default.

After a couple more drinks, we walked, talked, and soon, against my better judgment, kissed. Oddly, on that night alone, he was a great kisser. I truly had no plans to sleep with him, but as I had just gotten dumped by Greg, I enjoyed tormenting him.

Very quickly, I had him wiggling lustfully on my hook. What can I say? He was always there, and though he didn't sparkle, he mastered the fine art of not offending.

After work, but before meeting Zoë at the Cobalt Colt, I stopped at home to find that the dog had defecated in the boudoir. I screamed at Numb. It looked at me shamefully, then I realized that I was actually the monster. The poor thing needed to be taken out. I should have dropped it off at the pound that morning. I cleaned up its protest dump, put a leash on the canine, and walked it around the block. It kept stopping, sniffing, and haphazardly urinating—just a squirt—on a million different artifacts of the street—lampposts, meters, the tree. Finally, it stared up at me soulfully as it dispelled a monstrous pile.

As I dashed away to meet Zoë, some civic-minded dude yelled at me to scoop up the poop.

"It's not my dog," I said sincerely.

"You're holding the fucking leash," he screamed back.

I grabbed a discarded Pennysaver and shoveled the load

into the corner garbage can. How did Primo do this? I never saw him scoop up his own shit, let alone anything else's. In fifteen minutes I was showered, re-dressed, and pushing open the door to the Cobalt Colt.

"What the hell happened?" Zoë asked as soon as she spotted me. It took me a moment to realize she was talking about Primo.

"I came home, and he was dead in front of the TV." I saved myself the embarrassment of explaining that I made his corpse dinner and got mad when he didn't eat it. I told her that I had called his mother that morning.

"How'd she take it?" She stirred her mochachino.

"Remarkably well," I replied, and suddenly wondered if June wasn't the beneficiary of a mega life insurance policy.

"I hope you don't mind if I ask you a question?" Some hairy Italian leprechaun had just imposed himself on our giant world.

"We're in the middle of—"

"Go ahead, dear," Zoë interrupted me. Her smile was pouty, her standards dwindling.

I watched her are–you–Mr. Right? face float to the surface like an ice cube in a punch glass. For several minutes, while this obvious gentile bantered incoherent imbecilic nonsense that in his world passed for wit, I watched as she blossomed under his attention.

"My boyfriend just died!" I finally blurted when I had reached critical mass.

"Oh, jeez, hey hon, I'm sorry," the Italian said. It was the only thing he said that made any sense.

"Do they know what he died of?" Zoë asked, still wearing her sensitive enchantress mask for the benefit of the stranger who listened on.

"Not yet. The medical examiner is going to call when he finds out."

"Hey, can I get your number?" the small stallion neighed at

her. As soon as she gave him the seven-digit combination to her telephonic safe, he took off like a burglar in the night. Even if she didn't know it, I knew she would never hear from him again. Too many guys nowadays were phone number conquistadors, too cool to go any further.

"What's your problem?" She pounced on me.

"He wasn't even Jewish," I pointed out.

"Don't you ever tell me what kind of man—"

"You distinctly said you were only looking for a Jewish husband," I shot back, adding, "In case you don't remember, my boyfriend just died. I'm entitled to some sympathy."

"Primo Schultz was the biggest piece of crap loser that this bogus city ever squeezed out!" she screamed.

"Excuse me, did I hear you mention Primo Schultz?" interrupted some coiffed, early-middle-aged pseudo socialite sitting at an adjacent table.

"Yeah," I replied, glad to have an opportunity to disconnect Zoë.

"God, I haven't seen him in ages. How is the swine?" she asked with a wide-open expression. She was sharply suited and professionally poised. Zoë looked at me, amused to see how I was going to tell her.

"He's not well," I began, feeling slightly jealous. "May I ask who you are?"

"He was my boyfriend nearly twenty years ago," she replied matter-of-factly.

"Twenty years!" Zoë kerplunked. We both looked at each other agape.

"You went to junior high school with him out in Brooklyn?" I assumed aloud.

"No, no," she corrected. "We both lived right here. Between First and Second Avenues, near the Ninth Precinct."

"You lived there together?" Zoë asked, pulling her seat nearer to the lady.

"Sure," she replied, "We went to Cooper Union."

"You're kidding." I had no idea that Primo had any kind of formal education.

"Well, he dropped out after his first year." Sounded like him.

"Wait a second," Zoë interrupted. "Primo was only thirty-five. He couldn't have been in Cooper Union in the late seventies." I had thought he was thirty-two.

"Thirty-five!" the Agnes B. deportee remarked. "He can't be a day younger than forty-two."

Looking at her watch, she stood up, dropped a five-dollar bill on the table, and was about to give salutations when I asked, "Where are you going?"

"Work. Give Primo my best."

"Primo's—" Zoë looked at me.

"Here." She pulled a business card from a small vest pocket that seemed to be customized for them. "Tell him I forgive him enough so that if he wants to give me a call, I might be able to help him out a bit."

"What do you do?" I asked, inspecting her card as she opened the front door of the bistro. She didn't respond. The gilded Romanesque lettering answered for her: "Barbarosian Gallery—Helga Elfman, Assistant Director."

"You should tell her," Zoë said as the art peddler stepped off the curb to hail a cab. I jumped up, leaving my coat and purse on the table, and dashed out the door. By the time I was outside, Elfman was already climbing into a taxi.

"Wait a second!" I grabbed the door before she could slam it behind her.

"What is it?" she asked, obviously thinking about her upcoming appointment.

"I . . . I . . ." The Middle Eastern cabdriver craned his thick ox neck to see me.

"Primo . . . he's . . ." Someone started honking. I jumped into the cab, slamming the door behind me.

"Five-twenty-five Madison Avenue," she told the driver, and then looked at me almost nervously, as though I might be a danger. As the cab zoomed west on Houston and the annoying recording by some older, out-of-work, barely known actor warned us to buckle up, I explained, "Primo died last night."

She gasped and placed an open hand over her mouth in horror. Tears came to her eyes. She took out a Kleenex, dabbed around her nose, and finally, ceasing to sniffle, took out her compact. At a stoplight, she refixed her makeup. I wondered where she got her eyebrow pencil, yet propriety forbade asking.

"This is sad in so many ways," she stammered, "it's almost impossible to count."

But I was dying to hear that count. I wanted to feel for Primo too, but hadn't, didn't, and couldn't. It wasn't that I didn't feel bad for him, I just didn't feel that his death was tragic.

Snapping her compact shut, she looked out toward the south side of Houston and said, "These streets here, I can't tell you how many times Primo and I walked them, back when you could get a loft for four hundred a month and you could still count the number of East Village galleries on your right hand."

"He told me he was in a band, and I remember him telling me he painted, but—"

"Oh, please! He couldn't play that awful guitar to save his life, but he was a gifted painter." The cab turned up Lafayette and proceeded up Park Avenue. "When the big art boom hit in the early eighties, it seemed to happen all around him. Everyone he knew—some of whom I believed copied his style—was having their works snatched up, but he couldn't get a single deal. It was uncanny. He was friends with Basquiat and hung out with Warhol until he couldn't bear them any longer. Amazing in this business how a person will be friends with you, will lend you money, let you stay at their place, even sleep with their girlfriend, they'll give you everything but help in selling your work." At Twenty-fifth the cabbie turned onto Madison.

"Where are his paintings now?" I wondered aloud.

"I don't know—he had this series of paintings that were superb. I know that he destroyed a lot of his old stuff. By the beginning of the nineties they must have reminded him of his failure."

Does good art become bad at the end of each decade? I wondered. "You couldn't help him?"

"Well, I loved him so much," she admitted. "And what does he do? What does the slime do? He dumps me on New Year's Eve 1980 for a sixteen-year-old."

She didn't need to say anything more than that. Getting dumped on New Year's Eve sounded awful. Soon the cab came to a halt. Helga Elfman tossed a ten-dollar bill onto the worn-through vinyl of the front seat and slid out the back.

As the cold wind snapped around the southeast corner of Fifty-ninth Street and Madison Avenue, I immediately awoke to the fact that I was without a coat or purse. Zoë was probably still sitting at the table with my things.

Helga took long strides. I trailed behind as if she was Mother Goose. Turning to me as an afterthought, she said, "Maybe you really should notify that Asian jailbait he dumped me for."

"Who is that?"

"That crazy Sue Wott. The Cambodian trollop."

If I had loved Primo enough would he have dumped me?

"I guess I'll let sleeping infidels lie."

"Well, they were married."

"Married?" The word ricocheted and reverberated. "Where is she now?"

"Call the Film Archives. They've showed those boring short films that she did."

"Do you really think I should tell her?"

"Sure, she should feel crappy along with everyone else," Helga replied.

She opened a large glass door and vanished, leaving me

shivering and alone on the dark Midtown sidewalk. Trembling and penniless, looking inside, I saw her standing at the elevator bank, facing away from me. I heard the *bing* sound. She had stepped into an elevator. I whipped opened the door and hopped in just as the doors were sliding shut.

"Unless you're about to tell me that yet another ex-boyfriend from years gone by is dead, our business is done," she said at close quarters.

"Actually, I was wondering if you could lend me ten bucks to get back downtown."

"If I learned anything from Primo, it was never to lend anyone anything," she replied. Pulling a ten from her purse, she handed it to me and said, "Call it payment for information."

"Thank you," I replied. We rode the elevator up to her floor together, and before the door opened, she asked, "How do I look?"

I studied her face. In it I could see deals and dollars swirling about. "Great."

"Let me know if there's a funeral or something."

I promised I would, and the door slid shut. It was goose-pimply cold out as I slid my arms into my shirt. I looked like a fat amputee as I grabbed a cab on Fifty-ninth. Back in the Cobalt Colt, it was as if I had never left. Zoë was sitting with a bald guy in his forties, smiling meaningfully. He looked like a detainee at a dental convention. I waited as she pamphleteered out her phone number. Afterward, he rose and left, probably to return to his wife and kids in Long Beach. Even on a bad day she could do better.

We paid the check and tried to agree about a restaurant. She wanted to try a new Chinese restaurant, Shun Tung's, on Fourth Street. I craved Middle Eastern on St. Mark's. We compromised in the center of Asia—going to Milara, an Indian restaurant on Sixth Street. Rice, unidentifiable meat that looked like chunks of clay swimming in a gummy brown sauce, a large bowl of cabbage tossed from the Cuisinart to the microwave, various cold sauces, a nonpunitive check, and an evening of strange-smelling burps. During the meal, I told her that I had learned that Primo was married.

"You're kidding?" she said.

"Some Cambodian girl."

Perhaps to pay final respects to the location of Primo's departure from this earth, Zoë walked me to my apartment. As we climbed up the stairs to my door, something was whining and scratching behind it.

"You don't want a dog, do you?" I asked.

"I'm allergic," she replied quickly, but I knew that she had never even owned a pet.

"How do you know unless you make the mistake of adopting one?"

"I just know," she concluded and left.

Early the next morning, long before the alarm, I realized what had kept me up the night before. The dog had torn the bottom out of the garbage bag for bones and whatever other scraps it could find. I realized that I hadn't fed it since Primo's death. I opened the cabinet above the sink and took out the dry dog food. I poured it into its blue bowl. I flushed the toilet several times to make sure it was clean enough for drinking. It was only about five in the morning, so I lay back down to try to salvage some slumber before work.

But the carousel kept turning. Slides were projecting. I relived the fateful evening that converted Primo from a torture toy to an ambiguous boyfriend. It was the sixth or seventh time we went out. We were in Tompkins Square Park, and he was rubbing up against me, attempting to kiss. We were sitting in one of the little cul-de-sacs, where I played him like a yo-yo, pulling him close and pushing him away. Inasmuch as he was Mr. Cool, the king of control, I have to admit that I was relishing the slow burn I was putting him through. Then something very bad occurred, the only awful thing that could have happened—the Gregor walked by. In his hairless, exercised arm was a skinny, anemic Gwyneth Paltrow type. He didn't say a word as he passed. They both gave a patronizing smirk, and I could see it in Greg's smug face: "You'll never do better than me."

Are all new boyfriends just bad reactions to past relationships, new poisons to kill off the old toxic lover and loves? I grabbed Primo, headed over to Horseshoe Bar on Avenue B, and started knocking back the three-dollar drinks from the hangover shelf. A booth opened up, and we slid in. Things started getting hot and heavy right there in the bar. Then we went to his place, and I got in way over my head. We saunaed the place up with our vapors, and soon crashed and burned beyond forgiveness. No AIDS test, no condoms, no holds barred. The next morning, after we showered and quietly parted, I started feeling that awfulness that followed mindless ga-ga sex with a stranger. Worse, Primo was someone I was essentially drawn to because of a strange disdain for him. The day was a slowly rising flood of shame and self-hatred. By evening, I felt like a full-fledged tramp.

The anger and lust and booze and sweat and loneliness had all just got the better of me, leaving me wobbly and wide open. When I heard his message on my machine later that day, I didn't want to speak to him. Primo must have thought that I was this little innocent, his blushing bride. What followed was a frenzy of messages that I fast-forwarded through.

It wasn't until a few days passed that I came home to find Primo leaning on a parked car across from my front stoop after work.

"Hi," he said, as I stood there hoping to miraculously disappear.

"How are you?" I had to say something.

"I'm here to apologize," he began and looked nervously to the ground. He stepped closer so that he didn't have to talk above a whisper. He seemed to be torn. "You haven't called me, and obviously something is wrong."

"I've just been very busy." I preferred the silent treatment. Sex and then no follow-up call.

"Obviously it's more than that."

"No, it's not," I stammered. Why couldn't he just leave me alone?

"Look, can we walk a bit?"

We headed toward Houston. "It took me years to realize that sex for men is completely different than it is for women. Sex is a big amusement park, and I guess the woman is the ride. But I think for women, it's something far more vulnerable, like a way of testing our trust. Like you would've liked me better if I hadn't done anything." My silence was intended as a confirmation of this. "I have this strange sense that you ordinarily don't go as far as you did the other night,"

"No," I confessed. I couldn't look up at him. He took my hand in his and kissed it.

"I'm not good at humbling myself, but I think the world of you. I enjoy being with you, and I was honored that you trusted me." He produced a perfect rose from inside his jacket pocket and handed it to me. It was all so tacky and wonderful.

"If you just give me the opportunity, I'll prove to you that you don't have to feel you made the wrong decision." Mr. Hallmark couldn't have stitched it up any better.

All that was just months ago, but now, probably because he was dead, it seemed like years ago.

Numb seemed to be in gastrointestinal pain, pacing, wincing, giving me that awful, wet-eyed look. It had to go bad. I rose, threw a raincoat on over my underwear, slid on sneakers, leashed the beast, and walked it.

Twenty minutes later, when the dog inscrutably found that ideal spot, it went. As I brought it upstairs, feeling the chill in my bones, I again vowed to take it to the ASPCA before the week was over. It was ten o'clock, and I was late for the job. The subways were jammed, the ride labored. The streets were packed and seemed too small for the city's swollen populace. After decades of being unpopular, New York was now the place to be.

When I arrived I was given a new workstation. Yesterday's desk had been taken by an earlier temp. I answered phones that no one knew the numbers to, and was given a cryptic document to fax to Siberia.

By eleven, I found the shadow of an opportunity to sneak into an empty cubicle to quickly check my messages. In addition to one from my landlord telling me that I was late with the rent, I received one from Primo's mother asking if I could call her.

I dialed immediately. "Hello, Ms. Schultz. This is Mary Bellanova."

"The medical examiner called and asked me to pick up Primo." I could hear her TV blaring in the background.

"Do they know what he died of?"

"Cardiac seizure."

"Did he say what caused it?" I asked.

"Oh, he said that he didn't believe that Primo knew he was sick in advance." She paused, as though she were trying to remember something. Then she added, "I've called the Malio Funeral Home."

"When is the burial?" I asked.

"He's being cremated."

"What are you doing with his ashes?"

"Actually, I was hoping maybe you could help me," she said. "He's spent the past twenty years living in that filthy Village, so it seems right that he should be spread there."

"Wouldn't you prefer to do it?" I asked, slightly perturbed with this strangely uninvolved mother.

"I'm wheelchair-bound," she explained. She sounded TV-bound.

"I'll be glad to—" I couldn't finish the phrase. She gave me her address and told me she would call me once she had possession of the urn.

"You know, Primo has a dog. You wouldn't be interested in taking him, would you?" I managed to squeeze in.

"I'm afraid of dogs," she concluded.

When I hung up I felt an instant chill, a fear at how life can be wrapped up so neatly. Clinging to the hope that Primo's life—and all human life—was not so close to oblivion, that a person could not be as easily disposed of as a goldfish, I remembered that Primo had a Cambodian ex-wife. I decided that I could tell her about Primo's death. And maybe she would mourn for this sad man.

Going through my purse, I located the name of the young divorcée, Sue Wott. I called information, asked the automated operator for a residence in Manhattan, and spelled the name out quickly. In a few moments the human came on and said that her name was not listed.

For lunch I went to a wilted, overpriced Korean salad bar near work and got a brown muffin and a black decaf to go. The free corporate coffee tasted like army surplus ink. Back at my anonymous desk I was given a pile of pointless documents to copy, a task obviously designed to keep me busy for the bulk of the afternoon. The Xerox machine at the office did not have an automatic feeder, and each copy had to be done individually. Feeling the futility of it all, I grabbed the phone, located an outside line, called information, got the number, and called the Film Archives on Second Avenue and Second Street, where Helga said Sue Wott's films had once been shown.

When the box office girl put me through to the manager, I asked if they knew of a certain Sue Wott.

"You must not be a regular," a male responded with a mix of pissiness and prissiness. "Otherwise you'd know that she hasn't had a film here in about ten years. I don't know her number anymore."

"You don't know if she's in the city anymore, do you?"

"She's a rock-and-roll diva now, thank God."

"Why thank God?"

"She's a nut. And since then she had that kid."

"Kid?" I confirmed.

"Yeah, about six years ago."

"You don't know who the father is?"

"No, and I don't want to know."

"You couldn't give me a clue of how I could track her down?"

"I remember someone saying that she was stripping."

"Stripping?"

"Yeah, in a striptease parlor." He asked, if I did track her down, not to mention him. I promised, and he hung up.

A striptease parlor. You didn't hear many places called parlors anymore. The word was dying. I returned to my Xeroxing, eager to catch up to my self-determined schedule. The shift supervisor stepped in to see me working at a frantic pace.

"You don't have to kill yourself," she said, pleased with my rapid rate of copying and collating, unaware of my sidetracking. I thanked her, and as soon as she stepped out, I called Zoë at work.

"It's busy here," she said in a whisper. "What's up?"

"Remember Primo's wife?"

"The crazy Cambodian?"

"Yeah. I heard she had a job as a stripper."

"Shake it, baby."

"Where would she strip in the city?" I asked.

Long ago, when Zoë first came to the city, she validated her deepest insecurities by doing a brief stint as a stripper.

"What was the bombshell's name again?" she asked.

"Sue Wott."

"She probably has an alias." Zoë had called herself Kitty when she stripped. "If she lived in the East Village, she probably hit either the Baby Doll or Billy's Topless."

Zoë's boss must have turned a corner, because she hung up without saying good-bye.

I called information and got the numbers for both Billy's Topless and the Baby Doll Lounge. When I called Billy's, the female bartender answered over the jukebox.

"Do you have a dancer named Sue Wott?"

"Who, what?" she clowned.

"Do you have an Asian dancer?"

"China Blue dances weekend nights." It was Tuesday.

"You probably wouldn't know if she was married to a Primo Schultz, would you?" She hung up. I called the Baby Doll. The music there was louder, the background conversation more grinding.

"Do you have a dancer named Sue Wott?" I asked.

"Never heard of her."

"Do you have any Asians working there?"

"Yeah, Minnie Belle."

"You wouldn't know if she's married?"

"Why, are you a Mormon?" He added, "She's divorced I think."

"What days does she strip?"

"Thursday." I thanked him and hung up. I called Zoë and told her I was going to pay a visit. Claiming that her life had been too peaceful lately, she asked if she could tag along.

Thursday after work, Zoë and I met at the Starbucks on Fifty-first and Broadway, and walked over to the subway, where we each used the last ride on our MetroCards and squeezed into the rear car of an overcrowded, poorly ventilated R train.

The doors slid shut and the stops filed off; Forty-second, Thirty-fourth, Twenty-eighth. More people got on than off, pushing Zoë and me closer together so that we were right up against each other. Tightly pressed together, she asked, "You don't think that you're going a bit overboard with this, do you?"

"What do you mean?"

"We're going to a strip club to meet an ex-wife of Primo's. I mean, you never showed this much interest in him when he was alive."

"He was never this interesting," I explained.

We got off the train at Canal Street, and Zoë led the way.

It was not even dark yet, and the streets below Canal were drained dry. A silent suspense built up in the few blocks we walked. By the time we reached Sixth Avenue, we both felt a bit nervous. Standing in front of the place, I noticed a stupidly misspelled sign that read, "sTopless Dancing." Zoë lit up a ciggy, so I did too, and we both took deep drags.

"I've never gone into one of these places," I confessed with a grin.

"Just make believe we're the toughest dykes on the block."

"Right on, sis," I said, exhaling my fumes.

Zoë pushed through the doors, turned left, and went inside. Instantly I felt eyes spearing us from all directions. The bar was filled with chunky, darkly dressed men facing fleshy feminine ghosts—strippers working for their tips. One, a robust Russian, was lying sidelong like a Botticelli, opening her wide marble thighs to show where the thin G-string held back a bundle of pubic hair. Another skinnier girl was sliding and straddling the aluminum poles. In contrast to the motionless male spectators, the women looked like a pair of human animals begging for food. I didn't think of it as degrading, particularly after hearing how much money they made every week. They were using as much as being used.

"Which one is Minnie Belle?" Zoë asked the lady bartender, an over-the-hill Latina with her boobs pushed up over her bustier.

"She just finished dancing. She'll be coming out in a moment."

Stripping was an anachronism. Girls stopped actually stripping in the fifties. Nowadays, they just wore strings and "danced." We both took stools. Zoë ordered a lite beer. Needing to stay sober, I went with a soda. The skinnier of the two dancers, who was in the middle of her routine, smiled at Zoë. She had almost no body to speak of, but she had an incredibly cute, girlish face and long blond hair. Zoë smiled back at her. The stripper waved Zoë over. I remained by the bar, far too nervous to move. After two songs, Zoë took a five from her purse and slipped the bill into the elastic band of the stripper's G-string. Some creep hooted.

The stripper grabbed Zoë's hand and wouldn't let it go. A Gloria Gaynor song came on, so Zoë stepped over to the aluminum poles that hemmed the dancers in and started shaking it with the blond. A few of the men started laughing and making adolescent remarks, but it didn't stop the two gyrating women. Watching the blond lift the hem of Zoë's skirt a few inches and simulate oral sex, one of the quieter guys started dropping a flurry of single dollar bills into the corral. I knew the only reason Zoë was acting this way was her compulsive disorder to be the center of all male attention.

After a few songs, I saw a gorgeous Asian girl wearing glossy black high heels step out from the center door. She had long black braided hair that covered her skinny rear. Her beautiful eyes with thick dark lashes checked out the man-infested darkness. She was wearing a checkered blue shirt knotted over a red bra.

Some boyish lad, who reminded me of a young Mickey Rooney, hijacked her before I had a chance to ask her about Primo. Another older fellow, who looked starched up like a marine, was waiting for her in the wings. Mickey the lad bought her a drink and started to talk to her. She listened and laughed easily, chugging down her cocktail. A big bull pigeon was chirping for the blond stripper to undress Zoë as their dance turned into a slow grind. I lit another cigarette and noticed that Mickey was only halfway done with his drink before Minnie Belle took the liberty of signaling to the bartenderette for a refill. The blond stripper was pulling Zoë's zipper up and down behind her back.

"When you dancing, sweetcake?" some half-wit asked.

"When hell freezeth over," I replied biblically and ordered a second Diet Coke.

"Well, considering the weather lately, this might be a bad year for that." He was cute but young, like a cross between Matt Damon and Ben Affleck.

"What do you do?" I asked, not wanting to waste any time. If he didn't have some entertaining artistic pursuit or wasn't pulling down at least six figures a year, I was going to abort this conversation in its first trimester.

"Unemployed," he replied good-naturedly.

"How are you hoping to pay for my refill?" I asked, deciding to see how far I could ride him before he would walk off.

"I saved enough just for that," he replied. If he wasn't cute, I wouldn't have wasted another moment on the bar stool.

"How old are you?"

"Twenty-three," he said. He must have been kidding.

"You got ID?" He showed me his driver's license. He wasn't kidding, which shot apart my belief that male lechery began at forty.

"I'm thirty," I told him.

"You look great," he replied, earning himself one big point.

"Where do you live?" I asked, wondering how far men came to see these dancing girls.

"A short happy walk from here." He lost half a point for that one.

"How big is your appointment?" I asked tiredly.

"My appointment was at three o'clock. A complete cleaning." He opened his mouth, showing off his pearly whites. "No cavities. My apartment, however, is a massive cavity, a lofty space waiting for your queenly presence." I noticed that mousey Mickey was escaping the deadly grip of Minnie Belle.

"I don't mean to be rude, but I have to scram," I said to the unemployed charmer.

"Here." He handed me a business card. "Give me a call if you want to go for coffee and talk." I took the card just as the starched marine was stepping up to the bat, offering Minnie Belle a drink.

"Can I speak to you a sec?" I asked, cutting him off.

"Wait your turn, sister," said the sarge.

"At ease," Minnie Belle said to the man, who was still in the Vietnam of the mind.

"Is your name Sue Wott?" I skipped ahead.

"There's a name I haven't heard in a while, and don't want to hear for another long while. She's out of the circuit."

"You wouldn't know how to get a hold of her?"

"We have a common friend, Lydia."

"Could you give me her number?" The sergeant was making angry guttural sounds.

"I'd rather give Lydia your number," Minnie replied.

"My boyfriend just died," I explained. "He was Sue Wott's ex-husband. I'm trying to find out if he was the father of her kid. If he is, I think she'd want to know."

"Last I heard she was in some all-girl rock-and-roll band— Nutty and the Sexy." I thanked her and gave her my phone number. Minnie was on to her next victim.

The youth I had talked to had vanished. His card read, "Alphonso Del Guardio, Jjd. LLC." I had no idea what academic degree these enigmatic initials signified.

I looked over to collect Zoë, but she was still flirting with the blond boneshell. She'd been nice enough to come to this pit with me, so I didn't want to interrupt whatever it was she had going.

I sidled up to the counter, where another barfly landed and started his buzzing.

"Hi," he gurgled. With waxy cheekbones, sunken eyes, and sucked-in lips, he looked heroin chic.

"Hi."

"Work here?"

"Hell, no."

"Want a drink?"

"Diet Coke with lemon." He ordered some imported suds for himself.

This one was strictly in love with himself, telling me his boring life story. How he grew up in Brooklyn with six brothers and a father who took the strap to him if he messed around too much, and how that explained what was wrong with kids today. This was one thing I had loved about Primo. He understood that nobody wanted their ear used like a toilet bowl. As this sad sack talked his heart out, I heard some maudlin Billy Joel song come bleating out of the jukebox. It reminded me of the time I was stuck chaperoning a bunch of old high school friends who blew in from Long Island. I had to guide them around the city, and for some reason Primo tagged along. Even they were having a dull time, so we dipped into some touristy Midtown bar.

While they were sipping their beers, Primo slipped off to the bathroom, or so I thought. A karaoke machine was rusting in the rear. He put a dollar in, picked up the mike, and started singing Billy Joel à la Sid Vicious. It was incredibly stupid and perfect all at once. The out-of-towners thought it was romantic. I started laughing.

"Yeah, it's funny, ain't it?" the barfly remarked, thinking I was laughing at his boring repartee. Maybe I was PMSing, or maybe I just felt trapped by this insufferable bore, but I found myself missing Primo gravely. Tears came to my eyes.

"Is everything all right?" the guy asked, concerned.

"I need to be alone." I went over to Zoë.

"You ready?" she asked. Her blond companion had finally evaporated.

Outside we debated getting a cab to the East Village. It wasn't that far away, and neither of us had worked out in eons, so we decided to stretch our legs.

"What was that little romance you had going?" Zoë asked, apparently noticing my interludes with the variety of sad male specimens.

"Me? How about you and Anne Heche?"

"Oh, please. I've known Chase for at least five years. We were just horsing around."

"You knew her!" I was surprised.

"Not well, but yeah."

"She looks about seventeen."

"She's loaded with preservatives."

We bantered our way through Soho and finally headed east. She asked me how my fortune cookie crumbled with Sue Wott. I explained that it was someone else, but Minnie Belle knew her and still had a common friend; she was going to pass my number to her. I dropped Zoë off at her place on the far side of Tompkins Square Park, on Tenth Street.

Avenue B was becoming a roulette wheel for gambling restaurateurs who figured that if they could offer an exotic cuisine and an interesting ambience, they could win the Avenue A crowd while paying a cheaper rent.

I wouldn't have been aware of these if it weren't for Joey Lucas. During the first three months of our friendship a few years ago, he twice invited me to these underpatronized dives. Now I associated two of the Avenue B dinners with two major depressions in my life.

Zephyr, which was located somewhere around Sixth Street, had a strange fusion of German and Arabic food. Like my relationship with Greg, it was costly while the service sucked. I remembered bellyaching about what a reptile he was while eating that meal with Joey.

"Don't waste your time," Joey counseled. "Move on."

The next time he took me out to dinner, we went to either Mediterranean or Baltic, or some such squalid piece of real estate from the Monopoly board. It substituted a quirky-looking interior for good food and service. I remembered sitting at the table drinking a lot more than eating, stuck in the doldrums of singlehood. It was just after I had been dumped by Greg. I was grateful to be with Joey that night so I didn't have to witness another evening turn to cigarette smoke in Zoë's ashtray bars.

"Believe me," Joey refrained, "it's painful now, but once the scar heals, you'll look back and wonder how you put up with him all this time."

"I know, " I whined, "but—"

The entire evening was that riff played in a million different ways. With each replay, I got drunker and more teary, until he had the good sense to taxi me home. When he tried to leave, I asked him if he wanted to watch TV. He must've sensed that I was lonely, because he stayed until I passed out, pulled a blanket over me, turned off the lights, and left.

I felt too embarrassed to return his call the next day, but a few weeks later, when he showed up at Starbucks, where I was working at the time, he ordered a coffee.

I gave him his drink and told him I was getting off in twenty minutes.

"Are you making a pass at me?" he kidded just loud enough for the woman behind him to hear.

"It's just another service we provide for our bachelor customers here at Starbucks."

"You folks really are friendly. I'll be sitting next to the window."

It was the week of the loud and smoky San Gennaro Festival, so after work we headed down Mulberry Street, which was covered with plastic archways laced with cheap Christmas lights. Overpriced mobile game arcades and vehicular grills blocked a slow-moving jam of dumb tourists. Pickpockets must have had a field day. By evening's end, when he walked me to my door, I first realized that I felt the psychospiritual indigestion that could only mean I had a serious crush on my former upstairs neighbor.

A few forgettable days passed. Neither Mrs. Schultz nor Lydia, the mysterious friend of Sue Wott, called. I kept meaning to put up notices to give away the dog, but as I procrastinated and took it to the various dogruns in the area, I discovered a new cache of available men—meaning a temporary home and short reprieve for Numb. I chewed Twizzlers and smoked up a storm, getting ready for the old dating circuit again.

One serendipitous bonus from the Baby Doll Lounge was meeting the youthful smoothy Alphonso Del Guardio. Out of disdain for sitting around and waiting to be picked up, I called him, and we agreed to have dinner and see a flick. We met early one evening at a Thai restaurant between Tribeca and Chinatown. He didn't look so bad in a nonseedy milieu. Over a steamy dish of pad thai, he asked all about me. I tried to be witty, light, and evasive—what every guy wants. He laughed a lot, and seemed aggressively interested. Afterward, since it was still early, we went for a walk. In Chinatown each of us got a cone of green tea ice cream; then we headed southeast, across Worth Street, over the Brooklyn Bridge to a movie theater on the other side.

Once we were above the East River, I popped the big question. "What do those initials after your name stand for?"

"You mean on my business card?"

"Yep."

"Well," he cleared his throat. "I have a graduate degree in paranormal psychology."

"What exactly is that?"

"Ever see the movie *Ghostbusters?*"

"You don't—you're not—"

"Have you ever felt someone was watching you while you were all alone?"

"Yeah, but it always turned out to be the creep across the courtyard," I kidded, hoping he'd tell me the truth, not "The truth is out there."

"The University of Minneapolis is one of three institutions in the country with such a graduate program."

"You are bullshitting me, right?" I stopped walking, refusing to take another step.

"I'm afraid not," he said, looking at me sincerely.

"So you're saying you can communicate with the deceased?"

"I'm not a clairvoyant, but yes, that's one of the skills I'm trying to develop." I looked him deep in the eyes; unflinchingly, he looked right back. Over years of watching stupid TV news magazines, I had seen video footage in which strange lights and shadows moved wispily across the screen, coupled with eccentric types who made claims of feeling their restless unincarnated souls. I immediately wondered if there was anything I wanted to say to Primo.

"What were you doing in that strip bar?" I asked, trying a different strategy.

"It was close and cheap. How about you?" He somersaulted the question back to me.

"My ex-boyfriend just died, and I was trying to notify his ex-wife."

"Ex?"

"Well, he was my boyfriend, but the relationship was falling apart."

We talked a little about past relationships. He told me that he dumped his last girlfriend about six months earlier, but now, after learning about his paranormalcy, I doubted him completely and wondered about his sanity. Why were guys like this always attracted to me? When we reached the halfway mark on the bridge, I stood against the railing and just looked south over the

Narrows. Under the setting sun, in the greenish brown waters, I could see Governors Island and Staten Island. A tugboat was passing one of those floating tourist traps that rounded the island—a Circle Line. I couldn't get enough of views like that. Alphonso slowly banked up against me and started pressing close. I could feel his throbbing urgency against my unexercised upper buttocks. I made a subtle sound that indicated a civil distance. He ignored it, pressing harder.

Reaching behind me, I poked him gently in what I estimated to be his beanbag.

"Ow!" he shouted and stepped back. Upon recomposing himself, he said, "I'm sorry."

"Just take care," I cautioned.

"I didn't mean I was sorry for rubbing up against you," he murmured back.

"For what then?"

"For the fact that those initials after my name don't mean anything."

"What do you mean?" I turned around.

"I snagged you." He laughed glibly.

"You're kidding?" I jumped back.

"I wish I had some kind of graduate degree," he said. "I do watch *The X-Files.*"

There should be a covert government agency that protects people from academic initials that don't stand for anything. Pissed, I stormed off. He raced and begged my forgiveness.

"Come on," he appealed. "I owed you that."

"Owed me it," I repeated.

"Sure, after all you put me through at the Baby Doll, then vanishing just when we started talking." I remembered dashing off when Minnie Belle became approachable, but I didn't know I had created some kind of debt. He had let his ghostly little lie last for about twenty minutes, bringing it to the outer limits of a practical joke.

"So, what exactly do you do with your life?" I asked after deciding not to walk away and just leave him there.

"Oh, this and that. I really haven't found myself yet." A cute guy with a fascinating career turned out to be just another slacker. Shit.

"How do you afford to live?" I inquired, trying to show my disappointment.

"Well, okay." He regrouped his thoughts and charged forth. "For one thing, I inherit. I have a modest trust fund right now, but when another one of my rich bachelor uncles dies, I should be getting a very nice townhouse, and when a third uncle kicks, I'll be getting a country house and probably a couple of cars."

"So you just spend your days praying for their deaths and watching game shows?"

"Not at all. I stay in shape." He slapped his loose polo shirt. "I have a lifetime membership at my gym. I can work out as much as I want, and I'm always reading. I go to the Strand every day. I have a library of books and videotapes."

What next? Was he going to impress me by making a cellular call? He continued dazzling me as we climbed down off the bridge and headed over to the Brooklyn Heights Twin. This coincidentally was my favorite cinema in the city. In this strangulating age of flavorless megaplex conglomerates, it was the last of the small, cozy, inexpensive theaters. We watched a foreign movie about a shy misunderstood girl who dated a loud misunderstood guy. Then we cabbed it back to the city. As the taxi idled in front of my rotting apartment building, I shook Alphonso's hand.

"Can I call you again?" he asked. He had paid for the dinner and flick, inexpensive as they were. Unless he was still lying, he should soon inherit all the resources of someone who was hardworking.

"All right." He leaned forward, hovered around my face for a moment like a mosquito looking for a place to sting, and finally gave me a peck on my cheek.

Over the course of the following weeks, he didn't call me, but Zoë—who asked me a million details about the date—insisted that I could do better. During the week, aside from temping, I cleaned out my account paying the rent and utility bills. I also put an ad up in the Off-Campus Student Housing Office at NYU: Female, nonsmoker, no more pets. Numb was enough. In doing this I took the opportunity to jerk up the price of my rent beyond half in order to relieve myself from some of my fiscal flab.

By Monday, my phone machine was loaded with homeless students. By Friday, I had interviewed twenty-two potential roommates and narrowed my list down to the two top candidates, who looked and acted pretty much alike. They both seemed perky and reticent. They claimed they had no boyfriends. Both resembled Winona Ryder with their nervous cute looks. The edge that Winona A had over Winona B was that she didn't make a nasty face when I told her that my boyfriend had died in the apartment. But when I called Winona A and told her she had been selected, she explained that she had already got a place. Winona B won by default.

"I'm sorry, but I got another place," the second Winona mimicked the first when I broke the news to her. I indiscriminately pointed to the next name on the list. It was a heavy, sweet-faced girl named Carolina. When I told her that she was my very first choice, she screamed in ecstasy.

"Can I move in tomorrow?"

"Do you have first and last month's rent?"

"Yes."

"Come in the afternoon."

In a way I was looking forward to having a roommate. Someone younger to pal around with, to watch *Oprah* and *Rosie* with, who I could laugh and cry with. The next day at nine, the doorbell rang. Carolina, whose name reminded me of rice, clumped up the stairs with a pair of chunky parents, each one carrying a large, colorful trunk. They looked like circus people.

"These are my folks, Marsha and Ross." They both said hi.

"The sublet was for one," I said groggily.

"They're just helping me." I didn't respond. "Here are the checks." She handed them to me.

I stood naked and groggy with a sheet over me, holding growling Numb with one hand and my sore head with the other.

"I wasn't expecting you until noon."

"Sorry," she said meekly.

"I hope this isn't going to turn into some passive-aggressive behavior pattern," I cautioned.

"It won't."

I took the checks and gave her the keys. Amid the bumpy rumpus of moved furniture, I slept for two more hours. All was quiet when I finally stepped out of the room. There was no sign of her, and for the first time since Primo had moved in, the door of the other room in the house was closed and shut.

The next time I saw her, she introduced me to her boyfriend, a tall mop-headed kid named Dorn. I shook his hand, and he smiled. I knew at once by his dialect, demeanor, and dress that he was gay. Carolina was unknowingly dating a sweet gay lad, yet it wasn't for me to tell. That was the kind of news that only life could teach her. I retreated into my room.

During the balance of our roommateship, we never watched TV or gal-pal'd once. The few times I saw Carolina, she was with Dorn. I wondered when and how she was going to find out the distressing truth.

Good roommates are born, not made. They are also neither seen nor heard. Carolina was pretty good on both counts. There were few signs of her existence: ever tightly curled tubes of toothpaste, ever smaller concentric circles of toilet paper. Fortunately for her, she never touched my food, and I never saw hers. The real test that she always passed was that most of the rent and half the electric bill were always on time. I wouldn't share my phone.

On that first day, I wanted her to feel comfortable in her new digs, so I leashed Numb and met Zoë in Tompkins Square for the annual Art Around the Park and Music Festival. She was dressed to lure. I deposited the dog in the run, and we watched a lineup of local bands and Beat wannabes in the portable bandshell. While listening to some obnoxious young kid reading off a laundry list of gripes under the banner of poetry, I recalled Primo telling me that the old Tompkins Square had a permanent stone bandshell, but the homeless slept inside it until it reeked like a cement armpit, so the city tore it down.

On one of our first dates, he gave me a walking tour of the neighborhood, pointing out where Jack Kerouac lived on Seventh Street, right down to the beautiful dilapidated outdoor theater in the East River Park where Joseph Papp supposedly performed Shakespeare back in the fifties before he had the Public Theater or the Delacorte in Central Park.

Zoë and I headed down A, where she bought a fruit smoothie, then we wove through the crowds along the west side of Tompkins Square Park where each artist was given a paper canvas and had only the length of that day to fill it with his or her labors. Zoë sucked her frozen drink out of a straw and made dismissive proclamations about each artist's day-long endeavor: "Silly crap, political crap, hippie crap—"

"Cut them some slack," I replied serenely. "They've been working on their canvases for less time than it takes for you to do your makeup."

When she ran out of art to criticize, Zoë started teasing me about my low writing productivity: "You need a boyfriend who'll crack the whip."

"Dating other writers is a bad idea." I spoke from experience. "They're either jealous of you 'cause you write more than them, or they taunt you 'cause you write less."

We finally parked ourselves in two over-upholstered, broken-down armchairs in the Alt.café on A. We both ordered decaf lattes while silently hoping that someone would stumble across us.

Forty minutes and two decafs later, this catty bitch named Cathy, friendlier to Zoë than me, sauntered in. She was a sculptress who never sculpted. She talked about her latest love interest—some twit named Phido—and how she was nervous he was just using her for sex.

"This is the time in the relationship when you should write down his bank account numbers," Zoë said while manically checking her makeup, "and try to get in good with his friends and parents."

"Why would I want to do that?" Cathy asked.

"That's the group he gets his opinion from. If *they* like you, *he'll* like you."

"Why the bank account?"

"I don't know," Zoë said, lifting her empty cup because it looked good, "just seems like a good idea."

"Also try to get him to a doctor for a general workup," I counseled. "You don't want someone who will conk out on you after a *Simpsons* episode."

Zoë suggested we all go to one of the local multiplexes and catch some birdbrained blockbuster, but I still hadn't gotten over the last Hollywood mega-gyp. There was no way I was going to shell out ten bucks to watch another two-hour video game. Zoë said she knew films were junk, but seeing one would give us something to gab and giggle about. Where the youths of yesteryear argued about Marxism and French philosophy, we had dumb films. She and Cathy called 777-FILM, picked a flick that started in twenty minutes, and headed over.

After the coffee shop, I browsed through several clothing stores, which confirmed that fashions didn't improve, the prices just went up. While looking through racks of "recycled vintage wear" and listening to lame nonstop rock tunes, I decided that life doesn't really get better or worse, but people do. As we get older and less naive, our expectations rise. That's when films, clothes, and other people start turning to crap. A few years ago, wandering through these alphanumeric streets, I could meet a half a dozen catty Cathys, mindlessly throw away a wallet full of cash on trashy Hollywood flicks and enjoy it all. I could wear stupid clothes, dance to studio-contrived music, meet an army of Primos and Alphonsos and Phidos, and just have a really good time. All that was over. Nowadays, if I could meet one entertaining guy, buy one self-respecting CD, find one decent, not ridiculously priced dress, and catch one engaging film per season, I was way ahead of the game.

Lightning-boltishly, I realized I had forgotten Numb. I dashed back through the audience of fashion casualties watching the live musical performance in the park and into the dogrun to find a goateed, pierced, tattooed slacker dude molesting my pup. Actually, the guy wasn't bad looking. His face came together nicely. His body was long and lanky. But the dark green tattoos that lined his muscular arms and the coil of silver earrings on both ears turned me right off. Looking up at me slowly, he asked the dog while rubbing its head, "Who's your mommy, huh?"

"Its mommy taught it not to talk to strangers," I replied with an unembarrassed smile.

"Not allowed to leave your dog unattended." He pointed to a billboard covered with rules.

"Give me a break." I took the dog from him. "I had to use the people run."

"Numb was playing solo for the past fifteen minutes," the cretin shot back. "Doesn't take that long to use the bathroom."

"You know its name?"

"'Course. Where's Primo?" His eyes searched about the teenage wasteland.

"He died. Want a dog?"

"No! Don't say that!" He started groaning and looked right

through me. Another person who made me feel emotionally superficial.

"How well did you know Primo?" I asked.

"I'd meet him here. We'd talk," he recollected. "He was living history; the guy met everyone and did everything." When he opened his mouth, I was relieved not to see a tongue stud.

"We're having a memorial," I said to prove my humility. "I'm trying to round up as many people as I can."

"Well, he was no Merlin." The tattooed man wiped a tear away.

"Who the hell's Merlin?"

"The homeless cripple on Sixth and A a few years back. You don't remember him? He used to sit in his sleeping bag reading for months on end."

"Sounds like a good boyfriend."

"Oh!" The guy spontaneously became inspired. "You should notify that blond girl, what's her name . . . Josie! He had a fling with her. I'd see them together a lot."

I didn't respond. We'd been dating for the past six months, which means he was cheating on me. I withheld my outrage and asked, "So where might I find Josie?"

"Who knows, any bar or bistro probably." Then, pausing a moment, he added, "Big dumb blond."

Glimpsing up at the billboard, I noticed one rule: "No Bitches in Heat." I was about to leave when, as an afterthought, I asked, "Do you know if Numb is a boy or a girl?"

He looked under it very carefully and declared, "Either your dog has a very small penis, or she's a girl." I thanked him and left with my girl dog.

When I finally got home, I found a message from Mrs. Schultz: "Hey, whatever your name is, I got Primo's ashes. I actually had them since Wednesday, but I just found your number. I was hoping that perhaps you could pick them up sometime."

Screw him, I thought, let Josie do it. I took a nap and had a strange dream: an attractive woman was standing completely dressed in a shower, but the shower turned into a form-fitting hole in the wet and wormy earth, and the water turned into a long black snake, maybe a python, and its long thick tail was whipping me in the face, whip, whip, whip. But it wasn't a snake's tail at all. Looking, I realized it was a man's hand. The beefy hand was smacking me while I was softly telling the man-hand I loved him. Awaking, I realized it wasn't entirely a dream. A strange voice was rambling on my machine, talking lovingly about Primo. I snatched up the phone.

"Don't hang up," I said grouchily. "Who are you?"

"This is Lydia," she replied. "Minnie Belle called and said you were looking to give Primo's ex-girlfriend a big inheritance." I considered giving her Primo's mother's address. With the fortune came the curse: she could have Primo.

"Minnie said you knew his Cambodian girlfriend."

"I'm kind of friends with Sue Wott, much as one could be. He used to call her Yoko Uh-oh, but I knew he was crazy for her. Her family made it out of Cambodia just before the Khmer Rouge killed everyone. I think he found that historical detail sexy."

"Sounds like him." He always went for women who were historically down on their luck.

"They had a real bad breakup."

"How did you know him?"

"I was her friend, but I became his paramour."

"What do you mean?"

"While he dated Sue Wott, I was a parallel lover." A hippie's way of saying he was cheating.

"You're not blond, are you?" I asked, wondering if this was Josie, the bitch in heat.

"No," Lydia replied and added, "You have to understand— Primo was a real environmental lover." I could hear that tie-dyed, self-righteous undertone in her wispy voice. "So what happened to him?"

"The medical examiner said his heart failed but didn't give a real reason."

"Alas poor Primo. All those free radicals. He was really something."

"A real asshole." I felt foul.

"You know what? I accept that," she replied. "But he was also an incredibly intuitive artist." One detail I noticed about flakes was how they hooked onto their own lexicon and were constantly using trigger words and abstract terms that sounded impressive but rarely meant anything.

"Primo had about as much intuition as a pigeon," I debunked. "And I never saw any of this bogus art."

"Not many people did." She knew better than to disagree with me. "If you're interested, I have some of his videos somewhere. I scored them with Philip Glass music and still watch them from time to time. They really are beautiful. Most were shot around sunset. The sky is incredible."

"I thought Sue Wott did all the films."

"Oh, she did," she explained. "But Primo choreographed with me, if you want to call it that. Jane Knonot in *Local Vocal* magazine called him 'the John Cage of dance,' but he was hardly that."

"Did he dance?" It was impossible to visualize him in leotards, let alone leaping around.

"If he did," she replied, "I never saw him do it."

"So what exactly did he do with you?"

"He got hold of an old camera and shot a series of videos in the summer and fall of 'eighty-five. He called them *The Elements*. He taped me with another dancer doing what he called Wave Dances. Then we did Storm Dances, Wind Dances, Sun Dances. He never got around to Snow Dances." A striptease in nature.

"Just imagine what he would have done in a hurricane," I quipped.

"Why did Primo's heart stop?" she asked. "Was it a heroic death?"

"If watching TV requires courage, it was."

"He talked about that, I think. Watching TV to death, maybe that was what he did."

"Not to sound—" I sputtered, and spurted, "How did you feel about cheating on your friend with him?"

"If you're trying to make me feel ashamed—" She finally started getting riled, but I didn't give a damn if she hung up on me.

"The infidelity doesn't bother me," I lied. "But while she was taking care of his child, you were—"

"She didn't have a kid back then. And for the record, I suspect Sue Wott knew that we were involved." She paused. "You have to understand, the early eighties in many ways were more akin to the seventies. No one had heard of AIDS or STDs. We were all trying to discover ourselves through our sexuality." She was using the generational "we," fancying herself as part of some cosmic clique.

"Do you know when Sue Wott dated him?"

"Roughly through the end of the eighties."

"When did you date him?" If that was the right verb.

"Around 'eighty-three. It was a June–October relationship. Whenever I see autumn leaves, I think of him. Would you like to know our song?"

"Not right now. I'm just trying to get a general time line of events." So there it was: while I was going to junior high, Primo was cheating on his postadolescent wife with her spacey, love-in girlfriend.

"Has there already been a funeral?" Lydia asked.

"There's going to be an ash blow." It sounded like a piñata party. "Do you know anyone else he dated?"

"Not really. I stopped bumping into him in the late eighties, when I moved to Williamsburg. I'd hear things about him from time to time, through the grapevine. The last time I remember seeing him was during his summer equinox celebration in 'eighty-nine."

"What's this?"

"He used to have equinox and solstice celebrations. Did he stop doing that?"

"He never did one while I was with him," I replied. My call-waiting beeped. I asked Lydia to excuse me a moment and switched on to Zoë. She and Cathy were in an ugly mood. They had just returned from seeing a spectacular big-budget turd. She assured me that I did the right thing by not going. Now they were going to see some crappy bands at Arlene's Grocery. Did I care to join them?

"When you're single," she explained, "you have nothing to lose."

"There was still sleep," I replied, and clicked back to Lydia.

"You wouldn't know Sue Wott's phone number, would you?" I asked, before I forgot the whole point of speaking with her.

"Sure," she said, flipping through her phone book, "but when she hears who you are, she's going to flip." She relinquished a number with a local prefix. She also took the liberty of announcing her own e-mail address, ninpoop.com, which I pretended to write down. She asked if she could have my address so that she could put me on her mailing list for the next time she had a dance performance. Sure, another postcard to throw out.

She also gave me her phone number and summed up, "Even though I hadn't really seen him in ten years, just knowing that he was out there somewhere, hustling up a buck, painting, or playing with some new rock-and-roll band, just putting his kaleidoscopic spin on things, well, for me, it's a day-to-day struggle between life and death, and life is slowly losing, you know?"

No, but yes.

She paused a minute, doing mental math, and then added, "Maybe that's how it's supposed to be. Once all the cool people that make life worth living are gone, maybe then death ain't so bad."

She hung up. I had never met the Primo these women

described. It sounded as if he had run out of Primo-ness by the time he got to me. Why did I choose a man who gave so little of himself? As I dialed Sue Wott's number, I couldn't shake this awful feeling that there was something wrong with me.

After five rings a machine picked up, and a blast of awful rock music exploded on her outgoing message, then a shrill but overly articulate voice yelled, "If you want Sue or Jane, leave a message at the beep, if it's you Chett Mazur—fuck off! In case you're lost, the audition is being held on the third floor of Context Studios." The voice said that this audition would be tomorrow between one and three in the afternoon.

I hung up before the beep. Context Studios was an old furniture warehouse that had been renovated into a recording studio/rehearsal space over on A between Second and Third Streets. Going to see her in person tomorrow seemed a lot wiser than leaving a message.

I turned off the light to go to sleep, but felt Primo lying there in the darkness next to me. I could still smell him and feel him. I wanted to simply bury him with a few tears, but nothing came. I hated myself all the more for that. Soon the dog came over and curled around me. I pushed it off the bed.

Joey rang my doorbell early the next morning, waking me up. Hearing his voice on the intercom, I buzzed him in and jumped back in bed. I could hear him walking up the rickety stairs, down my hallway, opening my front door, and entering my bedroom. He planted a cup of coffee and croissant on my end table and sat on the edge of my mattress.

"What time is it?" I mumbled, unable to focus. He was petting Numb.

"Eight-thirty?" he said, looking over at my clock radio. "I'm here to inspire you." He must have figured that I was still in my post-Primo depression.

"You're not going to tell me *crisis* is the same word as *opportunity* in Swahili, or some crap like that?"

"Not unless *dead loser boyfriend* is the same phrase as *good riddance.*"

I sat up and sniffed the coffee, grateful that he remembered I didn't take sugar and just a touch of milk.

"I never understood what you saw in him," Joey said, rising in his boots and buttoning his blazer back up.

"You just got here. Want to climb in bed?" I asked nonchalantly.

"Love to, but I got a business appointment," he said. "I just wanted to drop by."

"I should be hungry around seven, if you want to bring dinner by," I said by way of thanks and good-bye.

He smiled, and showed himself out. As if the entire occurrence were a dream, I went back to sleep.

My inner alarm clock went off at one that afternoon, and I

bounced up like a Pop Tart in an overwound toaster. I had to go to the band audition and confront the legendary Sue Wott. I pulled on my grungiest clothes, which were too tight and made me look bustier than I was, walked the dog, drank Joey's now-cold coffee, and dashed back out to Context Studios. A handwritten note taped out front read, "Auditions for Bassist for Crazed Beaut."

I rang the bell and was told to come up to the third floor. In the elevator a mix of dancers, actors, and musicians were going to various studios. I got out on the third floor, which was loud with muffled music.

"Hey," squawked an early-middle-aged woman with a long neck and round peroxided-spotted head. She was standing in the doorway of a nearby room. "What time is your appointment?"

"I'm here to see Sue Wott," I explained.

"What's your name?"

I told the ostrichlike lady and was informed that my name was not on the list.

"What list is that?"

"Aren't you here for the audition?"

"For what?"

She gave me this fed-up look, and I just knew that if I nodded anything but yes, I'd be told to fuck off, so I said yes.

"Weren't you given an appointment?" As she held up her hands, I could see every finger was hooped with a huge silver ring.

"No," I said politely, playing ball with her.

"Well, just have a seat, and if someone doesn't come for their appointment, you can fill it."

She pointed to an old sofa and vanished back behind the door of the rehearsal space. Along the couch was a squad of about six unwashed denizens seated side by side, probably wishing they could all be elsewhere. I was the oldest in the group. I noticed that I was the only one who didn't have a chewed-up bass case. I slouched against one of the worn arms of the sofa, the last place to perch.

"I'm not here for the audition," I said to the others in the group, hoping to give peace of mind to this competitive gaggle.

Before I could get too uncomfortable, the door of the audition room cracked open, and we all could hear human screeching: "I don't give a fuck how you want to play it! This is *my* audition! The day you start a band and I come for try-outs, you can tell *me* how to do it!"

"Fuck off!" Another shrill female voice rebutted. A door flew open and a Joan Jettish lookalike stormed over to the elevator, toting her bass.

Following her, a tall, slim Asian terror marched over, her hair swirling all around her like a small brunette typhoon. The anarchistic gang of bass players tightened into a unified chorus of petrified auditioners.

The bandleader marched over to us and gave a razor-slashing smile: "Let's get this straight. If any one of you can't take orders, the elevator's over there." She thumbed behind her, which was actually the opposite direction from the elevator. "You're here to do as I say. If you have any problems with that, don't waste my time."

She then turned heel, threw open the beaten plywood door that she came from, and vanished back inside.

"Fuck this." One of the girls rose. "I heard she was bonkers, but this is insane."

"You're right," another girl concurred. This one had a rainbow of dyes in the outer fringe of her volcano haircut. The two girls headed down the stairs. After a minute, a third, green-haired leaf fell from the withered tree of that autumnal sofa.

"I guess that just leaves us," I said, smiling to the two masochists seated next to me.

Just as I was about to lose the last of my courage to speak to the tiny terror, the door flipped open and the spotted ostrich chirped at me, "Hey, Natalie Merchandize! You're on."

"They're ahead of me." I pointed to the two girls seated next to me. I was hoping to catch Sue on the way out.

"We're waiting for someone in that studio," one of the girls volunteered.

"What? Why didn't you tell me?" I asked one. She shrugged; the other looked utterly vegetated. The two were shiny examples of the pernicious effects of rock and roll.

"Where's your instrument?" the peroxide abuser asked before I stepped into the tightly insulated rehearsal space.

"If I can just speak to Sue for a moment?"

"Come on." Peroxide beckoned me inside the claustrophobic chamber that was packed and coiled with cables like a satellite about to be launched into outer space. Sue and another girl were casually holding their weapons, chatting.

In every high school, each year, there is a group like this. They are the trailblazers, the first to do a variety of things that include being caught smoking in the girls' room, having sex with the bad boys, moving to the cruddy city, and if they're really lucky, like Sue, dropping a kid.

"She's the next," Peroxide introduced me as she climbed into her seat before the drums in the rear of the tiny room. "I didn't get a name."

"Shit, can't you do anything right?" Sue flicked her aside with her eyes and asked, "So who the hell are you?"

"My name is Mary Bellanova. Are you Sue Wott?"

"I don't remember a Mary Bellanova."

"I . . . I just thought if I came by—"

"Where the hell is your bass? What did you plan on doing, humming your audition?"

"No, it's just—" Only at that moment did it occur to me that I actually did own a bass: it was Primo's old instrument, still sitting in my bed room.

"Use Marilyn's," Sue Wott said. A bass case was pointed out

to me by the drummer. It looked small, black, and rectangular, like a child's coffin. I took it out and pulled the leopard-spotted strap over my neck. A small teardrop-shaped pick and two wads of yellowish gum were under it. I weighed it in my hands; it was tighter and heavier than my old folk guitar, but its weight offered a glossy authority. Placing my fingers along the neck of the bass, I pressed the strings to the frets and gently twanged them. Then I plugged a cable from the guitar to the foot pedal and made sure it was in tune, all under the scrutinizing eyes of Sue Wott.

"Ready," I said.

"This is Norma J." She singled out the ostrich lady, who was barricaded behind a stainless steel fortress of drums. I smiled meekly. She extended her drumstick for me to shake.

"Okay, this number's in E," Sue explained and pushed the play button on her demo cassette player. I listened to a bass guitar keeping beat with the drum, and I knew without a doubt that I could do it. I played with the pretaped tune for about three minutes.

"Do it against the drums," she instructed.

I did so. Sue played the tape for about five more minutes and then stopped it.

"All right," she said, "let's do it live." She turned to the girls around her; they all played together, and I joined in. After about five minutes performing, she shouted out orders: "Jazz it up," Then, "Keep it tighter," Then to me, "Play against my beat."

I did as told.

The music was so loud that every time we stopped, I heard a faint ringing. I realized I was the only one not wearing earplugs, and instantly figured out that those yellow wads of gum were old plugs. At the next break, I rolled them into tight little points and slipped them into my ear canals.

"Can you sing backup?" she asked. I nodded yes. She sang, "I wondered could he . . . get a woody?" then said, "Sing it like that when I nod my head, *capisce?*" I *capisced*. She sang the song from the top, I accompanied on the bass, and when she nodded, I sang out the refrain with Marilyn, "Could he . . . get a woody . . ."

"This isn't karaoke, do it softly," she instructed as we kept playing.

"Okay, now go down to D." The entire band went over this song a couple of times.

"Okay, play a D, but do it in this octave." Again I did as told.

After another minute she said, "Don't make it so poppy, punk it up a bit." We played it amateurishly awhile until she shouted, "More together!" We strummed to the beat of Sue's commands for about five more minutes. Looking at the blanked-out faces of those around me, I had to bite my lip to keep from smirking. All the other girls had their wills rolled, tossed, and respread into a Sue Wott's Special pizza. It didn't feel so much like a rock-and-roll audition as a drill for the West Point Marching Band.

We took a break when the lead guitarist subconsciously revolted, strumming chords against her will, asserting something strangely reminiscent of creativity. When I saw Marilyn under the bright lights of the outer corridor, I noticed the series of tiny holes around the fringes of her nose, lips, and ears. It was as though she had been run through a threadless sewing machine. It wasn't till later that I learned that she clipped enough non-stainless-steel studs and rings through her face to fill a tackle box. They had leaked into her love canal, causing toxic shock and a systemic infection. Since then she had forsworn all the hooks and barbs of piercing fashion and had decided to let her holes heal.

"Thanks for the use of your bass," I said as we returned to our places in the rehearsal chamber. Marilyn nodded silently and vanished somewhere.

"I'm sorry for yelling out there," Sue Wott announced at the conclusion of the final tune, "but I couldn't believe it. That dyed black bitch was trying to change our number as if *we* were *her* backup!"

"What nerve," I said, trying to keep my sarcasm to myself.

"What other bands were you with, hon?" The tired ostrich spoke slowly.

"I was with the Fuck Yous, and before that I was with Spontaneous Inventions," I spontaneously invented.

"I knew the Fuck Yous from the Bay Area about ten years ago," the acoustic guitarist mentioned. Aside from her seam of holes, she had a buzz cut, surrounded by a fringe of evenly longish blond hair.

"I knew a Fuck Yous from New Orleans," Sue added.

"This was a local Fuck Yous," I replied.

"You'd have to dress sexier," Sue commented, "but you know that."

"Sexier how?"

"You know, low-cut tank tops—see-thru slips are even better. Miniskirts, go-go boots, whatever."

"I don't know." I laughed, nervous.

"You got a nice body," Sue asked. "You shouldn't be afraid to put it out there."

"Could I talk to you alone?" I asked her, hoping to talk about Primo and leave.

"Not right now—I need to talk with the rest of my band, and then I'll call you back. We need a few weeks. Then I'll talk to you as long as you like."

"Fine," I replied.

As I took the elevator down and headed back home, I asked myself why I had never brought up Primo. It was the sole purpose for my being there, and I could be as assertive as the next nut. It wasn't until I got home that I fully sorted out what had happened. A touch of it had to do with Sue Wott's intimidating tone, and to some degree I enjoyed being with a clique of girls. The idea of winning any kind of contest was a real ego boost; but the bulk of it was the romantic spell that every fool in this neighborhood came under—to be in a successful rock band.

Over the course of the week, I waited for her to call to see if I was in. Yet the more I thought about Sue's call, the more I thought about Primo. All roads led back to him. Several times I lifted one of his boxes up, intending to chuck it, only to put it down again. I wanted to get on with my little life. Every night in my head I'd break up with him. And every damn morning, his cool, lifeless body was right there with me when I woke up.

Joey was immensely supportive, as usual, but I had to limit seeing him. Over the past few years, after my breakup with Greg, he attached himself as a kind of transitional boyfriend, taking me for supportive dinners and upbeat movies. Occasionally after a dinner or walk home, I would look at him with a lingering smile; once I even kissed him just a moment longer than I should have. At the end of our dates, he would tighten his face awkwardly, wish me good night, and hasten away without even a kiss. I partially held Joey responsible for my Primo relationship. Instead of properly playing the boyfriend field, I hung out with Joey far too much. I was intent on not doing that again.

Gung-hoed by Zoë the man-eating shark, I joined in her ongoing campaign to net a husband. Initially we did the bar scene—Flamingo East, 2A, Brownies, and Horseshoe. On those occasions when she finally got into a good one-on-one talk with a guy, I would grab a *New York Press* and wander off to a candlelit table. There I would fortify myself for a life of celibacy by reading the "Women Seeking Men" ads. All of them seemed cutesy variations of "SWF—Attractive, intelligent, great attitude. Will consider anyone. Just call."

Even though I could never stand them, I went to every BYOB East Village party I was invited to, which came to about one per week. I would hold a bottle and stand next to Zoë, who invariably had some guy to chat and laugh with. The challenge was in not peeling back the beer label or munching down too many chips, and ultimately in drinking the booze before it got flat and hot in my sweaty hands.

Strange fruit fell from boring trees at these weekend get-togethers. I was asked to pose nude in public by one photographer, offered a role in some off-off-Broadway play because I had "the look," and got pitched a job to work in the most cynical of all places—a video store. Even though I never really knew anyone at those parties, every guy I'd speak to would know someone I knew, and that person would invariably be someone I couldn't stand.

At one party a guy who immediately struck me as another Primo approached. He wasn't too ugly, or old, but inasmuch as he was neither upbeat, nor ever really depressed, he was on the bland side. His real strength lay in his inexplicable interest in me. We talked for the sake of talking for about twenty minutes before he finally got around to asking for my number. I asked him for his number instead.

As he scribbled it down, he blurted, "If you're not interested in me, you can just reject me now. You don't have to beat around the bush."

"Frankly," I said, speaking from under the slightly embolden-ing parasol of two gin-and-tonics, "I'm still in the rigor mortised stages of a relationship."

Smiling, he held out the torn top of a matchbook that held his lonely seven digits.

"So." I felt buzzingly courageous and decided to test him. "What exactly do you see in me?"

"Is this a riddle?"

"I know it's a ridiculous question, but do you just want to get laid or what?"

He looked at me honestly and said, "It's one-thirty in the morning, you're good-looking, you seem bright, and circum-stance has put you here. I hope that's the answer you were look-ing for." In other words—get laid.

I drank down two more G&Ts, three more than I should have. When I finally stumbled home at about five in the morning, feeling more than slightly loaded, I reviewed the "Impressions" poem Primo had written for me. He never used the word *love,* and never disclosed any of himself. It was a typical male concoction—smoke-and-mirrors flattery, three-card-monte emotions, and sleight-of-heart trickery—all designed to score. I lay in bed feeling like a supreme idiot.

I was either bingeing or purging on Primo. I had a Primo disorder. I angrily curled up in bed around my new pillow. It was the first purchase I had granted myself after he died. Drunkenly I meditated that although the cushion never gave me a Valentine's Day card, it hadn't slept with another girl, nor was it hiding some dark, mysterious history. This pillow had no veiled exes, no covert kids. I fell asleep and gave birth to bitter and forgettable dreams.

I woke up the next afternoon with a hangover spinning me like I was tied to an overhead fan. I brushed, showered, made a cup of decaf—I had read somewhere that caffeine was related to breast cancer and hypertension—and braced myself before my phone. I went through my phone book and called Primo's mother back. I was on a strange ride, believing if I tossed him to the wind, I'd be free of him forever.

"Mrs. Schultz," I began when she picked up. "I was wondering if I could pick up Primo today?"

"What time?"

"In the next hour or so," I said.

"Do you need directions to get here?" Yes. She gave me overelaborate subway instructions: Take this train to that stop, get in the second car, don't use that exit, go up these stairs, don't talk to the newsstand guy . . .

I left the house and made the mistake of walking down St. Mark's Place, the overbelly of the seedy East Village. I passed immigrants selling stupidly emblazoned T-shirts, white teenage beggars better dressed than I, tourist bars, and fast-food stands. I crossed Cooper Square to Broadway, where I almost got broadsided by one of those red double-decker tourist buses. Who let those things out of England?

While waiting on the subway platform for the train, I began noticing red spots on my skirt—someone else's bloodstains from a punkfest I attended a while ago. Even if my shirt was clean, it was way too downtown, far too trashy and revealing for where I was going. While trying to get my mind off my poor fashion choices, I realized some cute guy was circling and seriously checking me out. I looked away in perfect contempt: I'd rather never meet him and always have his love than the other way around. The distant lights of a train were visible at the end of the tunnel. A moment later its doors slid open.

The subway wasn't too crowded, but it smelled woozily of perfume and vomit. At the Prince Street stop I dashed into another car, and resentfully counted off the stops as the train slowly made its way into the middle of bulbous Brooklyn. Why did I have to come out to see this mother? I never even saw her while I dated her cheating son.

I followed the directions and finally spotted the house. It was surrounded by a brown little lawn and carless driveway. A thorny tree jutted over the bug-squished screen door. I couldn't see Primo growing up here. I checked my face in the front-door glass. I was transparent and unwashed. I rang the incredibly loud bell, fixed my lipstick, and finger-combed my lifeless hair. Soon I heard thudding sounds coming from deep inside the house, reminiscent of a B horror flick.

The door mysteriously opened, and out wafted the odor of dead pigeons—a smell I knew well from my airshaft. From out of that swampy darkness, Mrs. Schultz edged forward in her high-backed, wicker wheelchair. I was on the set of *Whatever Happened to Baby Jane?* An elderly lady, drunk on cosmetics, extended a pale gloved hand. She wore a colorful floral sundress that extended down over her knees. A white bandanna was knotted around her loose chicken neck. Her silver hair was bunned up. The woman had no real resemblance to Primo, or to anyone else I had ever met.

"You must be Primo's little pal," she said, as if to dissolve any sexual involvement, which was fine with me.

"And you must be his mother." I tried to act like a soap opera character.

"Come on then," she said, backing up her chair.

When I entered, she closed the door behind me and pointed

me down a narrowing hallway. Several dusty oil paintings were squared along the faded floral wallpaper. They depicted empty gray cement sidewalks that looked like the streets I had just passed to get there. I didn't compliment them; false flattery was my last line of defense. I wondered if Primo had painted them.

Creaking behind me in that scary chair, she herded me into a large living room. Upon the shining oak table, which smelled freshly of Pledge, sat only one stark item, a perfectly sealed package. Its dimensions were roughly six inches square. Printed on a computer label under the logo for the Malio Funeral Home (which was twined around a calla lily) was the phrase, "The Remains of Primo Schultz."

"Did you have any problem finding the house?" she asked. All I could think was, Poor Primo.

"No."

"Are you hungry?"

"No, thanks." She motioned me forward into another room. I rose and walked to a closed door. "This was his room. Open it."

I did as told and found a bruised and lonely little space, dominated by a large bed surrounded by drawn curtains. On top of the made bed and small desk were the same kind of yellow-and-blue banana boxes that Primo had left behind in my house. There was a stack of obscure magazines that included *Howard the Duck* comics and old *National Lampoon*s. In the corner was a decal-covered guitar case, also electric. Between the desk and the wall were assorted cellophane-wrapped canvases, presumably his paintings. The one noticeable omission for a Primo Schultz room was a TV.

"This is my little museum to Hal." I heard the wheelchair squeaking across the wooden floor behind me.

"Hal?"

"That was his given name." I guess I should have figured that one out. I picked up an old journal called *Trouser* magazine and flipped through it.

"I don't know what half of this stuff is," his mother said, shaking her head. "I never really went through it. I don't know if it's garbage or valuable."

"I guess it was valuable to him," I muttered without thinking.

"I mean, it really was kind of selfish for him to just die. I mean, I'm seventy-two years old, but I can't afford to die yet."

She kept talking, as if trying to make Primo's ghost feel guilty. I turned her off and scanned the room. There was evidence of a hectic, youthful life. A collection of ticket stubs on a bulletin board, tacked there hastily twenty years ago and fated to remain there for what would probably be the next fifty years. They were from various hip concerts he'd attended during the late sixties and early seventies: Television, Captain Beefheat, and Rush were among them. There was a ripped ticket to the Bangladesh Concert. None of them had admission prices above four dollars.

I flipped through what looked like the first edition of *The Whole Earth Catalogue.* Under it was a yellowing rubber-banded stack of brochures announcing:

END THE WAR IN VIETNAM RALLY
12 Noon
Saturday October 12th, 1971
Washington Square Park

It was clear that he was supposed to hand them out but didn't—probably why the war dragged on. Yellowing pages gave mini-reviews of the band he was in during the late eighties, Infant Mortality. I found a stack of cassettes, presumably a demo the band put together. The name of the tape, "DO OR DI," was printed in generic white address labels. There were cards with gilded lettering announcing a group show where his artwork was scheduled to appear, and a stack of multicolored pages entitled "THE NATIONAL POETRY MAGAZINE OF THE LOWER

EAST SIDE," dated from the early eighties. Mrs. Schultz rambled on as I kept flipping until I made a real find, a poem:

THE SUE WOTT ACHE

Despite a worldkinds telling and detailings
and meticulous recordings:
of symptoms, signs, and syndromes,
of its palpitations, pustulations and abrasions,
of its scabs, blood flows, of its impairments and impalings,
of muscular deterioration, of neurological disintegrations,
of its endless clottings, twitches, stoppings and failings,
no doctor yet can calm the pain
not even a soothing balm has been discovered
to relieve the inflamed affections
of a brusquely uncoupled lover.

It was a better poem than the one he wrote me, and now it was too late to dump him—at least figuratively. On the other side of the page was that goddamn line drawing, no different from the one of me. Instead of circular eyes, hers opened like zippers. It was difficult to believe that the rock-and-roll despot I had auditioned for—such an absolute terror—could inspire this yearning. I located another poem delightfully entitled, "Fuck You Fuck!" that read:

Go ahead—Kiss to your heart's content!
—it won't make you any goddamned younger
or any more in love.
And I can laugh much longer
while thinking how the both of you can't believe
either hasn't or will ever kiss another
to wilt and wither this one.

My eyes started growing misty as Mrs. Schultz murmured, "Christ, I'm starving. You hungry, dear?"

"Sure," I replied politely. Remaining thin and attractive in America was a chronicle of hunger.

She spun in reverse, turned ninety degrees, barely missing a glass cabinet, and zoomed into the kitchen like a Pakistani cabbie. I followed. She ordered me to take down a can of StarKist Tuna. I removed it from the cupboard, but confided to her that I didn't really want tuna.

"In my day we ate as given," she muttered, told me to open another drawer, and instructed me to take out a box of Entenmann's cinnamon rolls. She told me how to open the box. She told me where the right knife was. She told me which plate to put the boring pastry on—the china, not the plastic. She criticized me for cutting more than a proper square.

"What do you want to drink?" she asked.

"Water," I said simply, because I didn't feel like being instructed in making coffee.

She asked me to bring the dish of crappy pastry into the dining room. So I sat before her and ate the week-old cinnamon rolls as she waxed on, trying to spin Primo's death into guilt. Her life would be lonely now. Who would call her for Mother's Day? Who would come over for Christmas? In the course of the next twenty minutes, while thinking of a way to get the hell out of there, I caught a glimpse of an old photo and saw Primo wearing a sailor outfit.

"Holy shit," I said, without intending to curse. "Was Primo in the navy?"

"No, that was his father."

"Oh, yeah. He does look older."

"We met during the war," she began. "He was so handsome. But he was not a stay-at-home type."

Maybe he just wasn't the stay-with-you type, I wanted to say. "Is he still alive?"

"I don't know. We divorced soon after Primo was born." She looked out the window. "You know how it is."

"Oh yeah," I replied. Fathers in this day and age have a way of vanishing. "Frankly, I always wanted a daughter," Mrs. Schultz eventually confided. "I always liked my boy, but it wasn't easy being a single mother. It was difficult dating. If I brought home a boyfriend, Primo would have a fit. I would have to find places outside to be intimate. Primo was such a temperamental child; he had an artist's temperament."

"With all the work he did," I said, pointing toward his grim cave, "it's a damned shame that he never made it."

"Yeah, well—" She looked off in the distance. "He came pretty close."

By the sad, faraway look in her eye, I sensed that she was done socializing. I rose, looked at my watchless wrist, and declared I had a rendezvous. Mrs. Schultz nodded, picked up Primo's ashes, and was about to put them in a Loehmann's shopping bag when she paused and looked at the neat, angular box containing the remains of her only child.

"Does anyone really believe for an instant that this is all that's really left of him?" She kissed the kraft paper that covered the box, pressing her tacky red lipstick onto it, then dropped it into a bag and handed it to me.

I bowed down and gave the old lady a quick embrace, which was really just a shoulder clench. She smiled and told me not to be afraid to call if I needed anything. I promised her that I would call even if I didn't need anything, which was a bold-faced lie.

While waiting at the Brooklyn station for the Manhattan-bound train, I flipped through copies of different fashion magazines. "Are you going to buy that?" the Indian newsstand operator asked. I closed the *Elle* and walked fashionably away. I battled sadness on the trip home, yet when we finally reached Manhattan and the train started filling up, my mood shifted. I remembered the line drawing Primo did of Sue Wott with the soft narrow slits. Asian eyes, I had read, were adapted to the snow-blinding climate of frozen Asia during the Ice Age. This was my ice age. Primo's line drawing of me didn't look half so attractive as the one he did of her—the girl of his dreams and nightmares.

If this wasn't bad enough, for about ten minutes while stalled in the White Hall station, some fat old hippie made goo-goo eyes at me. His short arms were covered with old algae-colored tattoos, and his big beer belly made him look like a lecherous bullfrog. I placed the bag holding the cube that was Primo on my lap to conceal myself as much as possible. It didn't stop there. When I got off the train, up to the light of day, it was as though I was on a harassment conveyor belt. First a row of street-lunching stevedores made comments as I walked up Eighth Street toward Kmart. At Cooper Union, a man walked right behind me, chugging out a series of vile anatomical comments. Perhaps lack of exercise and crappy eating habits make a fellow horny. If this male annoyance unit had a nutritional breakdown label, his fat calories would definitely have exceeded all other items.

When I finally opened my door, the answering machine had just clicked on and was recording a message: "Good news. We've picked you."

It was the target of Primo's affections—Sue Wott. I snatched the phone off the horn and said, "Can I ask you a few questions?"

"You don't have to pay a percentage of the band's operating expenses," she explained. I could hear a kid screaming in the background.

"Is that your child?" I asked politely.

"Yes, but he's not part of the deal."

"Who's the father?" I asked in that interstice of levity.

"A man. Are you Crazy and Beautiful or not?"

"Can I think about it?" I asked, looking at myself in a hand mirror.

"No, I need an answer right now."

"Now?"

"We already booked space and have a date lined up. I would've called you earlier, but we had to hear from one last girl in the Mica Shits."

"You picked me over someone else?" I couldn't believe it.

"Sure, but they couldn't follow orders and you had bigger boobs, so you won out."

If she were male I could sue her, but because she was a brash chick I could only ask her where and when they were meeting: two tomorrow afternoon at the same studio where I had auditioned.

"And bring your own bass this time," she growled.

"Two in the afternoon! How about during weekdays?"

"We're mainly planning to rehearse in the evenings. I'll see you tomorrow." She hung up. I lay down and, while trying to decide whether or not to take a nap, I fell asleep.

It was early in the evening when Joey woke me up on my machine, saying that he heard there was a great restaurant in my neighborhood, did I want to join him. I picked up. Of course I did, only in these classy overpriced mess halls where you got to wear a nice dress and tasteful makeup and have waiters treat you like a queen, only then did I feel like I had any worth. An hour later we met outside the Gotham Diner, where he talked about the travails of his long day.

"At the collection agency?" I asked, slicing up a segment of leek in a wonderful mustard sauce.

"Yeah, it's amazing. People think they can just take the money and walk."

"How do you collect the cash?"

"Mainly through lawyers—we get a ruling, and then we'll put a lien on them or grab their wage or tax refunds."

"It sounds depressing."

"It is for them. But hey, they should be thinking about that before they place the bet."

"What bet?"

"I always think of the money as a bet. Life's kind of a gamble, isn't it?"

"You are such a philosopher," I commented. After dinner,

dessert, aperitifs, a stroll to my apartment, a walk of the dog, and television, there was the joy of sleep.

Late the next morning, I thought about looking for a better job. I also thought about shaving my legs and waxing my bikini line. Each seemed equally inconceivable. By one-thirty I was out the door, heading to the first band rehearsal of my life.

I inspected Primo's old Fender Bass. It was tattooed with odd and torn stickers. Under its neck between the last two metal frets were scratched *E, A, D, G.* I didn't have an amp, so I couldn't hear the actual sounds that twanged out. I was running late, but I grabbed a cup of coffee downstairs.

I followed the path I took to the audition, down the street, into the old building, up the rickety elevator to the third floor. The little room was like a decompression chamber, packed with three girls and their supplies. They were playing when I showed up. After they finished their little jam, Sue said, "You're allowed three latenesses, and then you get fined a dollar for every minute. That's how we do things, you dig?" I didn't respond, and she wisely didn't push it.

What the fuck was I doing here? I wondered as she screamed at Norma, "Are those drumsticks tuned up? Finding the rhythm from you is like getting a pulse from a heart attack victim."

When Marilyn started laughing at the little insult, Sue turned on her. "You came in too late and stayed too long. And by the way, we're supposed to begin at E, go up to A, and then back to E, remember?" Sue played in E on her acoustic guitar as she sang the lyrics: "Don't jerk off beforehand." Then to A—"Then go limp and blame me-e-e, man . . ."

Noticing me looking at her in amused horror, she asked, "Hey, new girl, I hope you brought your pick?"

"Cool it, cupcake," Marilyn replied.

Sue didn't respond. After this short, abusive break, equipment and people were squeezed to one side. A space was created to stand, and a worn-out practice amp was pointed out for me. I strapped on my bass and plugged it into an extra distortion pedal that Marilyn had that allowed me to modulate my sound.

Sue discussed the type of music the Beautiful and the Crazy were trying to attain; some hazy point between punk and pop. We played four songs. Even though it was my first session, and I hadn't played since college, the looseness of the band was not all my fault. Norma missed beats. Marilyn was frequently out of tune, and Sue kept forgetting her lines, which was unforgivable, considering she wrote all the damn songs.

After an hour of instrumental torture, we stumbled and bumbled through the remaining four songs. All were faintly accusatory toward men, but the level of sarcasm and wordplay redeemed them; "Colder Than a Witches Tit" and "Poontang You" were among my two favorites. One tune, "The Ache," was loosely based on Primo's insulting poem to Sue. After a second hour, when two of the simpler songs had been shaped and polished into something discernible, Norma started dropping her drumsticks. Sue called a fifteen-minute break and asked her drummer if she was able to continue. Overly ambitious, Sue had rented out three hours of rehearsal time, far too much for attention-deficit-disorder-suffering East Villagers like ourselves.

Sue gave Marilyn five dollars and told her to buy us all some coffees and a box of Pepperidge Farm cookies. I wondered where Sue got her cash, and if she was still stripping—or maybe it was from all her late fees. Before we began the second half of our rehearsal, Sue stared at my instrument. It was covered with fading and peeled decals from years gone by.

"Holy shit," she finally broke through the gaze of contemplation. "I recognize this." It didn't even occur to me that she could trace it until she said, "This is Primo's fucking Fender!"

"Primo?!" I said fearfully, and had this strange fear that she was going to throw me out of the band.

"Where the fuck did you get it?" She picked it up like an old acquaintance with whom she'd had a bad falling-out.

"He sold it to me," I replied.

"You know him?"

"Someone introduced us. He was trying to get some money quickly." I knew she'd recognize this as Primo's style.

"The bastard!"

I considered telling her about his demise—this was my opportunity to come clean—but in that instant I didn't want to jeopardize my band standing, so I innocently asked, "Did you know him?"

"Aside from being my husband through most of the eighties, he screwed two of my friends as well as my sister, who I still don't speak to." She didn't mention child abandonment or non-payment of child support, which comforted me.

"Did you love him?" No sooner had I asked this than I regretted it.

"You know what love is," she embarked as she stepped into my personal space, "Love is a contract, and he never fulfilled his part of it."

I was dying to ask her if Primo was the father of her Amerasian kid, but she clapped her hands loudly and announced that she had to talk to everyone. She filled me in on their upcoming events. In two weeks we were scheduled to play at Mercury Lounge, then a few days after that we were going to have a showcase performance with two other girl bands, including Emily's band, Crapped Out Cowgirls, and Purple Hooded Yogurt Squirter.

"Don't you think we should practice more before going out?" I asked.

"We're going to rehearse about a half dozen times before the Mercury show," she explained. Tomorrow we'd meet again.

Norma the geriatric punkster lived on Second and Seventh, so we tiredly walked east together. Sue and Marilyn, the human pincushion, headed north. Once home I checked my messages. Alphonso, the ruffian I had met in the strip joint, asked for a rematch. I was too tired to think about it.

My most wonderful and awful moment with Primo were one and the same. For my twenty-ninth birthday, only about four months ago, he took me out for one of the finest dinners I had ever masticated. It was at the Royalton in Midtown. I actually purchased a dress for the occasion. He wore a nice suit. Where he got it and what became of it afterward, I could only wonder. Knowing that I'm a closet carnivore, he ordered the most expensive cut of meat on the menu, something I never could have done without guilt.

"You have to remember this day," he said with a sneaky smile.

"I thought thirty was the big birthday," I said.

"It's really twenty-nine," he corrected.

"Why?"

"Twenty-nine celebrates the last of your twenties. Thirty is to celebrate the decade to come."

While we ate, a beautiful, heavy rain fell like a string of pearls from the heavens. Afterward we walked all the way back home down Fifth Avenue along those dark, washed, and empty streets and we only saw about two people. It was as if everyone had left the city; we were virtually alone in New York that night.

When we finally got to the front door of my apartment, he handed me a small velvet-lined box.

"What the hell's this?" I said. What I really meant to say was, Who are you? Where is Primo?

"It's a wedding ring," he said, beaming. "An expensive one, too." I later had it appraised at six hundred dollars, which for him was a moderate fortune.

"So when are we getting married?" I kidded, knowing there must be a catch.

"We just did," he explained, as we headed through the grimy hallway to the apartment door.

"Just did what?"

"No one stays married nowadays."

"So what are you saying?"

"I'm celebrating our time together. We are whatever we are. That ring commemorates these last few months together. If we last another fifty years, or break up in the next ten minutes, that ring celebrates it."

When we got inside, scented candles, expensive wine, exotic incense, intense kissing, and then better-than-average lovemaking followed. The ensuing sleep was like falling backward down a clean and bottomless elevator shaft.

Looking back at it, the whole thing, every detail, was an incredible setup. He had planned almost every move. The way a clever serial murderer carefully plots each crime, Primo had collected and stashed away his weapons of seduction. By the next morning, however, the dream was over. The prince was his old froggy self. He never did anything even remotely romantic again. I don't know how many failed relationships taught him how to play all the strings of that one orchestrated night, but it worked. It was the best evening in our relationship, or for that matter any relationship I ever endured. It was a diamond solitaire of an evening. I don't wear jewelry, so I put the ring he gave me in a special place. Initially I thought of it as a keepsake, but now it's a warning. That wonderful evening was nothing but a terrific con. I put up with relentless sloth and selfishness all in hope of just another perfect night like that—an evening that would never come.

That was why I had to ask the medical examiner if it was possible that Primo secretly knew in advance he was dying. If the answer was yes, it would have been the single cruelest act any man ever perpetrated on me. But since his death was unplanned, Primo was only another typical male who for some reason gave me one great evening and then left.

The more I thought about Primo, the more I could imagine of his yellowing past: he was nothing more than one of many skinny, shabby teens in those multipocketed green army jackets you'd see in the news footage marching in antiwar rallies in the late sixties. Or one of the nameless, faceless fans who'd crowd into the old Fillmore East and Academy of Music. Or getting beer drunk in Max's Kansas City in the early seventies, maybe even putting on bells and plats, blow-drying his hair for that sweaty bend in the late seventies and early eighties when cocaine discos were puke-chic. I could see him pressed along the velvet ropes of Studio 54, or the Peppermint Lounge or the Mudd Club, but rarely being allowed in. Just a living Xerox, a piece of human wallpaper for decor in a flashback.

The next exhausting day at work was slow. While sitting at my desk waiting for something to do, I fell into a deep and beautiful sleep. Another replacement, lower on the temping pole than I, called my name and said the supervisor wanted to see me. She was a swinish lady with a rusty tin can for a heart and a bulletproof perm. I figured that she must have seen me sleeping.

"Mary, your work here has been getting shoddy," she said, not even complimenting my snoring.

"What work?" I asked sincerely.

"The work we give you here."

"You mean Xeroxing and answering the telephone?" I asked and unintentionally yawned.

"Don't take that attitude," she replied. What attitude? It would have been a lot smarter if she said the obvious; there was no work. Sleep at home.

"So where's this heading? Am I fired?" I asked, fitting my head into her guillotine.

"I don't like this," she replied. "I hate having to let someone go. I mean, you're a good person." Her voice started breaking apart. "I've known you for a couple of months now." I couldn't believe it, the demon had a heart.

"Look, don't sweat it. I've been fired before," I consoled.

I saw tears trailing down her villainous nose. I couldn't believe she was crying. "They suck," she finally muttered.

"Who?"

"The executives here. The only reason they're forcing me to fire you now is because if they wait another two weeks, they'll be forced to give you unemployment insurance."

"That does suck." I sided with her.

"You should fight them tooth and nail," she advised. "You know what, just come in tomorrow, make them call the police on you."

"It's okay, really," I comforted her. I would have preferred if she was her usual bitchy self; then at least I could hate her. I spent the remainder of the day stealing as much stationery as I could carry. When I called home for my messages, waiting for me was a shocker: the Gregor said he was getting married, and he wanted me to attend the wedding. As if he knew about this one, there was also a consoling message from Joey, asking if I was around tonight for dinner. I called him back to accept his invitation. When his machine picked up, I said, "Dinner is fine, tell me where and when." Then I dialed Zoë and we small-talked. Several times I almost mentioned I was in a band, but I caught myself; it seemed important to our relationship to give the constant impression that I wasn't doing anything with my life. She finally mentioned there was an office party after work.

"It's not office party season," I noted. "Why is your office having a party?"

"Not my office," she shot back. "It's *Burnt Out.*" That was the hot new downtown magazine with attitude. Its guiding concept was a weekly schedule of events and places for young people to get laid.

"Is there an open bar?" I needed to know. Otherwise all I could hope for would be free back issues and that was not going to help keep me awake.

"Free domestic homegrown ale till the wee hour of seven o'clock," Seven was not a wee hour. She sounded like she was reading the description off a comp. "It's at Gulliver's. You know, the new Irish pub on Fourth."

"Let's go." At five o'clock the office door popped open like a mouth, and I was gulped down the esophagus of an elevator and dispelled out into the intestines of streets. A couple of blocks of zigging east, a couple more zagging south, a few clothing store detours, one stop at the Body Shop, and I was there.

Zoë wasn't. I considered waiting out front, but when I heard some guy say, "Hey you!" I was beguiled. It was the pierced, tattooed dog rights activist I met at Tompkins Square.

"Numb better not be alone in the run," he joshed.

"No, she's at home crapping on my floor."

"So do you work for *Burnt Out?*" he asked.

"Yeah, I pieced together the fascinating movie schedule in their last issue," I kidded.

"Did you really?" He seemed intrigued.

"I could have," I replied. "All it involves is transcribing Movie Phone."

"Listen, don't knock basic competence," he retorted. "Most people can't even pull that off."

He was right, but I still had to nod in dismay over this awful truth. Some booming rock music started playing, which instantly obliterated the fine art of conversation, and we spent the next few minutes trying to communicate in charades. I was sure that living in New York had destroyed at least 20 percent of my hearing as I found myself repeatedly saying, Huh? and What? Finally, through silent consent, we elbowed our way up to the swarmed counter. Both of us drank the one free beer they had on tap.

"What are they celebrating anyway?" I shouted, still wondering where Zoë was.

"This," he shouted back, holding up the ale in the colorful plastic. "It's a promotion for the new line of beer." It figured. Since no one ever did anything in this city of millions, there was nothing to really celebrate but celebration itself. If this city was truly drained of all these act-alike morons who never tried to do anything important with their lives, there would be no apartment crisis. In fact there wouldn't be a city; there'd be about eight interesting, hardworking people who probably would be all jealous of and mean to each other. Since I wasn't one of those chosen eight, I wouldn't be here either. This compelled me to scream to the tattooed freak, "Are you some kind of artist type?"

"Sure," he replied over the ridiculously loud music. "There's a lot of artist hype!"

I was beginning to suffer the claustrophobic pang that comes with speaking to a stranger for too long. I feared that he might believe in some way I was beholden to him for the remainder of the party. Before I could find any graceful way of departing, he managed to extract two more plastic cups of beer out of the fray. I chugged mine down quickly.

"You know," I said, feeling the reckless effects of the dark brown ale, "if you take all those ridiculous pins out of your ears, and have those tattoos zapped off with lasers, you wouldn't look half bad."

He nodded yes, pretending to hear. I no longer felt bound to him, just the beers. This time I reached into the piranha tank and escaped with two more drinks. When I handed him a cup, he mouthed the word *thanks.* We knocked glasses and drank.

"Forty years ago," I piped up, "you'd be a beatnik. Thirty years ago, you'd be a hippie. Twenty years ago you'd be a John Travolta clone." He nodded and reached into the throng of arms and hands and pulled out yet two more beers. We were really on a roll.

Zoëlogy finally pulled up alongside. But it was just after seven, and the beer now cost ten bucks a cup.

"I'm getting the hell out of here," she declared, not aware that I was liquored up and linked to a tattooed man.

"Hey, I know you," Tattoo Man said to her with a big drunk smile.

"Who the fuck are you?" she shot back.

"He's with me," I hollered. The CD player stuck, hiccupping the same musical syllable over and over. Zoë growled, turned angrily, and pointed toward the door. I headed out, and Tattoo Man followed.

"I didn't want beer anyway," she said grumpily once we were outside.

"What happened?"

"The bitch at work insisted that I stay late, she said I wasn't working hard enough."

"The bitch set you up," Tattoo Man responded thoughtfully.

"I got canned, but I joined a band," I rhymed accidentally, divulging my secret.

"What brand?" Tattoo Man said, still suffering eardrum trauma.

Drunkenly I realized that if I gave the whole tale of how I joined a band just to meet one of Primo's exes, I'd sound insane, so I airbrushed my remark. "Delmonte is a brand, but I was canned from my job."

"I know about a job in publishing," Tattoo injected. Both of us ignored him.

"I'm starving," Zoë moped.

"Me too," I said, drunkenly empathetic.

"I have a friend who cooks at Veselka," the drunken man said. "I can get us some retail food."

"Veselkbucks?" Zoë said. A movement of inveterate invertebrates had been calling it that since the old diner had morphed from the greasy old Eastern European dive into the greasy new overpriced dive.

"I can always go for pierogis," I heard myself drunkenly say.

Like a toxic fog, we drifted east to Bowery, pausing briefly in front of Bowery Bar for any celebrity sightings, and then twisted north. While we walked, Zoë talked to me about how much she hated her boss, her work, and men in general. Occasionally when Tattoo Man would try to insert a remark, she would make insulting remarks and mimicking faces when he wasn't looking.

"You know what I like about you two?" Tattoo coughed up, when we reached the corner of Seventh Street. We listened, waiting to be praised. "You aren't those aerobic-neurotic types that work out at the twenty-four-hour Crunch on Lafayette all night."

"Are you saying we're fat?" I asked, always braced for an insult.

"Not at all."

"What's the matter with you anyway?" Zoë said, still angry about missing out on free booze. "Why are you so eager to fatten us up at Veselka?"

"I'm not eager." He threw up his skinny hands.

"Then why d'ya say we aren't thin when we are?" I slurred.

"I just saw that girl pass, and—" His finger stabbed the air.

"What girl?" Zoë demanded, her suspicion heightened to near paranoia. Both of us were craning about for this phantom rival.

"What's your name?" I asked, not meaning to sound menacing, but sounding it nonetheless.

"Howard."

"What a jerky name!" Zoë fired back. "How old are you anyway?"

"Twenty-ninish."

"What's all the crap on your arm?" I asked callously, inspecting the tattoos. "Looks like gangrene—chop it off."

"We're thirty, How-wa-a-ard!" Zoë ranted. She was averaging because I was still twenty-nine but she was thirty-one.

"Do you like older women?" I slapped him on the arm.

"Hey!" He rubbed his shoulder.

"Hay is for horses," I kidded as he stepped away from us nervously.

"Where you going, Twenty-nine?" Zoë said, turning his age into his nomenclature. She advanced while he tripped backward. Since he was tall and lanky, the kind of person who *did* work out at Crunch at all hours, he twisted around like a snake and bounced back to his feet, prancing away like an upright horse down Seventh toward Second Avenue.

"Hey!" I called out, confused by it all. "Where the hell does he think he's going? Get him!"

"You promised us a fucking meal!" Zoë galloped after him, giving her own rogue twist to corraling a man.

"Get the hell back over here!" I screamed, and started laughing at the ridiculousness of it all. I was too drunk and filled with pee to press on. Zoë, however, was not amused. She continued after him. As he raced by McSorley's, the asshole jock bar of all time, a fratty group of thugs spotted Zoë running after him, with her long mane of blond hair trailing. One of them grabbed Tattooed Howard and pinned him against a sports utility vehicle.

"He stole your purse?" the lead date-rapist type asked.

"Yeah!" she said, trying to catch her breath.

"No, I didn't!" Howard replied, holding his arms up.

As one of the frat brothers pressed the poor Tattoo Man's throat against the car door, a bigger one looked over to Zoë as if her blond feathery hairdo was God's evidence that she could tell no lies.

"He owes us a meal," she explained earnestly, which was sort of true.

"What's this, dine and dash time?" one of the secondary jocks said to Tattoo Man.

"I didn't eat a thing," he said, still waving his hands up.

Another suburban dude reached into Howard's pants, pulled out his wallet, and took out all his paper cash, handing it to Zoë.

"That's mine. You're robbing me," Howard clarified.

"Just ten bucks should do it," Zoë said, "Two plates of pierogis." She took the ten dollars and instructed them to put the wallet back in his pocket and send him on his way.

"Come on," one of the frat boys called to Zoë from halfway up the block. "Come in here, we'll buy you a drink."

"Thanks," she yelled back without turning around. "But I don't drink with assholes."

It was the first time I ever saw her refuse male attention.

"He was just so smug, wasn't he," Zoë said more than asked. Smugness and glibness were egregious sins to her, the uncrowned princess of insecurity.

"You mugged him," I said, still laughing but dismayed by the weird spectacle.

"He'll get it back." She was mildly amused yet still pissed.

"When? How?" I asked, staring across the street at Cooper Union.

"Karma," she replied, as though this Buddhist notion were some kind of vast ATM system that collects and dispenses money according to fairness without so much as a fee. I was still snickering at the event, drunkenly muttering about being arrested for robbery, when I looked over and realized that poor Zoë was crying.

"What's the matter, hon?"

"I'm just pissed that I missed the bar."

"Really? You're crying 'cause you missed free beer?"

"No, the goddamned temp supervisor cow yelled at me in front of everyone and called me lazy."

"You're *supposed* to be lazy. You're a temp!"

"It's more than that. It's everything. Bullshit life. No boyfriend. Past thirty. Nothing." She recomposed herself, and we both decided we weren't hungry after all. We walked around the flat, overly-hyped East Village and agreed that they should just turn it into a big boardwalk and amusement park. We made another right down Third Avenue, passed the cruddy peeling tenements, made a right on Fourth Street, passed pods of business school graduates thrilled to be dining like artists in the Bohemian

Village. As we walked down Fourth we passed the last enclave of street Latinos, holdouts from the old East Village days. Ultimately we wound up at the same corner we started from, on Fourth and Bowery, walking in a large pointless rectangle.

"You know," I finally got around to saying what was on my mind, "what you did to that guy was . . . well, I see him at the dogrun all the time."

"I know," she replied.

"How do you know?" I asked.

"I don't know, I just know," she replied, taking out her compact and fixing her makeup to cover her tearful microburst. "I see him around too."

"Well, he really isn't a bad guy. So the next time I take Numb for a walk, I'm going to give him the ten bucks back." She understood what I was getting at. Opening her purse, she took the ten dollar bill out and shoved it in my palm.

We didn't talk about anything for a while as we floated like barges down the car-streaked streets. I intuited we were pondering variations of the same question: If we lived our standard seventy-seven years, we would be dead by about 2050, and what difference would it make?

"Oh! You want to see the Captain Kangaroos?" she said excitedly.

Maybe we weren't wondering the same thing after all. She remembered that this hot new local band was playing at Coney Island High that night, so we headed over there. But it turned out the Captain Kangaroos were playing at Mercury Lounge, so we headed over there. When we arrived, through the small group of people orbiting outside, I spotted Bobby Sox, the tall, sexy black man who worked the door. We exchanged hellos, and Zoë gave him a kiss. In his deep, bellowing tone, he said he had heard the unfortunate news of Primo's premature passing and expressed his condolences. I thanked him and ventured inside. Zoë stood around and flirted with him awhile. The price of all the free beer was stoically waiting on the bathroom line for about ten minutes. When I finally relieved myself and exited, I found Zoë returning from the tiny auditorium in the rear. She explained that the band had already played, and they were now putting away their instruments.

We broke apart for a while, and each of us greeted our own small clique. For me that involved two girls, Lizzy, one of the few genuine female waitresses among the gang of transsexuals at either Stingy Lulu's or Lucky Chang's, and a righteous black mama, Vivica, whom I recurrently met on the party circuit. Each of them was one spoke of a separate wheel of people who had come to see the band du jour—the Captain Kangaroos. Now all were clearing out. I also spotted my bandmate Marilyn and dodged her, lest Zoë come over and discover my bandification.

In a few minutes I was sitting alone, sucking an overpriced, watered-down gin and tonic through a tiny red straw as some underage MBA hit on Zoë. I watched her in the distance talking, nodding, smiling, nodding, smiling, slowly reeling this guy in like a two-hundred-pound fish on a hundred-pound line. The guy was wearing a formal suit; other than its artificial claim to power, it hid the fact that he looked about thirteen years old. This manboy was Zoë's ideal of masculinity, some adolescent sadist to dominate her. I could see what was going on in that hormonally imbalanced head of hers. Despite the fact that she was the most cynical of all East Village's jaded and alabastered creatures, she secretly went bonkers when the film *Titanic* came out. She looked like a bloated, peroxided Kate Winslet, and this freaky kid was her asymmetrical, problem-skinned Leonardo DiCaprio.

As the beer from the *Burnt Out* party finally wore down in my system, but before the G&Ts could kick in, I began to feel pissed off at Zoë for all the venom she'd shot at Tattoo Man. I was just starting to feel attracted to him. Despite all the dye in his skin, I liked the way he looked, the way he got me beer without my asking, and the fact that he let me recreationally attack him, which was my principal source of amusement with most people these days. Now that Zoë was free of all her sourpuss anger, she was receptive to this cardboard cutout in a suit. In the back room, after the Captain Kangaroos left, there were three other bands playing that night. The first two bands had electric banjos, and they sucked. The last one, which featured a moaning sound track, sucked even worse.

We were better than them, I thought before I could catch myself, referring to the Beautiful and the Crazy. As my energy dipped amid the lullaby of explosive tunes, I found myself drifting off to sleep.

"You know, you'll get a job without any problem." Zoë had appeared out of the darkness. She must have presumed that my slumber was born of depression about losing the crappy job. Behind her, like a six-foot puppy dog, was the suit boy. She was holding his hand like a leash.

"You're looking for a job?" the suit asked in a reedy, arrogant little voice. "I'm the manager of the Kinko's on Houston Street. I have a day shift that just opened. You can work for me." Ugh!

Behind the suit was a grinning Asian man who kept staring at my worn-out shit kickers. I wasn't sure if he was friends with someone, so I didn't respond, and he eventually receded back into the void.

"Oh, giving her a job would be so wonderful," mooed Zoë to her latest love farmer. She was taking intermittent sips from his Sam Adams.

"It's not the job that depresses me," I finally revealed. "It's Primo."

"That was her ex-boyfriend," Zoë updated her nitwit.

"I mean, his dog, his belongings, even his remains are in my apartment. I can't get rid of him. Even his exes seem to be everywhere. And he was such an asshole. I found out he was cheating on me."

"What are you talking about?" she asked.

"Tattoo Man said he slept with some dumb blond named Whorzy." I appropriately mispronounced the offending name.

"You're kidding!" Zoë said and started laughing.

"What's so funny?"

"I wasn't laughing in amusement." She paused. "Forget it."

"Forget what?" I asked.

"You know what you should do?" Zoë began again, but laughing again, she caught herself, covering her mouth. "I can't say it."

"What?" asked her postadolescent poster child. She whispered into his ear for about ten minutes.

"Tell me," I said, not really interested.

"It's way too wicked," the suit deemed. "It's the kind of thing you'd regret in the morning."

"Let *me* regret it," I said, resenting the fact that Zoë had sacrificed me so that she could get closer to this Retardo Leonardo.

"Where do you take dogs?" he hinted, adorably in the know.

"The pound?" I guessed.

"No! the dogrun." Zoë snickered. "You should dump Primo's ashes in the dogrun!"

"Yes!" I screamed. It was so perfect. I bolted up. "Let's do it right now!"

"You can't do it now," the suit replied. "The park is closed."

Closing Tompkins Square Park was the basis for a bloody police riot ten years ago, but I didn't give a damn. "I'll pay the fines if we get caught."

"Let's go," Zoë said and gulped down the remains of his beer. We dashed out the door across Houston and up First Avenue, sprinting the entire way as though we might forget the idea.

As we passed through the streets, I learned that the suit's name was Jeff and that he was dressed in Geoffrey Beene. I asked them to wait downstairs and dashed up. When I threw open the door, the dog barked and cried and did a two-legged jig around me as I fumbled for the boxed Primo. I was about to slam the door behind me when Numb dashed out, so I brought her with me, down the stairs, and out the front door.

We scurried through the Eastern European housing projects snaking along the bench-lined walkways where old ladies kvetched about their aches and pains all day. We hurried down Fifth Street between First Avenue to A and then north, passed the all-night Korean mega-market, and arrived at the closed gates of Tompkins Square Park. Although I hadn't brought a leash, Numb was good about not crossing the streets without me.

There were still a lot of people hanging out on the southwest corner of the park, and we didn't want to get arrested, so we headed down Seventh Street, up B, and finally came to the dissolute eastern border on Ninth Street, where the dog was narrow enough to squeeze through the vertical bars. Zoë and I leaned forward and flopped over the chest-high gate. When Jeff jumped over, his suit jacket flapped open, and on his nice blue shirt I saw the word *Kinko's* sewn over the right pocket in bright blue thread.

"This alone is a sixty-dollar fine," he pointed out nerdishly.

At about a hundred feet into the park we were in the dogrun, and I took out the brown sack filled with Primo. As I carefully cut the tape and began tearing into its layers, Numb dashed around, sniffing traces of piss and crap. Finally I removed the cardboard box. Inside, a heavy glass jar held his remains.

"Maybe this isn't such a good idea," Zoë uttered, perhaps sobered by the desolation of the park.

"Why not?" Jeff shot back.

"He was also capable of being quite sensitive." Zoë grew maudlin.

"Oh, please," Jeff replied. "He was a mega-sleaze."

"You didn't know him!" I snapped. "He was twice the man you are!"

"Hey, lighten up!" said Zoë. "He was just trying to be supportive."

"At least he was an artist, not some wannabe accountant."

"Screw you," the suit shot back. Even in my rage, I noticed his lack of imagination in returning an insult. "Just because I'm wearing a suit, I'm guilty. For all you know, I'm an unemployed poet who just left a funeral."

"He's right, you know." Zoë stood by her just-met man. "You're thirty years old. Time to get over the 'down with the establishment' crap."

"I'm twenty-nine and don't need to hear some yuppie-looking geek judging someone he didn't even know."

"No one ever uses the term *yuppie* anymore," she *re*-replied.

"Screw this!" Jeff stuck by his trusty catch-all phrase.

"Relax, both of you," Zoë said, but it was too late.

"No! Screw this! I don't need this." Jeff marched out of the dogrun and back over to the gate.

"Goddamn it, Mare! I liked that guy," Zoë said.

"Hey, at least I didn't mug him for ten bucks."

She turned and rushed out, pursuing her Lego Blocks boyfriend. I was glad to be alone with Primo and his dog. I unscrewed the top of the heavy little jar and looked inside. He looked like some kind of powdered mix. But even if by adding water and stirring I could bring him back, I wouldn't. I considered resealing the jar and heading home. But impulsively, I tossed the powder into the air. Numb thought I was playing and jumped into the cloud that was Primo. With her canine jaws wide open, the dog got a mouthful of her old owner. Then Numb looked around, puzzled at how something that seemed solid one minute was invisible the next. She shook off the powder and sniffed about. Primo was now a permanent part of the dogrun.

When I heard a distant siren, I feared that we were going to be arrested. I collected all the incriminating evidence—container, box, and wrappings. Numb and I left the run. En route, I stopped at the big Korean mart and, as if I hadn't consumed enough booze, bought a bottle of Miller Lite. I opened it and took a long swig as a cop cruiser passed down A. It slowed to a halt in front of me

"Hey, lady," called the cop on the passenger side. Except for a couple late-night stragglers, the street was empty.

"What?" I asked and wondered how in the world he could have known I was in Tompkins Square Park.

"You got some kind of ID?"

"What did I do?" I said, earnestly. Femininity was a useful tool that, unfortunately, I had simply run out of at the moment. Straightforwardness was allowed at times. Wit, however, always threatened them.

"No open liquor." He pointed to my bottle. This "quality of life" law was suddenly being enforced along with other statutes that had been notoriously overlooked for prior decades. Harvard Professor Wilson's landmark study concluded that if you scratch a petty criminal, a hardened felon lurks underneath: ergo, no beer. The cop told me to pour it out. I just did as told. No sudden moves. It wasn't worth arguing with the police. Primo used to say they always won and sometimes left you aching.

"What's your name? If you don't have any outstanding warrants, I'll let it walk with a warning." He was merciful. I stated my name, which he slowly typed into his little dashboard computer.

As I waited for the result, I noticed CPR decaled on the side of his new white squad car: *Courtesy, Professionalism, Respect.* That was all I ever wanted from a boyfriend. Since I had no bench warrants for turnstile jumping or jury evasion, he let me loose.

"Is that your dog?" The doughnut dipper pointed to Numb, who was leaving her urinary tag on the side of his car.

"Did she crap?" I asked, looking around for a turd to fetch.

"No, but she's supposed to be on a leash."

"Oh, yeah. I have it at home."

"Well, walk it home by its collar, or I have to fine you."

I was just a grab bag of illegality tonight. I demonstratively held the dog that Tattoo Man declared as a female. The cop drove off, having made the city a better place. The dog looked up at me sadly like she'd done something wrong. I gave her a hug and let her go with a warning. Together we walked home.

The next day I woke up early but had no job to go to, so I went back to bed. I got up again in the early afternoon to the phone ringing.

I helloed groggily.

"Hey Mary, it's time for our second date."

"Fine," I said without the slightest clue of whom it was. "When and where?"

"You tell me?"

"Dinner?" I asked and wondered if it could be someone I knew from school.

"Dinner sounds great," he replied. I wondered if I had ever slept with whoever this was. "Where shall we dine?"

"Where did we dine last time?" I inquired, figuring that might release the necessary information.

"You mean the Thai place?" he shot back. It was Alphonso the Inheriter, the paranormalist I met in the strip club.

"Let's not go there again. How about somewhere in the area? How about seven o'clock at the Sushi Garage between First and Second Avenues."

"I don't know it."

"You can't miss it. It's a big garage on the south side of the street. Oh, but I have rehearsal at ten o'clock, is that okay?" In other words, are you going to be pissed for buying me dinner without so much as the possibility of getting to first base?

"That's all right, if we can get together by seven."

"See you then."

Soon as I hung up, I suffered the acute and divine epiphany of being jobless. It was the modern equivalent to what medieval monks recorded after weeks and even months of starvation and sensory deprivation. I lay in bed and watched the moments break into phenomenal particles of panic and could actually see the divine crack of God's ass as he completely turned his back on me. I rose, dressed, grabbed doggy, and went to the ATM where I checked my balance. Doing some basic math, I realized that I had about three weeks before I would be in debt. I got a *New York Times* and a cup of coffee and brought the dog back home. Flipping through the classifieds, I looked for employment. I saw a couple of lousy-looking, tele-sale jobs and realized that this was going to be a real disaster. I cringed at the thought of having to start the whole job search again, updating my bogus résumé, finding a costume that made me look responsible and professional, and then, worst of all, making calls and going for torturous interviews. Instead I turned on the TV and watched some white-trash sex nuts charging at each other on the *Jerry Springer Show.* For all the country's political sensitivity and moral outrage, we secretly hungered for pornographic gladiator fights. Numb put her chin on my knee just like she used to do with Primo.

Bored, I decided to peek into Primo's stack of banana boxes. I opened the top one. It mainly contained his clothes: novelty T-shirts that said things like "I'm with Stupid," endless plaid flannel shirts, boxer shorts, and various distressed denims. The second box was filled with "edgy" trade-size paperbacks that every cool dude in this neighborhood owned; the banal Beats, the usual hip crime novels, Charles Willeford and Jim

Thompson. At the bottom of the box, predictably, was a half-drunk pint of Jack Daniels. The last banana box contained his files: letters, articles, photos of him posing playfully with various strangers in front of local landmarks—the black cube, the old Orchidia restaurant on Second Avenue and Ninth, the old Saint Mark's Theater. There was a newspaper clipping depicting him raising his fist defiantly during one of the Tompkins Square protests. I found a birthday card from Sue dated 1982, wishing him a Happy Thirtieth. When I did the math I instantly realized with horror that he was forty-six. Then I located a second birthday card from someone named Reno, also wishing him a Happy Thirtieth. This card was dated 1986.

Evidently he had rolled the mileage meter back more than once. Toward the bottom of the box I unearthed another birthday card—from 1973—which wished him a Happy Thirty-Two, and I knew for a fact that he wasn't that old. He had rolled the mileage forward as well. I excavated a small yellow envelope that contained diamond-shaped blue pills. Upon rolling them into my palm and inspecting them, I concluded that they were relatively new. I wondered if they were some kind of recreational drug or a medication. I slipped them in my shirt pocket, intending to check them out.

I kept digging through the box, sifting through scraps, articles, bills, receipts, and clippings. To my surprise, I ferreted out a yellowing manuscript held together by a broad rubber band. It appeared to be hand-typed and was entitled *Cuming Attractions,* by "Primo Teev." Real clever. As I flipped through it, scanning some of the pages, I saw that it involved two girls, Daniella and Virginia, and some lecherous downstairs neighbor, Floyd. Occasional passages of florid prose leaped out from the otherwise crass and mechanized pornography. The copyright date at the bottom of the first page read 1979. The final page was numbered 256. On top of everything else, Numb's old owner was a pornographer, making me feel gladder still that I had expelled his lusty dust in the dogrun.

I turned the TV back on and again picked up the classifieds, but it felt like a weight in my hands. How long could I exchange the priceless years of my youth into thirteen-dollar-an-hour pay-checks and grind that into nothing? I felt like I was paying my dues over and over for a membership into hell. Primo's death had truly smacked me with the awful realization that all life even-tually comes down to is an unexpected fuck-you ending.

The one awful option to sidestepping the hell of tall glass skyscrapers and stilted behavior was the Kinko's on Houston Street. I could apologize to suit boy and work with a crew of Gap Kids, five and ten years younger than I, Xeroxing documents mindlessly. At least I wouldn't have to totally restrain myself, because losing that job wouldn't really matter.

I picked up the phone and called Zoë's work number. Someone else picked up her line, another temp who was prob-ably temping for a temp. When I asked for Zoë, I was told she'd been shipped upstairs with no forwarding extension.

"Damn."

"She'll be back down here briefly in about a half an hour to collect her things, but then she'll be going right back up," the temp added.

"Can I leave a message?"

"An incredibly short one." I could hear other phones ringing in the background. I asked for her to call me. Then I dressed and went out to the kitchen to see if my never-present roommate had left any interesting tidbits in the fridge. On rare occasions, there was a box of cereal and I could usually sneak a cup without her noticing it. But as I helped myself, the dog started jumping underfoot, almost knocking me down. She was stir-crazy and desperately wanted out.

"All right," I finally conceded. It was inhumane to ignore her.

I tried leaving a message on Zoë's home answering machine, but even that wasn't picking up. I didn't want to miss her. So in case she called me, I left a message for her on my outgoing message: "Zoë, I'm sorry about last night. I was just depressed about being unemployed. I was wondering if you could help me by calling Jeff and seeing if I can still get that job at Kinko's he mentioned. Thanks." Beep.

Numb was deliriously happy when I clipped her leash on, bouncing around the apartment as if she were having an epileptic attack. Once downstairs, Numb pulled immediately to the right, while I wanted to go left. I bought a cup of coffee at the Arab newsstand and headed toward Tompkins Square Park. Due to Numb's fetishistic sniffings and pissing, I kept getting yanked by the leash, spilling hot coffee on my hand and wrist.

"Goddamn it!" I finally screamed after a searing burn. I yanked the leash so hard, I unintentionally flipped the poor creature into a backward cartwheel. I rubbed her while profusely apologizing. I simply didn't have the patience to handle a pet. Numb, however, looked up at me with such incredible forgiveness. Even though the dog was thoughtless and egotistical, she had the profound gift of being able to absolve sins, something most people couldn't do. This compelled me to kneel down and give the beast a hug. We finally walked the remaining distance, and I let her loose in the run.

From the benches inside, I spotted the unchained chain gang—at least, that's what I called them. They were a dispirited collection of young men and women who marched out of the park's sole administration building. All wore plastic red vests and dragged bags or brooms. They separated to clean the four corners of the park. When I first spotted this battalion of civic workers, I thought they were volunteers, but upon close inspection it was obvious that they lacked the prerequisite zeal, and I never saw the same worker twice. One member of this club, a girl who looked to be in her late teens, opened the dogrun gate with one of her canvas-gloved hands, while in the other she carried a black plastic bag. I watched her as she walked around collecting garbage that got blown behind the benches. I was seated in a section away from most of the other owners as she came by. When she looked at me, I gave her a friendly smile and said, "Mind if I ask you something?"

"Shoot."

"Are you serving a community service sentence?"

"Yeah, for a few weeks."

"What was your crime?"

"Prostitution violation," she said matter-of-factly. I nodded sympathetically. "But, hey, I'd rather be out here working on my tan than inside some bullshit office somewhere."

She made community service sound even better than temping. She asked if I had a cigarette. I told her I didn't, and wished her well. She walked off, finished her rounds, and exited the run.

After ten minutes, Numb came running to me, hiding behind my legs. A long, bony dog that looked more like a fish with legs, maybe a whippet, came trailing after her. The anorexic canine kept sticking its pointy probe of a snout up poor Numb's wide ass until it had enough. I was half hoping to meet with the Tattooed Man—Zoë's mugging victim—so I could apologize, but he never showed up.

When we got back home, I found my message light blinking and hit the replay. Zoë intoned, "All is forgiven. Go to Kinko's and make copies."

She was going to call Jeff to secure the job. This gave me about five seconds of delight until I realized that it meant I'd be working at Kinko's.

"Hi Mary," the next message unspooled, "this is Joey. How about din-din tonight?" I left a message on his machine that I had a date tonight, but we had to get together soon. I needed him to have me psychiatrically cosigned as non compos mentis and assume legal guardianship for my joining of a band just to meet an ex's ex. Does a double ex cancel itself out?

I headed down to Houston and walked a couple of blocks east to the strange new apartment building, Red Square. It had a clock tower with its digits all screwed up and a ten-foot statue of Lenin inciting the slacker masses from its rooftop. On the ground floor was Kinko's. Jeff was wearing his official light blue cotton button-down shirt with the Kinko's logo. He probably had a cabinet full of them. How did he resist the temptation to sew a *y* over the *o?*

"Jeff?" I called out to him as he was replacing the ink cartridge of one of the machines.

He came over and softly said, "Zoë called."

"I want to apologize about last night," I commenced insincerely. "I was pissed and drunk, I'm really sorry. You were right about me being an idiot to judge you."

"I figured you weren't feeling well." He smiled coolly as if I were an annoyed customer. "The pay starts at eight bucks an hour, but we have a graduated pay scale, and you can work your way up."

"Sounds good," I lied. A loud electromechanical squeal sounded as if James Cameron's Terminator had just been bit in two by Steven Spielberg's Great White Shark.

"Christ, Lionel, what in the hell are you doing!" he shouted to one of the Kinkettes manning a large machine that looked like a space-age washer and dryer. Jeff popped open the hood of the apparatus, made some mechanical adjustments, closed the top, and came back over to me.

"That Lionel is not the shiniest lure in the tackle box," he said, amusing himself greatly.

As with all of Zoë's boyfriends, I did not like this guy. He gave me some forms to fill out and told me to "report" for work the next morning. Nine to five, Monday through Friday. I would come to work, I thought to myself, but I didn't *report* for anything.

I had some time before my dinner with Alphonso, which I used to review my latest literary endeavor about two salespeople who fall in love while working at a Gap. I worked in a Gap clothing outlet for two weeks during my junior year, but only began writing the story recently. It was a silent scream of working with all those gapheads. The two characters talk compulsively about clothes, cut, color, and fabric, but are unable to communicate about much else. The redeeming quality that keeps them together is that they both suffer the same emotional limitations. They end up going to the guy's apartment. With its polished wooden floors and recessed lighting, it looks like a Gap store. The girl just happens to have with her an album of photos filled with her friends, who all look like Gap models, just sitting expressionlessly against white backdrops. One friend looks exactly like Kate Moss. After tediously discussing courduroys versus khakis and denim jackets versus leather, they end up folding into each other, having wrinkle-free, drip-dry sex. Both fake loud orgasms and shortly thereafter get married. However, they never have sex again. (Both secretly hate its wild messiness.) But they do forever share a love of pocket Ts in assorted colors and jaunty baseball caps.

At seven I glopped on some blush and eyeliner to convince the world I was a female and headed out. The handsome fraud was standing in front of the place with a mixed bouquet of flowers—four bucks at the Korean greengrocers. I didn't mean to be an ingrate, but I didn't want to tote them, nor did I own a vase.

We went into the Sushi Garage, a former plumbing supply warehouse, and ordered some sushi rolls and saki. He talked about some action movie I would never see while I dipped my sushi pieces in a blend of green mustard and soy sauce and gobbled them down. Then he ate while I talked about being in an all-girl band. He smiled and nodded, not particularly interested. After we were done, the waiter put down the check, Alphonso put two brand new swollen-headed Andrew Jackson bucks down, and out we walked.

"Where's a good bar?" he asked.

It was eight-thirty, and I had to be at rehearsal by ten, with no interest in fuzzing myself with booze. Figuring that he seemed safe and looked cute, I took a risk.

"Want to come up to my place?"

"Sure," he replied.

As we headed upstairs, I reminded him that I had to attend band practice tonight, so we'd have to end things early. He said fine. As soon as we were in my apartment though, he grew somber. The dog raced up but was reluctant to lick him, just giving him a weird eye.

"Does he bite?" Alphonso asked. I told him no.

"You mind putting him in the bathroom?" He got right to the point, which I half-liked and did. We went into my room, sat on the couch, and looked at each other. I knew exactly what he was thinking: How could he go from this awkward silence to kissing? From kissing things were clear: feeling, stripping, and sex. But how do you get into the damned kissing, especially if there is no precedent? As best as I could recall, all we did on the last date was rub.

"You mind if I turn on the TV?" he asked, which turned out to be a stroke of genius. I consented, and he did. A video compilation called *Animals That Attack* was on. It was a collection of scenes in which animals attacked people, but not too seriously. Each time an animal took a chomp at a human I jumped back, inadvertently grabbing him, which allowed him the opportunity to do likewise. At a commercial I realized that during the frenzy of ferocious bites and maulings, he had slipped a hand on my breast.

"I should produce a show called 'Hands That Attack.'" He removed the sneaky hand.

"Can I kiss you?" he asked.

"Well, let's see." I picked up a copy of *YM* magazine that somehow had found its way into my house, and pretended to read aloud from an article: "'How to break past that awkward opening to the first kiss. Be playful, and amid a flurry of jokes and giggles he can slip you a kiss. Or with a few inexpensive scented candles and soft music, set up a more romantic mood so he can gently kiss you on the lips."

"Where does it say that?" He looked over my shoulder.

I looked up, and he realized I was joking. He nodded awkwardly, and we waited, as though for a bus.

Finally he cleared his throat and said, "How many Vietnam vets does it take to change a lightbulb?"

"I know that one," I replied.

"You weren't there, man!" he punchlined and started kissing me.

To the growls of stressed-out animals savaging their once beloved trainers, we exchanged affections. His pursed lips pressed too hard, his wagging tongue was hot and soft like warm sushi, but I enjoyed the accompanying rub. He had large hands and well-toned muscles. I let him slip his hands under my shirt, but I resisted allowing him into my bra. Not because I didn't want him too, but because sex was all about pace, and if I just opened up to him, it wouldn't be worth anything. I had already set up concessions on this date. I was going to permit him bra-access and maybe some minor touching, but no way would my clothes come off, and I certainly wasn't planning on sex yet. I'd made that mistake too many times.

Without asking, perhaps trying to give me a cue, he took off his shirt. Aside from the gloss of sweat, I could see that he had several creaky and incredibly amateurish tattoos.

"If you take your shirt off," he offered, "I'll rub your back."

"Rub over the shirt," I countered and lay belly down on the sofa. He sheepishly rose and started his rub. Looking over, I realized that it was already 9:53.

"Oh, shit!" I had only seven minutes to get my bass and ass to the rehearsal space. I tried getting up.

"Hold on there, little lady," he said forcefully, still positioned on my lower back.

"Get off, I got to run!"

"You're not going anywhere. I bought you dinner and spent the past two hours tenderizing you."

"Get the hell off me!" I shouted.

"You can't leave me like this, babe." He had me pinned down; I could feel his erection grow against my buttocks.

"Are you crazy!" I shouted.

"Okay, get a grip, Alphonso," he coached himself. "Get a grip, boy."

I heard him take a deep breath and then slowly release it. Finally he rose off me. "I'm sorry, Mary. It was just a bit sudden for me."

"No problem," I replied, turning away from him, buttoning up my clothes.

"Now, I didn't do anything I shouldn't've, right?"

"Right."

"We got no problems here, am I right?"

"You're absolutely right," I replied, restraining a genuine fear. He pulled on his shoes and shirt.

"I'm hoping we can pick up from where we left off." He smiled, happily trying to erase his pathology.

"Me too," I replied.

"Should I wait here for you?" he asked, as though I would trust him alone in my apartment.

"I'm probably going to be a while," I said politely.

As I rose to go, I noticed him do something strange. He took out a new twenty-dollar bill and stared at it. I had this awful sense that he was considering giving it to me as if in compensation. He slipped the bill back into his pocket.

"Okay, later then," he said and silently exited. I locked the front door, locked myself into the bathroom with Numb, and thought about the evening.

Awakening to the fact that I wasn't raped and late, I dashed out.

"It's ten-fifteen!" Sue caught me at the elevator.

"Please, I was almost date-raped."

"Date-raped?"

"Well, date-massaged." We entered the padded cell of the rehearsal studio, took our places, and played. I strummed while Norma drummed and Sue hummed, reviewing our set of songs. For twenty bucks an hour, Context Studio gave us a small, dimly lit room with a five-drum set, three small practice amps, and a cheap PA system.

What bothered me most in there was the smell: the decomposing foam rubber didn't merely absorb the noise but also the sweat and dander of generations of East Village musicians. It was the aroma of burned hope. Whenever I went to rehearsal, I could imagine the musically inclined kids who over the years had streamed through these studios on their way to the many local musical venues and then, eventually, off the face of the earth.

Tragically I still needed that awful hope, that belief that something finer and grander would come out of life. After years of writing, my labors amounted to being published in three tiny magazines, *Oblivious, Nada Quarterly,* and *Off The Ledge.* No one I knew had even heard of the magazines, let alone read my stuff. I was suffering from validation anemia. I needed something to hope for so badly that I was willing to play a guitar in the middle of the night while being abused by an ex-boyfriend's ex-wife in the process.

After the last guitar chord finished resonating, I dashed down the stairs and back to my apartment. The dog mugged me at the door, wanting love and attention, but I was out of both and was in bed by twelve-fifteen. Only to be back up by seven-thirty. By nine I was under the fluorescent lights of Kinko's, ready to be a copy whore for little more than minimum wage.

What was foremost in my mind when I took the nowhere job was that I would be able to add another chapter to my great skinny work, *The Book of Jobs.* After the first day, though, I knew I had to churn this story out quickly before I went bonkers. Working at this particular franchise meant wearing certain clothes: khakis, the blue shirt emblazoned with the company logo, a bright red apron (fellas wore black ones), and a plastic name tag. It meant standing behind a long stretch of unbroken counter performing one of five boring tasks: computer services, order placement, order pickup, cashiering, or fax services. I was bombarded with questions, from the varieties of binding (velo, hole-punched, staples) to the different types of paper (résumé or executive, card stocks, or pastels).

I found myself repeating: "Working from a single original, each page on white paper is eight cents per copy. Once you go over a hundred copies, the price drops down to four cents." If I felt sarcastic, I'd add, "Thank you, come again."

The most popular East Village colors—for band announcement cards and wheat-pasted flyers—were Lift Off Lemon, Cosmic Orange, and Fireball Fuchsia. Of course there had been a reduction of these flyers since His Honorable Mayor (not an artistic bone in his body) was cracking down on street-corner advertisements.

The one nice perk to this job that relieved me from the tedium was a cute guy named Scotty, a manager who had a palpable crush on me. Watching him work was amazing; he was like an idiot savant with Xerox machines. Once, while we were understaffed, I watched him doing several complicated jobs simultaneously, juggling three machines without double-copying a single page. Unfortunately, he had the personality of a blank sheet of bleached Hammermill paper.

Jeff proved himself an unwiped derrière by making sure that each Xeroxee received a Customer Comment form with their receipt. This was one of the reasons I ceased hanging out with Zoë, since she became an accessory to the suited manager. We still talked every day on the phone, but that first week my social life was reduced.

The most enlightening phone call I had that week was with Emily, the Bonnie Raitt protégé. Without telling her I was their latest addition, I asked if she knew anything about the local band, the Beautiful and the Crazy.

"Sure, the disoriented Oriental," she joked. "She's nuts. I was at that performance in Coney Island High when she beat up her old bass player."

"Oh my god," I muttered, not having heard this tale.

"She's crazy, but the band's actually good. For a while they seemed to be going somewhere, but first Sue had a kid, then the drummer OD'd and had to go into rehab." That sounded like Norma. "Then Sue had that fight with the bass player she threw out. But when they're good, they're really good. Very military, no fucking around. Why are you asking?"

For a minute my tongue twisted in a million different directions as it looked for a place to run. I didn't want to lie, but I didn't want to tell her I was this band's latest victim. Finally I hid behind the line, "I just saw these flyers for a bass guitarist."

"Do someone a favor," Emily advised. "Tear them down."

That week Numb became my best friend. Together we strolled all over the neighborhood, hitting all the big shit-ins, at every park, square, and schoolyard from Chinatown up to Stuyvesant Town. I learned a lot about dogs that week. While in the East River Park, I watched her roll joyously in a filthy pile of leaves, only to find that she was rubbing on top of a dead rat, something dogs do to disguise their smell. I also discovered that male dogs hump each other as acts of dominance—apparently they are eternally struggling for social position. But the greatest revelation occurred in a schoolyard on Eleventh Street, when the dog pulled the leash toward a hot Dalmatian bitch, and I saw this red thing that looked like a fleshless pinkie shoot out of her furry undersection. Numb was a boy.

I felt like a widowed parent in this new dog owner clique. A few of the owners who recognized Numb asked me what had become of Primo. I would tell them the sad truth. Ironically, the one place I couldn't bring myself to go was Tompkins Square Park. It wasn't from fear of meeting Tattoo Man, whom I still wanted to compensate and apologize to, but something worse. If I had not been mildly intoxicated, and pissed off, I would not have consigned Primo's ashes there. With each passing day I felt increasing guilt about the impetuous spreading.

After rounding out my first week at Kinko's, I was awakened late Saturday morning by the ringing phone. The machine picked up.

"Hi Gloria, it's June . . ." It was Primo's mother, confusing me with one of his other ladies. "You're not going to believe this, but the funeral parlor called. The fuckers gave us the wrong ashes, and we have to return the old ones."

I snatched up the phone before she could hang up and said, "I already spread them!"

"Well, unspread them, dear," Mama said. "They're someone else!"

"Who?"

"A dentist from Syosset."

I told her I'd do what I could and hung up the phone. No good turn ever went unpunished.

I dressed slowly, filled the dog bowl with pebble-like food, and thought about filling my own bowl with it. Saturday was always a sucky day for breakfast. There are no specials, and all the restaurants are bogged down by tourists.

I grabbed Numb and checked the batteries of my Dust-buster, then went downstairs for my usual cup of coffee. I bummed a cigarette off a teenager and headed over to Tompkins Square Park. A Salvation Army food truck was parked on Avenue A, giving cups of soup to a bedraggled line of scraggy homeless. I half considered getting a cup, but saw no other women in line. I headed over to the dogrun.

While pit bull and fox terrier owners sat inertly on the benches, I smoked my cigarette and paced around, mindlessly vacuuming up the earth. Over the black iron gate near the archway leading to the General Slocum Steamboat Disaster Memorial I spotted the peroxide teen, the convicted prostitute I met earlier. She was holding a broom, chatting with a large, older man. I operated my Dustbuster and watched as he spoke to her. He was growing more intimate with her by the minute. Now he placed a hand on her shoulder and caressed her.

"You know, everyone else picks it up with a plastic bag," said some skinny kid who shook a baggie in my face.

"Not me," I said, still siphoning up Primo.

"You must have a hell of a clean house." The kid collected his Jack Russell and took off.

I vacuumed like a crazed housewife and watched as the teenage public worker set her broom down and walked off with the older man. Apparently her community service went beyond all standard calls to duty.

"What the hell are you doing?" It was none other than Tattoo Man.

"Oh, shit." I stood up, turning off my little Dustbuster. "I've been hoping to find you. I wanted to apologize to you."

"It's okay."

"No, it's not," I replied, dipped into my pocket, and extracted a crinkled ten-dollar bill. "This is yours."

"I was never mugged by Ally McBeal before." He smiled as he took it. "If you chicks get any more powerful, guys are going to shrivel up; our muscles are going to atrophy. " I chuckled politely. "So what is this, a sorority prank?" He was referring to my vacuuming of the earth.

"This is even more embarrassing than accidentally mugging you. On the same night as that little misfortune, I got loaded and chucked Primo around here."

"You mean his ashes?" he asked. I nodded. "And now you feel guilty?"

"Yes," I replied, "but worse. It turned out to be some other woman's Primo, and she wants her was-band back."

"You are kidding."

"The freakin' funeral director accidentally gave us the wrong remains, and now we have to do an ash swap."

"That's a lawsuit."

"It's easier just to sweep him up and get out of this loop."

"How much did Primo weigh when you spread him?" Tattoo asked.

"He was heavy. With the jar he was about twelve to fifteen pounds." I figured he couldn't weigh much more than twice what he weighed when he entered the world. Tattoo Man popped open the back of my Dustbuster and looked inside. A few ounces of granulated dog shit had accumulated in the collection bag.

"This is going to take me all day, isn't it?" I frowned.

Tattoo Man walked over to the garbage can and pulled out a large plastic soda cup, which he emptied. He scooped up a cupful of dirt, dog humus, and wood chippings and offered it. "There you go—Instant Primo."

I took the full cup, which marked the end of my toil, and thanked him. His large dog came over and shoved his nose in my crotch.

"Hey!"

"Fedora!" he yelled and pulled his dog, sending him scurrying back toward the barking clique of canines. "I've trained him to do that to girls who rob me."

"You know, I really am sorry about what happened the other night," I said.

"You didn't do anything. It was that other girl," he murmured.

"I'm glad you remember that."

"Hell, I even know why she did it," he mused.

"Why?" I asked.

"Oh, nothing," he said and smiled demurely.

"No, what did you mean?"

"I didn't mean anything. Forget it."

"What are you reading?" I asked, peering at the stack of pages tucked under his elbow.

"A manuscript," he said tiredly.

"Friction?" I kidded.

"Only friction can be this bad."

"Are you a writer?"

"No, a reader."

"A reader for what?"

"I've been freelancing for a while. I got suckered into doing a bunch of reader reports for a small press."

"Sounds cool."

He yawned editorially. "Believe me, there are few things more tedious you can do than read this crap."

"You don't work at Kinko's five days a week," I replied.

"Christ, you work in Kinko's?" He looked at me with renewed disrespect.

"I got fired from my temp job about a week ago, and I just didn't have the nerve to shlep back up to Midtown."

"I kind of know what you mean. I have claustrophobic attacks just riding the damned subway." Midtown is a terrifying place filled with pantyhose wearers and overblown department store windows.

"Well, I'll get my courage back soon, because Kinkoing is even worse than temping."

"A Kinkoer makes a thousand copies, a temp makes only one," he lamented aloud, which led to an awkward pause.

"So what did you get your pointless degree in?" I asked.

"English. I was supposed to be an important young American writer."

"I was supposed to be an important young *female* American writer."

"If you want to do reader's reports," he offered out of nowhere, "I can get you fifty bucks a pop."

"I'll read your crappy manuscripts," I said hungrily.

"Give me your phone number. I have to run." I scribbled it down for him, thanked him for collecting the cup of Primo, fetched Numb, and returned to the apartment. Once there I poured the dogrun matrix back into the glass urn, then boxed and taped it up as best as I could.

Telephoning Primo's mother, I informed her that I got about as much of Primo as I could and probably the remnants of a few other crematees as well. I recently read that half of Truman Capote was dusted in New York, and half in L.A.

"Who are you, please?" she asked, disoriented. Once again there was a television bleating in the background.

"His former girlfriend," I replied.

"Sheila dear, is that you?" she asked.

"Yes," I replied. What was the point? A person didn't need to be senile to confuse the names of all the girls Primo had impaled.

She gave me the phone number of the family who possessed the granulated package of bona fide Primo. I dialed and listened to the phone ring. His damned mother couldn't even remember my name. There was really only one reason I was going through this again; guilt for what I did the first time. I never should have accepted his ashes, nor should I have dumped him in the dogrun. In a strange way I was actually glad that I had a second chance.

"Hello." I heard a rickety female voice.

"Hi, this is . . . I have ashes that I think belong to you."

"Oh, you have my Edgar!" I heard her perk up. "We were so worried. I just heard that eighty percent of all ashes get cast to the winds, whereas only sixteen percent go into statuary receptacles."

"What happens to the other four percent?" I asked.

"I don't know—I suppose they get lost in the mail or something." I wanted to say that at least one percent get drunkenly dumped in places like dogruns.

"So you're going to put Edgar's ashes on your mantelpiece?" I inquired.

"Actually, call us romantics, but we were married for sixty-one years, and we agreed that we wanted our ashes mixed together. Until I die, I suppose I'll put him somewhere, but afterward we'll be salt and pepper together again." That sounded so sweet; unfortunately, it would never happen. "So, how shall we do this?" she questioned.

"Well, I'm kind of busy," I said, trying to imply that I had no intention of hauling myself back out to the unwatered lawns of Brooklyn ever again.

"My son Lewis is about to drive into Manhattan. How about I have him pick his dad up?" she asked. For her age, she had a lucid grasp of proper nouns.

"Terrific."

We agreed upon a time—ninety minutes from then. It was laundry day, and that gave me just enough time. I picked up Primo's manuscript, *Cuming Attractions,* leashed the dog and dashed out with my bag of clothes. As the corner machines groaned and spurted, I gave his pages a closer read. Even though most of it was dreadfully generic, I really admired his industry in punching out an entire manuscript. Primo's tragic flaw was that he squandered his energies in pursuit of petty goals. My greatest problem in writing was the day-to-day perspiration. I never had any shortage of inspiration, but I never liked to sweat.

As I folded my clothes, I heard a thunderclap. I headed back home just as the first drops came down. Some Avenue A troglodyte, seeing me pulling my cart, started trailing after, singing that nitwit song, "Isn't it ironic, don't you think . . ."

"No, you're moronic. You really don't think," I sang back to him.

Just after I hauled my laundry bag upstairs, the doorbell rang. It was Lewis, ready to pick up dog-poop Pop. I dashed downstairs. He was a middle-aged daddy longlegs in a funereal black suit.

"Why was he opened?" He asked as we did the handoff. He had noticed that the package was resealed.

"I just wanted to have one last look," I replied and took the real Primo package.

"All ashes look alike," he scoffed.

"But unhappy ashes are unalike in different ways, " I paraphrased Tolstoy. He shrugged and departed.

Back upstairs, I noticed with unparalleled joy that there was a message on my machine. Without thinking or knowing why, I put the package of granulated Primo in the fridge and played back my machine to hear the tattooed man: "Still interested in writing reader's reports? If so, call me; if not, you can call me as well."

I called him back, and he asked if I wanted to meet him with Numb in the dungrun in an hour.

"It was raining when I last went out."

"It's cleared up now," he replied. My call-waiting beeped. I asked if he could excuse me a moment. He did. Zoë was on the other line. In a soulless tone, she asked what was up.

"Not much," I responded. "Usual."

"I'm sorry I haven't seen you in a while," she replied. "I've been busy." It was always this way; Zoë was a classic slave to love. When she was single, I was constantly buffeted with phone calls from her. Now, in a fleeting relationship, she evaporated into her man.

"Everything's just dandy," I assured her, and explained I had someone on the other line. She sounded relieved at being able to exit quickly. I switched back to Tattoo Man.

"Still there?"

"Yeah," I heard him say over his speaker phone. He snatched up his phone, and his voice came in more clearly. "Listen, would you have a writing sample?"

"You mean, like a college paper?"

"That would be fine."

"I did a paper in philosophy on the relationship between technology and morality."

"You don't have any lit papers?"

"I did a forty-seven-page study on the Soviet satirist Yuri Olesha."

"Bring that," he concluded, but before we said good-bye the call-waiting beeped again. We agreed to meet in forty-five minutes at the dogrun, and I pushed to get the other call.

"Opaline tonight at eight?" It was Joey, proposing dinner.

"I have to read a novel, write a reader's report, and go to band practice."

"Band practice? What weird cult have you joined?"

"It's not completely what you think."

"Well, you can tell me what I think while you eat. You can be in and out in half an hour."

Aside from my ongoing desire to fall asleep in his strong arms and hairy chest, the only time food was an art form was when Joey took me out for dinner. I accepted the offer and hung up.

I rummaged for nice clothes and decided on a Gap skirt and a black pullover. I spritzed on some of Primo's sandalwood musk and pulled a comb through my ruin of hair. Although I was twenty-nine, I didn't look a day older. With this renewed confidence, I went through my filing cabinet, miraculously located my old college paper on the great silenced Soviet writer Yuri Olesha, then grabbed the dog and headed to the park.

Several days a week the southeastern border of the park became a farmers' market. Pickup trucks were filled with fruits and vegetables, peddled by rugged folks in overalls. Their display tables were abundant with greens and other vibrantly colored gifts from the fields, bits of soil still visible in their roots. It all served as a valuable reminder that not all food was cellophane wrapped, boxed, frozen, or cooked in invisible-kitchen restaurants by strangers. The fruits and vegetables looked delicious, but I was fairly certain that my digestive tract had so thoroughly evolved that it could only accept hyperprocessed crap; it would reject this raw prehistoric food.

At the dogrun, I waited and watched the dogs carousing in their customary circle, forever play-fighting. Occasionally a small dog would try to dominate a bigger older dog, or a nasty dog would assert its insecurity by going after a weaker dog just to have something to bully. It compelled me to wonder where I was on the social totem pole.

"Hey," I heard behind me and looked beyond the gate to see the tattooed man, Howard, standing there with his Weimaraner in one hand and a large gray envelope in the other.

In a moment he was through the double-gated pen and then in the dogrun. As our dogs sniffed each other, the painted man sat next to me.

"You've never written a reader's report, have you?"

"No."

"Here." He gave me a sampling. It was one page long, starting with a brief synopsis of a crime novel called *The Heist:*

This is a thriller about two ex-cons, Scrawny Ronnie and Bug-eyed Bob. When the novel opens, they are in Attica together where they share cells and quickly learn that they have a great deal in common. While passing the time by discussing certain crimes they had performed, they realize that they had both contemplated breaking into a big ganglord's house. He's a violent man named Tuna who is filthy rich and ruthless. They each realized different aspects of the score that the other did not know. Ronnie has access to logistical details such as when the ganglord and his crew go out. Bob knows the layout of the compound, and that the upper floors are more vulnerable. Since they are both scheduled to go up for parole toward the end of the year, they agree to join forces and attempt to pull off this one last big heist. . . .

I skimmed through the remainder of the report to the commentary. "Although the prison scenes are slightly clichéd, they aren't bad. The passages outside of the big house, however, read like a badly rehashed mix of Elmore Leonard and Carl Hiaasen. While at times amusing, and even touching, the two central characters are indistinguishable and unsympathetic. . . ."

"Indistinguishable and unsympathetic, that's always been my problem," I said, reaching for the packed envelope containing the manuscript while handing him my graduate school term paper.

For a few minutes, we each flipped through the other's work. The novel I was to report on was called *The Manstrument,* by Tech Web. The title sounded German; the author's name sounded like a computer. Toward the middle of the 250-page manuscript, I started seeing references to the eponymous instrument.

"Is this a horror tale?" I inquired.

"Who knows?" Howard commented, but holding up my report, he said, "This looks excellent."

"It got an A in a Soviet satire class."

"You might be overqualified."

"Don't worry, I've grown stupid since I left school."

"Well, this should put some cash in your bra," he kidded. He asked how long I thought it would take. I optimistically told him that to read it and type out a one-page report should take a day.

"Hey, lady! You think that just 'cause you're young and sexy, you don't have to clean up your dog's crap?" I heard a familiar male voice behind me.

"All I have to do is click my fingers"—which I did—"and I'll have every male in this cage competing to fetch it."

It was Joey standing outside the black gate surrounding the dogrun; a very large, very thick Italianesque man was standing alongside him. Joey leaned over, and we gave each other a peck on the cheek.

"What are you doing here?" I asked.

"Just passing through the park," he replied.

"Who's your little friend?" I asked of his towering associate, who looked like he'd stepped off the set of *The Sopranos*. He had deep ruts and scars in his cheek; and black hair greased back.

"This is Sammy." Sammy nodded demurely and looked away.

"Joey, this is Howard," I introduced the two of them. They shook hands with a smile.

"Joey's my old upstairs neighbor," I said to Howard, and to Joey I explained, "Howard is my latest employer."

"It's a pleasure," said Joey. "I'll see you later." He was off.

"Well, I think we just concluded our business day," Howard the tattooed man said.

"I'll have the report ready by tomorrow," I assured him as I got Numb back on his leash.

"If you finish it, I'll give you another novel."

"Great."

"You know, I don't want to pigeonhole anyone," Howard said just as I was about to walk off, "but your former neighbor, who by the way seems like a very nice man, is in the mob."

"If you judge people by the company they keep, you'll understand why I have to dash abruptly." He chuckled as I walked away.

I took doggie home, sat in my most comfortable chair, and started reading. After four pages, though, I fell fast asleep. This was not entirely the fault of the book. I was addicted to prickly, mile-a-minute audiovisuals. If sexy hulk courtroom lawyers weren't prosecuting the only women they ever wanted, or hot ER doctors weren't using internal paddles on the heart of the only lover who ever jilted them, I quickly got bored.

I was awakened by Carolina and her gay boyfriend, Dorn, opening the front door. This caused the dog to spring to his feet, which somehow incited the phone to ring. I answered. Alphonso invited me for a walk. I told him I couldn't; I had work to do. Besides, our last episode had freaked me out, and I had decided not to see him again.

"Can't I drop by your home?" he asked.

"I'm just walking out the door."

"Where to?" he pressed, unable to get the hint.

"Some coffee shop in the area, probably," I said, free as a condor.

"How about dinner?" he cut ahead.

"I'm already booked," I explained.

He finally took the clue and said that he hoped we could get together again soon. Hastily I threw on a blue shirt and a black skirt, pulled on my pair of Kenneth Cole shoes, and went out to read the manuscript. Initially, I headed down to the Cobalt Colt, but dreaded the idea of bumping into Zoë. I couldn't get over what a hypocrite she was, dating that bore Jeff, repressing her wonderfully assertive nature.

I deviated to Limbo on A. Feeling rich from the manuscript

money I was about to earn, I ordered a latte and started reading. Within five minutes though, a fortyish, sinewy blond woman stopped before me. Her tightly defined muscles looked like thick branches of ivy swirling around the trellis of her tall, bony body. She was holding a cup to go.

"You're not the Mary Bellanova who dated Primo Schultz, are you?" she asked stylishly.

I virtually dropped the manuscript I was reading. Anonymity was all I really had. "How did you know?"

"It's on your shirt." I looked down and realized that, without thinking, I had thrown on the stupid Kinko's shirt, complete with my name tag pinned to it. In other Kinko's stores, employees only had to display their first name, but Jeff, going over the top in his quest for managerial posterity, made us list our full name, which left us vulnerable to obscene phone calls from disgruntled customers.

"I'm Lydia. We spoke." This was Minnie Belle's friend, the tiny-brained dancer who initially gave me Sue Wott's number.

"Hi," I said, instead of *shoo!*

"You're so pretty, which I have to confess is not what I expected from our conversation."

"How kind." Sarcasm.

"Did you scatter Primo's ashes yet?"

"I'm still conducting my investigation," I replied without even thinking about what I was saying.

"Did you ever speak to Sue Wott?"

"In fact, I did," I said, wishing I could delete all files of my existence from this person's cerebral hard drive.

"You know I meant to call and tell you, you should speak to Norma," Lydia advised.

"Who the hell is Norma?" The flow of girls never ended.

"They played together in a band."

"Wait a second, is she a tall girl?" I felt myself freeze.

"Yeah, short-cropped hair with leopard spots." It was definitely Norma the comatose drummer. With my joining, Sue should just rename the band Primo's Exes.

"They were married for about a day."

"Norma and Primo were married!"

"Sure, Primo was married like four times."

"WHAT!"

"I think only one of them was love."

"What about the other three?"

"One was green card. One was to get out of Bali."

"Bali, the island?"

"Yeah, I don't understand it. Oh! I think one of his wives was a lesbian."

"He married a lesbian?"

"Yeah, a modern downtown performance artist. He did it as a favor. So she could get an inheritance. Her grandfather's will specified marriage."

"And why did he get married to get out of Bali?"

"I don't know." She smiled. "When are you consigning him to the four winds?"

"I should be ready to spread him in the next week or so."

"Call me when you do," she twittered and departed.

I tried to start reading *The Manstrument* again, but it was too difficult. I tore through a copy of *Jane* and kept thinking about all those matrimonial relapses when Primo said, "I do."

"Mar-e-e-e-e!" called out a shrill female voice that sounded almost like a drag queen. It was from a phony from way back, a scary Gila monster named Lianna, who was actually friends with Delphi, my triple ex-boyfriend, pre-Greg. I cringed as I smiled, and tried to let all my muscles go limp. It was moments like this when I couldn't resist slipping into the world of wild exaggeration. I casually mentioned that I was secretly engaged to a Scandinavian and I had finally finished writing my working-class novel, which was under consideration at Pelican Publications.

It was all about making Delphi rue the day he ever dumped me.

After Lianna slithered away, I gathered my things and hastened out. I never had luck in Limbo. I was always intercepted by limp people. I headed up A, into the grungier Alt.café on Ninth Street. There, to my surprise, was Gilda, a modern dancer I worked with a few months back at the Astor Place Starbucks, while writing "The Coffee Wars." She was tall, clever, and strong. Guys would line up like bowling pins, and she would knock them down with her contemptuous insults. Working with her was always a blast because she used the customers as butts for her jokes, and most of them never even knew it.

"My God! I can't believe it's really you!" She was in the throes of steaming up a mocha latte. Without finishing the task, she grabbed my hand over the counter and complimented me on how good I looked. To the dismay of the awaiting customer, I did likewise. She came from around the counter and gave me a spine-crunching hug.

"I don't want to be rude—" the caffeine-starved patron began after a few seconds.

"Which you are being," Gilda finished his statement with a professional smile. She went back and served the guy his coffee, and then told me I could have anything I wanted, which meant two sugar-free brownies—one now and one for later—and a decaf cappuccino. We hacked up old times, carped about some of the twits that we used to work with, and snickered at pranks that we played on perfect strangers.

"Hey, are you still dating creepo?" she asked with her trademark candor. "You know, he came on to me."

"No, creepo died," I replied. It had to be Primo.

"Died!" She couldn't believe it. "No one ever dies anymore."

"Well, he did."

"Wait—I take that back. Someone overdosed here a while back," she remembered.

"Where?"

"In the bathroom," she replied, pointing to the back of the joint. I made a mental note not to pee there.

A clutch of heavy-footed out-of-towners tumbled in, each requesting ridiculously overpriced cappuccinos with special additions. I retreated into the insulated, overly air-conditioned back room, where I took a seat in one of the sunken leisure chairs, which looked as though it had been reclaimed several times from the sidewalk. I took out the manuscript and made another stab at reading the weird quasi-horror mystery called *The Manstrument.* Considering the amount of money I was getting paid, it would only be profitable if I could get through it quickly.

It began: "Beatrus was not a pretty girl. As a child she was small and hunched up like a lady bug. Her little face was hidden behind folds of puffy pink flesh, and dotted with a galapagos of ever-shrinking moles like a series of still-forming planets."

Beatrus grows up, does well in school, graduates in the top of her college class, and is accepted to an Ivy League law school. Upon graduation, she is snatched up by a corporate law firm, where she quickly moves up the ranks.

"Excuse me," someone asked, compelling me to toss a flurry of pages into the air. It was a slight Asian girl.

"What!" I shouted back angrily. The book was pissing me off.

"Nothing," she replied, dashing out.

Eventually, while assessing the estate value of one client— a freshly dead matron named Else Lancet—Beatrus wanders through the many floors and labyrinthine rooms in her gothic mansion. One hundred and seventy-seven pages into the tedious book, she finally stumbles across the goddamned "manstrument."

Under a tarp and layers of dust, Beatrus finds an object that sounds like the torture device in Kafka's "Penal Colony." It appears to be an old armchair, but underneath it has a series of coils that finger out like knuckles loosely coordinated to parts of the body, including a strange cap that pulls over the head. What the manstrument does is still unclear.

Since it was a quarter to eight and I was due to meet Joey for dinner, I skipped ahead and found that after many pointless pages, she finally sits her ass down and uses the "manstrument."

"Hello, Mary," said a familiar male voice. It was Alphonso, local man of mystery.

"What are you doing here?" I asked, but knew the answer; he was stalking me.

"Just passing by."

"Well, coincidentally, I am passing out," I responded. I hastily packed up my papers and raced out. Gilda, under siege by bistro-maniacs, shouted *ciao* as I raced past her with Alphonso at my heels.

"So are you pissed about our last meeting?" He got right to it as we headed down Avenue A.

"A bit."

"You have to understand, it was so sudden for me, and I like you a whole lot," he unraveled. "You're really smart and clever. You think I don't pick up on that, but I do. I appreciate you."

"Well, thank you."

"So, don't guys like me get a second chance with ladies like you?"

"What do you mean, guys like you?"

"You know, guys who fuck up a bit."

"You frightened me."

"What did I do?" He sounded tense. "I didn't do nothing."

"Coming up to me in there." I indicated the Alt.café. "That alone freaked me out."

"Hey come on, it's a public place."

"But something tells me you weren't just passing through."

"So I'll admit I had my periscope up for you. What's wrong with that?"

I shrugged and nodded.

"You got into my head."

He reminded me of Travis Bickle out of *Taxi Driver* with a trust fund, but telling him that would not be constructive, so I kept up my walking pace.

"You know," he went on, "I know I got problems with control, but the only control I ever wanted to exert with you was self-control because you are so foxy."

Thankfully, as I stepped up on the curb of Sixth Street and A, I spotted Joey waiting out in front of Opaline for our dinner date.

"Hi, Joe," I called to him in a help-me-please tone. "This is Alphonso."

"Hi there," Joey said, extending his hand.

"Who the hell are you?" Alphonso said, immediately threatened.

"Who the hell am I?" Joey said in a breezy easy tone. "I'm the guy who rips you a new asshole if you so much as go near this young lady again. That's who I am." Joey smiled. Alphonso smiled back. Then I realized they were connected. Joey was still holding Alphonso's hand.

"We have to run," I said, trying to gracefully separate them.

"How long you in for, buddy?" Joey asked Alphonso.

"What the fuck are you talking about?!" Alphonso yelled. He tried to jerk his hand away, but Joey grabbed his forearm and pulled the younger man closer. In a low tone, he explained, "I don't even want to see you near her again. Do you understand?" He released Alphonso.

"What the fuck are you going to do?"

Joey didn't respond; he just gave a look that made me wonder who he really was.

Alphonso turned to me and said, "FUCK YOU, BITCH!" And he dashed off.

I felt my heart racing as Joey asked me, "Are you okay?"

"Yeah."

"You didn't know him very well, did you?"

"No."

"Were you intimate with him?" he asked calmly.

"It's none of your fucking business," I shot back, still trembling.

"I don't mean to pry, it's just that that man was in Rikers."

"How do you know?"

"You didn't see his prison tattoos, his mannerism?"

"Were you in prison?"

"I'm a retired corrections officer," he disclosed for the first time. I stared at him in shock. I vaguely recollected him in a uniform when I was younger. "He's not going to bother you again. Once you got their numbers, these guys are cowards."

I nodded my head limply and thought about the evening I was alone in my apartment with Alphonso. He could have raped me.

"If you're not feeling well—" Joey said.

"No, I'm okay," I interrupted. I was really hungry and had been looking forward to a classy meal all day.

"Come on." He led the way. "Tell me about this band business."

Opaline restaurant was down a flight of stairs into what looked like a basement. Walking through a narrow lounging corridor, we emerged into a large room with a mezzanine against the far wall and a luxurious bar to the right. A line of overhead wooden fans slowly turned by a network of belts and pulleys gave the space a tropical, colonial feel. A glass skylight looked out under the starless New York sky.

The maître d' showed us to a booth on the upper mezzanine. We both took off our coats and sat across from each other. Joey positioned the candle on the table before me. I thought he was looking at my Kinko's shirt, but then I realized he was studying my face.

"What drinks can I get you folks?" an overly-friendly waiter asked.

"Johnnie Walker Black, straight up," Joey said, and looked at me.

"I have to stay up late tonight—just water."

"You sure?" Joey asked.

I nodded yes. "Band rehearsal," I explained.

"Which is possibly the only thing worse than dating an ex-con," he concluded.

"I initially did it to tell this girl that Primo died. She was his ex-wife."

"Right, so where is this heading? Are *you* a stalker?"

"Not really." The waiter came back, surrendered the menus, and placed a goblet of water before me. "Well, maybe just a bit." I smiled.

"How long ago did Primo break up with her?" Joey asked.

"About ten years ago."

"So why are you even bothering?" he said, exasperated, as the waiter set down his Johnnie Walker. Joey took a quick sip off the top.

"Well, when I went out to Primo's mother's house in Brooklyn, I found a published love poem, which was touching. But I also found a hate poem after she dumped him, which demonstrated beyond all doubts that he loved her deeply. Deeper than he ever loved me. She was the love of his life. I suppose my vanity insisted that I find out why." I closed my eyes to hold back a tear.

"So I return to the original question," he said coolly. "Why did you join this band?"

"Well, I didn't mean to. I kind of got sucked into the audition, and then I started playing with them"—I took a sip of my water—"and liked it."

"What does your mother say about this?"

"She doesn't know." I smiled just at the thought of her hearing the news. It was almost worth telling her, but not quite.

"Look, if you're doing it because you like the process, that's fine. But every clown and his brother is in a band. It requires a hell of a lot of time, hours that you can be working on something with a better return."

"Like what?"

"Like your writing," he replied. He swallowed the remainder of the scotch and added, "Look, I don't want to piss on anyone's parade, I just want to be helpful."

"I appreciate the advice, but I kind of know it. It's just a lark for the time being. I know I'm either going to get sick of it or get into a fight with warring Sue Wott. I'm just enjoying it for the moment."

"You're a lot steadier and smarter than I was when I was your age," Joey assured me with a smile. When the waiter came back, we both ordered fish. Joey got the broiled salmon; I ordered the seared tuna. Joey also requested a second Black Label and asked again if I wanted a drink. I declined. He stared at me with a weird smile.

I assumed that he was amused by the fact that I was in a rock band.

"I remember when you got that." He touched a point on my forehead. I knew he was referring to a tiny scar that I got as a little girl. In the dim room, I knew one could only see it if one knew it was there.

"I was about three." I had fallen down a flight of stairs and cut myself.

"It was a week after your fifth birthday," he corrected. "I went to the hospital with you."

"You went to the hospital?" I said mildly astounded.

"Well, maybe not to the hospital," he recanted. "But I remember you going to the hospital." The waiter brought his second drink.

The dinner with its surprisingly large portions went down too quickly. I kept forgetting to take smaller bites and chew at a more leisurely pace, something I intended to do when the entrées were over fifteen bucks. Usually the more pretentious the restaurant, the larger the plate and the smaller the amount on it. It wasn't just the food I was there for but the entire royal treatment. It was an event, like going to the theater without having to suffer through two hours of boring nonsense. I loved being served and attended to like I was a celebrity. The waiter took our large white plates away. Joe, under the age-old impression that coffee was the cure for drunkenness, ordered a cup. Since I still had to be awake for rehearsal, I got one too. We split a slice of chocolate cake that was rich enough to kill a diabetic.

"What do you got there?" Joey said, referring to the unfinished *Manstrument* manuscript I placed on the empty seat next to me.

"A horrible horror novel. I am supposed to write a reader's report for it."

"You're getting paid?"

"Not enough. Initially I took the job out of curiosity, but now I'm hoping it'll give me the confidence to finish my book."

He laughed and observed, "You join a band for one reason and stay in for another, and here with this manuscript it's the same thing."

"Things start out one way and then turn out being another," I summed.

"I know exactly what you mean." He laughed and looked off. "I sure as hell never thought I'd be living the life I'm in now."

"Amen to that."

"Tell me about your book?"

"I hate talking about my writing."

"Did it start out as one thing and turn into another?" He always seemed so totally amazed at me, which I suppose was a key reason that I couldn't help but love him.

"I told you about it, remember?"

"Oh, this is the group of stories about people working at the mall."

"Sort of, it's employees working in different franchises and their relationship to their jobs."

"You know, I don't mean to—" He caught himself. "No, forget it."

"What?"

"Well, when you first told me about this idea, I remember thinking this but not saying anything."

"Go ahead."

"What's so interesting about a bunch of people and their jobs?"

"Until the last twenty years or so people got a sense of pride and even identity out of their jobs. They had careers. My generation, though, consists mainly of people who despise their jobs and have to find other things to look forward to."

"How big is your book?"

"Small." I held up a space of about a half an inch between two fingers. "Around a hundred and thirty pages."

"What franchises do you skewer?"

"I don't skewer any of them. In fact some of the people love and fight for their franchise. I have a guy who works in one coffee franchise who attacks the managers of a nearby Starbucks and Pasqua's 'cause they're doing better than his small chain."

"Oh, I like that one."

"Thank you."

"You might be onto something. People need something to live for, even if it's just a bet. They make nothing into something." He took another sip of his coffee, then, pulling his chair up to me like a child, said, "So tell me another story."

"Well, my first story in the collection is about an African-American girl who works at a McDonald's, and her life is falling apart."

"Blacks got it tough." Real humility.

"Nowadays the preferred phrase is African American."

"All right, go ahead."

"When the McDonald's she works at has a week-long special

on Big Macs, she meets a senior citizen who is kind of a homeless person—"

"An old fart who's a bag man," he politically incorrected, just to needle.

"Anyway, with just friendship and common sense he helps her get her act together, and of course his name is Mac."

"I like that," Joey said suddenly. "The guy is kind of—" He didn't finish the sentence. "How does it end?"

"After the hamburger sale is over, he vanishes."

"So the guy is a magical hamburger. Sounds sad. I'd love to read your stories," he said and took a roll of cash out of his wallet. "Where are you going now?"

"To Odessa's to finish reading this and then off to practice."

He walked me up the block, which was buzzing with riffraff and rock-and-rollers. Then, giving me a peck on the cheek, he said good night and told me to call him if any unsavory boyfriends appeared. I ordered a tea in the rear of the overlit diner, where the greasy fumes filtered through my hair.

Back to *The Manstrument:* Over time, Beatrus, the lonely probate lawyer, keeps returning to the secret mechanical chair, which turns out to give her power-infusing acts of sexual fulfillment. Several chapters go on about her weird, freaky fantasies, and how the manstrument doesn't merely understand and cater to them but even surpasses them. Although the evolution of her fantasies was interesting, I found it patronizing to read a male's take on female sexuality. I skipped ahead to see the result of all these bizarre orgasms. Beatrus starts losing weight, her skin clears up, and she begins to shine. As she senses a greater interest from the guys around her, she buys a new wardrobe, gets a hot new makeover, a vogue hairdo, and seems to have a newfound power. Although guys start making overtures to her, she has learned the trick of surviving without them.

One man, however, tickles her fancy. Hendersen, a handsome rogue, is utterly infatuated with her. The only problem is, he is the adversarial attorney, representing a group that is contesting the will of Else Lancet, owner of the manstrument. Skipping ahead, Beatrus decides to take a chance and get down with the lawyer. He in turn snoops about and discovers her autoerotic secret, but in so doing, he inadvertently breaks the sacred seat. The big stupid finale occurs when Hendersen is faced with the awful dilemma: he can make love to Beatrus and manually infuse her with power, or he can deny her love and win his case. He nails her, sacrificing his profession, but they end up living happily ever after together.

At a quarter to ten, I left a buck on the table and dashed out. I walked hastily past the scruffy homeless and unwashed urchins that give Avenue A its vomitous charm. I barely had time to fetch Primo's trusty rusty bass and dash off to Context Studios. In the same way a bad meal lingers on the palate, the book haunted me with its pointlessness. No chair ever made love to me, not even in my dreams.

I rang the bell at Context Studios, but no one buzzed me in. After five minutes, as someone was leaving, I entered and jumped nervously on the tired freight elevator, which slowly lurched upward. I braced myself as we leveled onto the third floor, expecting Sue Wott to scream about my being late. When the attendant threw open the door, though, a touching sight was awaiting me. Sue Wott was sitting on the fleabitten sofa, gently rocking a beautiful child in her lap, whispering silly things into his ear, stroking his soft fine hair as only a mother could. As I walked up to them and looked for the young boy's resemblance to Primo, I felt myself melt into a smile. He looked so handsome, and I couldn't tell if he was well-behaved or just tired. His cute little arms went up as he yawned, and he smacked his little lips together. I watched as his mother gave him a tiny kiss.

Then she looked up at me: "What the fuck are you so happy about? You're five minutes late," the bitch said softly, torpedoing my mood. "We're all in there waiting, paying for your lazy ass—in fact, you're fined five bucks!"

"I'm broke," I said tiredly.

"I'll take it out of your cut," she retorted.

I threw open the door and entered the space. Everyone quickly readied their instruments as Sue ran down the rehearsal program.

"First we're going to go over some changes to 'There's Slime in My Bucket'—I want to try it with more of a back beat. Then we're going to do 'Fuck You 'Cause You Can't,' but this time we're going to do it right—understand, Marilyn?" Poor Marilyn understood.

We began rehearsing and worked our way down the list, replaying the songs and parts of songs over and over. After two insufferable hours of her prima donna-ing, we took a break.

Norma stepped out for air, cigarettes, and other motivational goodies. Without asking permission, I came along. A green-grocer was right downstairs. She silently selected her items and dropped her bill on the counter.

"So, how long you been playing?" I asked politely.

"Since 'seventy-three," she said without looking at me. Norma had this timeworn defeated quality, as though she taught Throwing in the Towel 101 at the Learning Annex. I could see the subtle signs of drug use on her vanquished face. I decided to cut to the chase. "So you know Primo Schultz?"

"It's a small, uncomfortable world." In other words, yes.

"I heard you played his bass too," I said with a smile.

"Who told you that?" I saw a spark of life in her Frankenstein cold eyes.

"I promised I wouldn't tell," I said earnestly. I didn't know how close she was to Sue, and didn't want to jeopardize tiny dancer Lydia's confidence.

"What did you hear?"

"That you were married to him."

"Oh that, that was Sue's bright idea. I had a job back then

with health insurance, and she figured if we got married, he could join my plan and get into a good rehab center. He was in it pretty bad back then." Another scam—it figured.

"So the marriage was bogus?" Like everything else in the man's fraudulent life.

"It started out as bogus, but—"

"But what?"

"Things got serious." That figured too. Primo couldn't even pull off a good scam. "Sue doesn't know about that."

"Well, she won't hear about it from me."

"You know," she said, giving her own twist to the Primo phenomenon, "sex for most guys is all about conquest or thrill, but for Primo, I always thought sex was just reassurance that you liked him."

Inasmuch as I had been cuckolded by the man, I was dying to know if this rationale included even a twinge of guilt for cheating on her best friend, but it didn't seem fair to reward her candor with guilt.

We headed back into the old building and up the elevator, where we caffeinated, nicotined, glucosed, and resumed our places for the second half of Sue's instructive abuse. Afterward she mentioned that we had only one more run-through before our big show at Mercury, and because of scheduling conflicts, we all agreed to come to rehearsal early. Staring at me, she said showtime would be at seven-thirty, and we should all make an effort to come on time. Then I watched as she packed up her few things. Norma and Marilyn grabbed all the instruments as Sue lifted her little boy in her arms, and downstairs we all went.

"Do you need any help?" I offered, feeling sorry for the tiny Primo, who was waking up so late from his deep sleep.

"Yeah," she replied. "I'm getting evicted. If you hear of any available apartments, let me know."

Marilyn and Sue piled into a cab, and I headed west with Norma.

Sunday I remained in bed, dreaming that my credit card debt was as easy to pay off as my sleep debt. I surrendered the mattress when I was unable to squeeze any more rest out of it, and jumped into my old swivel chair, flipping on the computer. I was eager to finish the reader's report and get paid. I flipped through *The Manstrument* and keyboarded out a brief synopsis, then delivered my verdict on Beatrus, the tortured fly stuck in Tech Web's web:

> This bizarre wish fulfillment of female isolation reads like something conceived in the last century without any of the gothic flourishes. Tech Web knows nothing about women. In fact, Tech would have had a far more interesting novel if he completely dropped the stock female victim and just focused on his erotic chair. It would have been amusing if a carousel of lovers sat on this vibrating throne. What if the President of the United States sat in the chair? Or if a gay person sat in it? Or Tech? How would the machine's fantasies change? Why was this a manstrument? Was there a womanstrument? If we discovered at the end that Hendersen was using one, and they each needed each other, the story might have balanced out. Otherwise the book seems to suggest that all a woman needs is a good screw. This might make an amusing R-rated *Twilight Zone* episode, but I personally would unplug *The Manstrument.*

As I was rereading, redrafting, and tightening up the report, the phone rang. When I rose to stretch, the dog jumped around me like it had won the lottery. It desperately wanted to check the new day's pee stains. I let the phone machine screen.

"Hi Mary, it's Zoë, you there?" I picked up.

"Listen, Jeff has a really sweet roommate named Psycho. He says when he saw you on that first night at the Mercury Lounge, he thought you were a dream."

"I don't recall anyone else that night."

"He says he remembered you. Says you were wearing cool shoes."

As best as I could recall, I was wearing the tacky white cowboy boots I almost always wore at night.

"He's sexy and available, and if you come with us, we can all hang out together." The idea of spending time with Kinko Kong while not getting paid—let alone getting felt up by some goofy, bootlicking roommate named Psycho—so that Zoë and I could babble between breast and butt squeezes struck me as repulsive.

"I'm going to have to pass," I said impatiently.

"What's the matter with you?" She immediately picked up on my disgust.

"Nothing," I said, reluctant to be the bearer of bad boyfriends.

"Bullshit, something's bugging you. Just say it."

"I think you're moving too fast with this Jeff guy."

"Things are moving fine. Thank you."

"And what happens when he gets tired of you?" I asked, committed to telling all. "He's going to dump you like they all do."

"Hell with you, Mary. Just 'cause you're not happy doesn't mean you got to piss on everyone else."

"Hey, you told me to tell you two months ago," I reminded. "You told me to warn you if you ever jump into the sack too quickly with a man, remember?"

"All right, so I'm warned."

She hung up the phone, and I felt a trace of guilt: she had gone through all the trouble to try to set me up on a date, and I didn't even have the decency to meet this clown. I called Tattoo Man, eager to see if I could trade my just-completed reader's report for fifty bucks and another manuscript. He picked up on the first ring.

"Hi," I commenced, "I finished *The Manstrument.*"

"How was it?"

"Crapament."

"You have the report done?"

"It's in my computer. Did you say you had another novel?"

"That's the spirit." Tattoo asked, "Can you meet me in the park in fifteen minutes?"

"Actually, I need a bit more time than that," I replied. We settled on half an hour. I jumped into the shower, took some of Carolina's many vitamins, brushed my teeth, and dressed. Then I grabbed doggie and dashed out the door. Downstairs I stopped at the Arabs', where I got a pack of American Spirits and coffee, and then took Numb to the Tompkins Square dogrun. I sat on the benches, slurped coffee, and smoked myself calm as the dog romped around with his peers. A homeless guy and a teenage girl both bummed cigarettes off of me as I fuzzed out and recollected details of that weird encounter with Alphonso the other night in front of Opaline.

"Hey, gorgeous." I turned to see Tattoo Man walking around the gates, entering the canine corral. He took a seat next to me.

"You okay?" he asked, picking up on my preoccupation.

"I had this weird situation the other day. I met this guy and we went on a date and he turned into a dangerous ex-convict."

"Shit, do you need a manly interdiction or something?" he offered timidly.

"Actually, that's the problem. I already had one. Remember Joe?"

"The gangster."

"He grabbed the guy and scared him off."

"Sounds good." He seemed relieved.

"It was just so smooth and proficient. I mean Joey instantly saw the guy for what he was."

"Sounds really good," he repeated.

"It was like something out of a movie. What haunts me is, how the hell did he know so quickly?"

"You think maybe your old neighbor really is a hoodlum?"

"Well, he said he was a corrections officer."

"So that explains it."

"But it just made me realize that I really don't know this guy. I mean he's been like my best friend for a few years now. He's had more than enough opportunities to sleep with me, rob me, even kill me. I utterly trust him, yet I just realized that I don't really know him."

"Well, I know a lawyer who has a private investigator who works in his office."

"Are prison records open to the public?" I asked.

"I don't know, but some things are public record, like birth certificates. Where is he from?"

"He said he was born in Hoboken—that's where I first met him, anyway." I handed him the reader's report along with *The Manstrument.*

"You know, the publishing industry is notoriously slow in paying its authors," he said.

"You're kidding." I was seriously strapped for cash.

"Tell you what," he said, taking the money out of his wallet. "I'll advance you this out of my pocket."

"Are you sure?" I asked, feigning timidity.

"Sure." He gave me the cash, then skimmed the reader's report as I traded a little of my own spirit for another American Spirit.

"Good, that should be fine," he said, upon completion.

"Who is this guy, Tech Web?" I asked.

"He's an Asian girl. She lives in the area. Her address is on the envelope."

"An Asian!"

He smiled at my astonishment. At that moment it occurred

to me that while reading the novel yesterday in Alt.café an Asian girl had interrupted me in the middle. When I was rather abrupt toward her, she jumped and ran. Could it have been Tech? If I had known Tech was some mousey little thing writing such a masochistically bold work—candidly discussing her pains, which now in retrospect must have been autobiographical—I would have hugged her and written a glowing report.

"Hold it a second," I said, grabbing the report.

"What?"

"I didn't know it was a woman," I explained.

"What does it matter?"

"It's different if it's a woman."

"All right, it's a man then, okay." He pulled the report from me. Then, as if giving me a new doggie toy, he said, "Here, have a field day with this one. It's written by a tall white man."

He handed me a slimmer manuscript. I took it out of the envelope. *Stark* by Elgin Freehold, looked weird from the very font. It had a freaky epigram from Aleister Crowley, a scary guy:

Not thirst in the brain black-bitten
In the soul more solely smitten!
One dare not think of worst!
Beyond the raging and raving
Hell of the physical craving,
Lies, in the brain benumbed,
At the end of time and space,
An abyss, unmeasured plumbed—
The haunt of a face!

This did not warm my heart. When I saw the subtitle, "Learning to Love It," I sensed I was in for a rough ride. Yet in the course of the past eight years of living in the East Village, I'd met girls who were strippers, prostitutes, and drug addicts. Girls who had done things that I regarded as unimaginable. If I couldn't just read a sicko novel for fifty bucks, I was pretty gutless.

"You can take a couple of days with this one," Tattoo Man explained. "I don't have any other books left."

"How did you get into this crap anyway?" I asked.

"What crap?"

"Doing reader reports for weird-ass novels."

"Believe me, these are better than coffee-table books." He shuddered at his own remark.

"Ever read one of these books"—I held up *Stark*—"and wonder if it's true?"

"A few years back. I read a mystery novel about a guy who kills and cooks his roommate, and then that guy on Ninth Street did exactly that. I completely freaked."

"A Hannibal Lecter type, huh?"

"No, killers are usually morons. If they were smart, they would just get their anger out by writing crappy novels."

"Christ, I hope that's not why I write." Tattoo Man had a meeting uptown, and since he couldn't handle the subway, and couldn't afford a cab, he had to start out early for the long walk. He said it took him forty seconds per New York block, so he could estimate distance pretty easily.

I didn't want to read the manuscript at home, so I headed back to Alt.café, slightly hopeful that maybe Tech would show up so that I could compliment her on her odd opus and apologize for being rude. En route I heard someone behind me yelling, "You there! Pardon! Hello there! Primo's executrix!"

I turned to see Helga Elfman hailing me from the backseat of a passing Lincoln Town Car that was being driven by a Russian immigrant in a suit. She made him pull over.

"Hi," I said, sauntering to the side of the car. I reflexively looked inside to see if there was either a bar or a television. There wasn't.

"You know," she said, dispensing with salutations, "I meant to tell Primo about this from years ago, but I think he was ripped off."

"What do you mean?"

"He did this terrific sequence of paintings he called the Age of Dissolution, that he said was a visualization of his disillusionment. It was a series of paintings of decadent technology that embodied this age, but with really weird twists—like flip phones that turned into bats and ATMs with tongues. He actually did an incredible visualization of the Internet that looked like the different rooms of a haunted house."

"So?" I wasn't in the mood to discuss modern art.

"They were engaging, passionate, original, thoroughly worked out."

"Could I see them?"

"Well, that's the thing—the collection was broken apart and sold off to private collectors. But I saw two of them being resold at the Erasce Gallery. The kicker is, they weren't attributed to him. That Sue Wott creature's name was scrawled at the bottom. She must have sold them as her own."

"I wonder how much she got for them," I pondered aloud.

"The two I saw were being resold for a thousand apiece."

"Did you know that she had a child by him?"

"Primo had a child?" She was astonished. "Wow, I could hardly believe he'd have the sperm count."

"Well, if she did get money out of him, she probably deserved it," I said in her defense. "And I know she's struggling now."

"Aren't we all," Helga concluded, utterly unforgiving toward the former lover.

Without a farewell, she instructed her driver to depart. I continued on to Alt.café. Gilda was behind the counter with a prepubescent supervisor looking over her shoulder. I knew enough to pass and wait until he was gone. Then I returned to the front counter, and she poured me coffee in an old mug and tossed me a colorless, odorless brownie. As I poured skim milk in my cup, she went on about her latest dance project with some vanguard group at the Ontological Theater at Saint Mark's Church. She talked about her latest difficulties as I scrutinized the rim-chipped mug, trying to find a clean place to land my lips. She was in a chatty mood, so I stood hostage to her freebies while she ventilated. Soon, thankfully, a busload of fools came pouring in, overwhelming her with cutesy orders. I slipped away into the recesses of the place to get down to work.

I took my seat, sipped the java, lit a cigarette, and began reading the *Stark* novel. Set in the late 1960s, it begins with a young parish priest, Father Harry Stark, who is giving a sermon in Rikers Island. Although the priest is fresh out of the seminary, he is as tough as nails, reminiscent of Pat O'Brien in the old clerical collar dramas.

"Here's the bottom line," he says to the flock of cons. "We are tested here by God himself. That's what life is, boys, and if God gave you a tough start, handing you rotten parents or lousy living conditions, then your reward will be that much higher in the end."

The reverend is soon appointed to a large, crumbling church in a poor, inner-city parish. At first all is fine—baptisms, weddings, funerals, masses, things grow a bit monotonous. But the confessions are interesting. In one scene, a serial Casanova confesses his seduction of various women: housewives, coeds, and shop girls. Immediately afterward an elderly gentleman pops in and confesses a trite act of impatience at a persistent beggar.

Over time, while he's asleep, Stark's dreams twist into a painful montage of the sins he has forgiven. Soon his daydreams turn as well. He ponders a series of questions that echo down to the core of his faith: Does confession truly absolve sin or merely alleviate the soul? Is recollecting someone else's sin a sin? Is the enjoyment of misery a sin?

Eventually Stark finds himself fantasizing about acts of petty thievery and minor cruelty. For the first time in his life, he has sexual stirrings. With these new fantasies comes a tremendous guilt. He soon goes medieval, punishing himself with petty acts of self-mutilation, branding his arms with cigarette burns and lacerating his fingers with paper cuts.

By the novel's end, the author completely derails the story. Stark uses the votive candles to set the church on fire. Though he dies in the process, he is righteous and rises directly to heaven.

I thanked Gilda for the freebies and headed home to write my report while it was still fresh in my head. As I zipped down First Avenue, I thought it was a shame. *Stark* wasn't bad. But the ending was too abrupt. As I opened the door, the phone rang.

I beat the machine to it. Jeff asked if I could come in to work at Kinko's right now, because Lionel had showed up dead drunk.

"No way," I shot back. "I didn't know you worked tonight." He was usually on in the daytime.

"I'm not working, but I'm trying to help Scotty find someone." Scotty was the night manager.

"Is Zoë there?" I asked.

"Yeah, but don't talk too long, I still got to find someone." A moment later Zoë got on the line.

"Hey," she said remotely.

"Hey," I returned. "Sorry about yesterday."

"No biggie."

"Well, you were trying to be nice," I reminded.

"I guess you were just trying to watch out for me," she replied.

"Well, I was," I replied sincerely, "but I guess I didn't have to be an idiot about it, did I?"

She made a remark about how we were going through an unusual Zodiac period. We were both Libras, and she avidly read the *New York DePress's* astrological predictions and reported them to me.

"So, you don't want to go on a double date with us and Jeff's roomie, do you?"

"Thanks, but the idea of going on a date with a guy named Psycho—"

"Not Psycho! Sako," she corrected. "He's Japanese!"

"Ohhhhh." That changed almost everything.

"He's a really nice guy. I swear it."

"What's he look like?" I asked.

"You know the actor Jackie Chan?"

"Yeah." I'd heard of him.

"He's like a younger Japanese Jackie Chan without the karate." There was a dearth of Asian-American actors for comparisons.

"I'm still mourning Primo, not right now." I paused, and then, to give her hope, I added, "Later, okay?"

We chatted about this and that, and she told me how much she was in love with Jeff, but of course, she had to say that because he was right there.

"He doesn't seem a bit . . . distant, does he?" I asked, politely.

"Yeah," she said immediately. "But they're all that way."

In a softer tone, she added that she couldn't really go into it. But if she could, I knew she'd let him off somehow: girlfriends were always revising and rationalizing their defective boyfriends. I heard Jeff asking her to get off the phone so that he could find a replacement. Conversation over.

I got on the keyboard and thrashed out the reader's report. After a reread and a spell-check, I printed it up and called Tattoo Man. As I heard his phone ringing, I spotted Primo's porn novel propped on a box in the corner.

The painted man's machine came on. I left the message that I had finished the reader's report for the second book and wanted to drop it off. I concluded with my euphemism for getting together with Howard at the dogrun: "Numb needs to take a dump."

While watching TV, I flipped through the novel *Cuming Attractions* by "Primo Teev," leafing through its stiff, stale onion-thin pages, glancing at all the typos, misspellings, lazy clichés and incorrect syntax. I was absolutely amazed that it went on for hundreds of pages. The older I got, the harder it was to even scribble out a shopping list.

To judge by the crooked yet deeply embedded type, it looked as though each letter was nailed deep onto the page. It was probably pounded out on some mad heroin rush. Another fly-by-night, get-rich-quick scheme. I remembered Primo telling me about an old friend of his who had worked in a porn-writing mill run by some freak who was later rubbed out by Sammy "the Bull" Gravano. Primo described how young kids, fresh out of NYU, anxious to see anything in print, even under a pseudonym, wrote the lewd crap standing up, typing it out on filing cabinets because they didn't have desks or chairs to sit in.

But that's not how I pictured this manuscript's conception. I could almost look through those sperm-tinted pages and picture Primo twenty years earlier, sitting naked, sweating, and trembling, a strict two-finger typist, punching the keys on some ancient Underwood reclaimed from the street. A ribbon and life desperately in need of a change.

Porn novels are no different from Harlequin romances, crime thrillers, or any other genre novels. The characters are usually stock and formulaic: the virgin, the seducer, the villain, the hero. Instead of romantic encounters or murders, they have their quota of sex scenes. It was easy to see why Primo was never able to sell it. Not only was it idiotic and loaded with errors, there were only four lame sex scenes in the entire book.

The phone rang. I picked up to hear breathing. I knew it wasn't obscene, but I gave the caller the benefit of the doubt.

"Mary."

"Joey?"

"Yeah, I'm sorry, I just ran up the stairs. Listen, I met a real sweet old guy looking for a dog." He had recalled me bitching about getting stuck with Numb.

"I should take you up on it. I can't afford him, and I'm never with him enough. I always feel guilty."

"So what's the problem?"

"I've bonded with him."

"So unbond."

"It might be a female thing, but once you've bonded, you can't unbond." My call-waiting beeped. I excused myself and clicked over to Tattoo Man. I told him to wait a sec and clicked back over to Joey. As though a thought was escaping, I heard him whisper, "But I don't bond." I wondered if he was thinking about his wife and kid.

"Joe," I said loudly, letting him know I was there.

"Oh, I got to run." He sounded embarrassed.

"You know my band is playing in a few weeks. If you want to come and see me perform, you're invited."

"Are you ever going to scatter Primo's ashes, or did you bond with them too?" he asked, slightly impatient. I was amazed how many unfinished details of my life he had retained.

"I just want to let enough time go by so that if this isn't him, someone will call me."

"Listen," he said in a calmer tone, "I'm going to be away for a few weeks, I'm traveling out West. I'll call you when I get back."

"Where are you going?"

"California, Vegas. Around. Business."

"We'll go for dinner when you get back. That way I can get my gift."

"What gift?"

"The gift you're going to buy me on your trip." That was my way of saying good-bye. I clicked back over to Howard, and we agreed to meet at the usual place. I collected the canine and the manuscript and bought a cup of coffee en route.

As I got into the inner gate of doggie hell, I saw him waiting for me, playing fetch with Fedora.

"You really go through these pages quickly." He flipped through *Stark*.

"They're actually great therapy," I confided. "When I see how bad everyone else's writing is, my own self-confidence increases."

"Everyone says that at first. But after you've finished your first ten manuscripts, and realize your writing still stinks, you'll get over that." He sounded as though he were speaking from personal experience. I handed him the reader's report. He gave me two twenties and a ten. Opening the envelope, he glanced at my report.

"Are there any new manuscripts?" I asked.

"No, thank God. We're all done."

"Done? I thought publishers were always looking for works?"

"Well, this is a contest for new works."

"A contest!"

"Yeah, the DLP Organization was left some money to set up a memorial contest. They put out calls for manuscripts in a bunch of journals and writing programs around the country and got about fifty submissions."

"What category?"

"It's wide open. It just has to be a first-time author submitting a manuscript-length work, around fifty thousand words. In addition to getting published, the author gets a five-thousand-dollar award."

"Holy shit." That should cancel both my credit card debt and the balance of my defaulted student loan. There was nothing like being broke.

"I got suckered into this insipid readers' project at a bulk fee. I needed cash bad," he explained. "Now it's over, and I'm free. And you know, you're lucky, the two manuscripts you got were among the better ones in the stack."

"So one of those two is going to get published?"

"Well, there were others, but they're about the same."

"Suppose I wanted to enter this contest?" I heard myself saying.

"It's too late," he replied. "Deadline was a month ago."

"There's no way you could slip a late manuscript in?"

"You have it now?" he asked.

"I can have it ready in a few days," I said hastily. I was one story short of being finished.

"Let me get this straight. You're going to spend the next three days writing a fifty-thousand-word novel?"

"Of course not. It's a collection of stories, I already wrote them," I revealed.

"I have to turn in these last two manuscripts tomorrow before five o'clock. Give it to me by then, and I'll say it got lost and I'm submitting it late."

"Tomorrow!"

"Hey, you're already four weeks behind the deadline."

"Shit." I thought about it and remembered reading in the *Paris Review* Writer's Interview series how French mystery writer Georges Simenon—who published over four hundred novels—had batted out his fastest potboiler in twenty-six hours. I had a little more time than that to write just one story—my Kinko's installment. It sounded so thrillingly impossible, I told him I'd have it ready for him.

Then, as I dashed home, I realized that I had band practice

tonight, and our big show at Mercury Lounge was tomorrow, on top of everything else.

I lit a cigarette, turned on the TV, and for the first time I played with Numb. There were just too many distractions at home. I threw on my clothes, grabbed a pen and notepad, and dashed out the door. Alt.café was too grungy, Starbucks too crisp. Limbo too cool, the Cobalt Colt was just right. When I walked through the door of the place, though, I heard a female voice declare, "Oh shit, well look what the colt dragged in."

I did not need to look up to know it was Zoë holding an espresso. She was having a smoke, not a good sign. She responded to my cigarette radar by saying, "This is medicinal."

Without a word she pushed back the chair across from her. I sat down and pointed out, "You're not allowed to smoke here."

"These are dietary."

Since I was an occasional sneak smoker myself, I restrained myself from saying that the weight slings right back afterward, plus you get a side order of cancer.

"How's the great love?" I queried.

"Still humming along," she replied with an unenthusiastic smile. The honeymoon looked to be over.

"How's doggie woggie?" she replied.

"He left me for another bitch."

We talked for another five minutes until she was done with her demitasse, and together we rose and exited. It wasn't until I was outside that I remembered the whole point in going there was to write a story. Other than setting it in Kinko's, I didn't have a clue what it was going to be about, so I was grateful to procrastinate.

We chatted our way up to Houston and over to Kinko's, our common link and sore point. She peeked in to see if Jeff was about, I waved to Scott the über-copier. He dashed over between customers.

"How's it hanging?" he clung tensely to dated clichés.

"Fine, how are you, Scott?"

"Just fine," he said sweetly, slipping his hands into his pockets.

I did likewise, where I found some gum. When I offered him a stick, he blankly responded, "I'd prefer not."

This remark reminded me of the Melville short story "Bartleby the Scrivener." Before the days of carbon papers and Xerox machines, scriveners copied documents by hand. This story is set in Wall Street offices of the 1850s. Bartleby is a quiet, hardworking copyist. One day, when told to do a transcription, he responds like Scotty, "I'd prefer not."

For Bartleby, this is a passive act of rebellion—he is a man, not a machine. His employer tries to understand his reluctance but cannot. When Bartleby is fired and told to leave the premises, he refrains, "I'd prefer not to."

He is eventually arrested and sent to jail. In the final scene, when his employer discovers him dead in the prison yard, he tells the prison guard, "He's asleep with counselors and kings."

My story would be a modern-day homage to Melville set in Kinko's, based on Scotty, a human Xerox machine who wants to work. He grows jealous and subsequently sabotages the newer automated machines.

"What's the matter?" he asked, seeing me smile uncontrollably, my eyes full of twinkles.

"Can I kiss you?" I asked in appreciation of his automatism.

"Sure," he said, baffled. I grabbed him and gave him a big lip-smacking kiss.

"Well, okay," he said, his head filling with blood. He must have figured his age-worn salutations sounded like love poems when he said them. With a new dose of confidence, he dashed back to the counter to attend an awaiting customer.

A group of skinny chicks who were waiting to have their

dance cards Xeroxed seemed to disturb Zoë. I think their thinness compelled her to ask, "Want to go for a run?"

"Sure," I replied, feeling elated that I knew what I was going to write about. We agreed to go to our respective homes, squeeze into our gym gear, and then she would pick me up. Numb gave me an uncomplimentary look as I pulled on my jogging bra, T-shirt, and leggings and waited for Zoë. During the last New Year's hangover, we both tiredly resolved and joined health clubs. But that was months ago, and to my knowledge, neither of us had gone.

"I have a guest pass, so let's go to mine," she said, which was fine. I was glad to go to another club first to lose a little weight before heading to my own gym.

Both of us were wearing trench coats and sunglasses over our getups as we walked the few blocks. When we arrived, the clerk looked at Zoë's ID and summoned up her computer file. It turned out she only had a week left on her three-month membership. A muscular, ponytailed, polo-shirted sales stud hoofed over with a clipboard and tried lassoing us fillies into renewing with him. No thanks. We escaped to the women's locker room downstairs, where we hung up our coats. Self-consciously we entered the large open area where men and women on black rectangular mats stretched their rubbery, slippery bodies. Zoë smiled, took a mat, and did something like a sit-up. I feebly followed her lead. We each did about ten of them before we just lay on our backs making groaning noises.

"Let's get our fat butts upstairs on that terrible treadmill before we have a coronary down here on the mats," she huffed. She was right. It looked less pathetic to die up there.

Tiredly we struggled up the stairs. Although there were no manstruments to mount, we had the good luck of finding adjacent machines in front of the ceiling-suspended television set. Neither of us had remembered to bring our headphones to hear the TVs, so we were only able to watch the music videos. Initially, ambitiously, we both plugged 6 m.p.h. as our running speed. After a few optimistic minutes, I almost slipped and was terrified of being dragged to death on one of those stationary devices. Zoë too was winded. The speed mysteriously slipped down to 4 m.p.h., and we both felt ourselves on a mechanical forced march clutching the front grip bar for dear life.

"What are you up to later?" Zoë said, grasping and gasping.

"Nothing," I huffed back, dripping. After ten minutes, Zoë jumped off her torture machine. I punched the pause button and—eureka! We were slim.

We both went back downstairs and put our old trench coats back on. Though we were sweaty, we both preferred to shower at home.

"Oh," Zoë said, instantly excited. "We're meeting with Sako tonight, before the party. You've got to come."

"I have to write tonight."

"Just for thirty minutes, so you can meet him and he can call you. I'm telling you, you're going to be so happy that I set you up."

"I don't want to be rude, Zoë, but if he's anything like Jeff—"

"I know you don't like Jeff. He's everything Jeff is not. You'll love him!"

I repeated that tonight was emphatically out of the question because I had to write. I couldn't tell her that I also had band practice.

"Come on, you need to eat anyway. It's not going to kill you."

"I'm going to be really tense tonight."

"All the better. Guys love a bitch. And this guy likes you. If you like him, you got a shot at something."

Probably as a subconscious form of sabotaging my literary submission, I consented to join them for a quick double dinner—ten P.M. at the yuppie Italian restaurant on the corner of Fourth and Second. Eat and retreat, I reiterated. She assured me that was fine.

It was seven by the time I got home. In addition to a hang-up call, I had two messages on my machine. The first was from Helga Elfman, who said that she had learned that Sue Wott had earned roughly three thousand dollars from the paintings Primo painted.

"With paintings that only a white man could paint and get nothing for," she said testily. "An Asian woman ends up making a bundle—that's the damned art world for you."

Numb was doing jumping jacks, giving me that fish-eyed look that said, if you don't get me the hell out of here and drain me, I'm going to piss on your shoes. So I forsook the shower and nap I desperately needed, leashed him, and gave him his ten minutes in the prison yard.

Before I got stuck owning a dog, I used to be pissed whenever I recovered a newspaper from a garbage can that had the pungent surprise of some pet's scoopings. Now I was the one always searching out a periodical to pick up Numb's gratitude whenever we went on walks. After he emptied himself, I took him back to his cell upstairs. It was time for rehearsal. I grabbed the bass and headed out. En route, I noticed the various peeled and bubbled flyers announcing the performances of East Village bands glued or wheat-pasted to buildings, street signs, and lampposts. Strange little phraseplays that at best made one smile: Zodiac Love Group, New Wet Kojak, Napolean Blown Aparts, and Mobile Homos were among the few.

"Early," Sue Wott observed with disbelief when she saw me. "You must be nervous about tomorrow's show."

"Actually it skipped my mind, but thanks for reminding me. I was looking for something to fret about." As we went upstairs together, I assured her that my being early was an unfortunate accident.

"I hope Norma comes soon," she responded, adding, "I usually pick her up on my way here. She's really bad with appointments."

When we got access to our tiny studio, we made small talk as Sue gathered the half-filled Styrofoam cups, paper dishes, and pizza crusts that had accumulated in the course of the rehearsal day.

"So how old is your son?" I began.

"Five," she responded. This surprised me; I was under the impression she had had her falling-out with Primo by then.

"I don't see a wedding ring," I said, hoping not to sound too much like my mother.

"You want to marry me?" she shot back. The girl was a land mine of domestic sensitivities.

"I was just wondering if you were a single parent."

"I'm half a parent," she replied without humor. "I have an extremely dysfunctional roommate, Jane, who—despite the fact that it's her apartment—pays off her half of the rent by babysitting."

"That doesn't sound too bad."

"It doesn't, does it? And yet, as it just turned out, over the past five months the fucking idiot has been living off the rent money instead of giving it to the landlord—surprise!"

"What does that mean?"

"You want to hear my whole crummy irritating story?"

"You can just cut to the chase, if there is one."

"The chase: Jane and I have an appearance in landlord-tenant court in a few days. At that point, if the landlord fights us we could be homeless."

"So Primo is not your son's father?" I asked, deciding to bull her entire china shop.

"You leave no stone unturned, do you?" she asked with a smile. "Actually, yes, he is the father, but that never bothered me."

"Why not?" I asked, since that was the question that had been pestering me above all else.

"Those idiots wouldn't let me in," Marilyn interrupted as she entered our chamber of horrors, shattering our gradual and fragile intimacy. As Sue and Marilyn chatted about this and that, I dipped out and went to the bathroom.

Norma showed up a bit late, which for her was early, and we got started. We'd made a habit of working on about half a dozen songs over and over during each rehearsal. All of them had vaguely the same riff constituted roughly by the same beat and a loosely similar melody. Norma, who seemed slightly feverish, kept overbeating or underbeating her drums.

"My nerves are bad tonight," she kept saying as she repeatedly dropped her fat chopsticks. She would take the opportunity to tighten one of the shiny lug nuts surrounding her drum, as if that was somehow the cause of her slippings.

While playing the last song in the round up, "Fuck You!"—the third song by Sue that had the word *fuck* in it—Marilyn broke a guitar string, and since she had replacements for every string but that one, we stopped fifteen minutes before the end of our session. Sue gathered us together to talk about tomorrow's show.

"We've all done this before," Sue explained to me. "I know this is your first show, but everything will be fine."

"I'm glad you have confidence in me," I replied, perhaps not sarcastically enough.

"She has it with good reason," Marilyn joined in. "You're a successful person."

"A successful person?" It was the nastiest thing anyone had said about me in hours.

"Sure, you haven't missed a single rehearsal. And you're not insane," she said sincerely.

"You didn't get stuck with a kid you can't afford," Sue tossed in.

"You don't drink, take drugs, or need some guy treating you like shit." Norma plopped her comments into this stone soup.

"Nowadays," Marilyn concluded, "that means you're a success."

An age of lowered expectations came with some ready-made benefits. Nowadays the standards had plummeted so far that I failed even at being a failure. I silently packed up. Nothing else was left. They had even robbed me of self-pity.

As Norma and I tramped up Avenue A, I commented how the alphabetized streets always struck me as temporary titles, as though some city planner had run out of names of statesmen and admirals.

"I once figured that they were named that way so that turn-of-the-century immigrants could learn the alphabet." The genesis of such things was a mystery: we just accepted what was there and worked with it.

By the time I got home, I was starving. It was ten-fifteen, and I remembered that Zoë and her trapezoidal boyfriend were dining down the block. With them was that Psycho guy, who had a mysterious crush on me. Even though I still had to write the Kinko's story, I decided to go—a free dinner was waiting, if nothing else. I brushed the city out of my hair, washed it off my face, pulled on some clothes that exuded happiness, and headed out.

The three of them were flickering under a candle, ensconced at a corner table. Jeff was yakking away as usual when I approached. Zoë was listening with an adoring smile, and this cute little Japanese man sat there making an attempt at not appearing bored, a detail that immediately charmed me.

"Sako, this is Mary. Mary, this is Sako," said Zoë, all of her real spirit flattened in girlfriendly servitude. I shook his hand, and as if I had pulled a chain, his entire face lit up. He looked adorable, so small and controlled, but I couldn't imagine ever sleeping with him.

"She thought your name was Psycho," Jeff teased.

"Like the Hitchcock movie," Sako said, and laughed.

"Sako is an interesting name," I stated, trying to white out Jeff's existence.

"It means William," Sako said calmly.

"William?" I repeated, unable to figure how he could extract a Western name from an Eastern one. He nodded.

When the large Egyptian waiter finally brought me a menu, everyone had already decided exactly what they wanted. As they listed their drinks and entrées, skipping appetizers, my eyes juggled through different dishes and finally dropped down on the eggplant parmesan, which I requested without cheese or oil. I didn't even want the eggplant, but I wasn't in the mood for meat.

"You know, just below this place is a gay porn theater," Jeff divulged. I had little doubt that he had frequented it in his spare time.

"Sako is getting his master's in film," Zoë volunteered, trying to normalize the conversation.

"At NYU?" I asked, smiling at him.

"Yes," he smiled back. "Actually, I just decided on a thesis."

"What's it on?"

"Teenage American films of the 1980s."

"Like John Hughes?" I sneered unintentionally.

"You know the works of Mr. Hughes?" He seemed genuinely astounded by my erudition. I smiled noncommittally.

"You should do a documentary on taking out the garbage," Jeff kidded shrilly, reminding me of the way dolphins balance briefly on their tail before flopping back into water.

"So do you like the program?" I asked, trying not to sound fatuous.

"You know another film you could do?" Jeff said to his own unclear amusement. "Do one on feet."

"Jeff dear," Zoë demurred with a tactful smile, instead of, Shut the fuck up!

Soon after everyone had drunk down the first carafe of wine and the second carafe was ordered, the bread basket arrived;

slightly reheated day-old buns and a small dipping saucer filled with medium-grade motor oil. Sako didn't touch it, going right for the wine. I nibbled slightly at the edge of one roll like a mouse. Zoë and Jeff gobbled down the rest. As the dinner unfolded, the conversation was a ridiculous montage of Jeff making grand declarations, which were usually obnoxious, Zoë politely trying to silence him, and Sako and I trying our best at navigating around both of them.

With every new word he said, with every understated gesture and demure facial expression, I liked Sako more and more. He was a proud little man, and that contrast turned me on. Yet despite his ingratiating mannerisms, his love of Americana made me wonder where things could really go. After we passed on the overpriced dessert tray, Sako asked, "So you're a writer of fiction?" reminding me that I was quite late for my rendezvous with my word processor.

"Actually, she's an employee at Kinko's, but who's counting?" Jeff joked.

"Go fuck yourself," I rejoined. It was time to write, and this was a superb opportunity to act insulted. I shoved my chair back so ferociously it fell dramatically to the floor, then stormed out. I had dashed across Second Avenue when I heard the faint mewings of someone behind me, "Mary! Mary!"

I turned to see Sako catching up to me.

"I am sorry, he is such an idiot," he struggled to say, referring to Jeff.

"I should just get used to it," I said. We walked in the street around a half-completed construction site.

"What are they building here?" He looked up at the still unfinished building on the south side of Fourth between First and Second avenues.

"These are the new efficiency apartments that'll turn this neighborhood into another one," I replied and decided to impart some trivia that Primo had once told me. "This used to be the

Andersen Theater. It was one of the old Yiddish theaters that lined Second Avenue back around the turn of the century. During the sixites it became a rock-and-roll palace."

"Rock and roll?" That caught his interest.

"Yeah, this was where Janis Joplin first played in New York."

"This, here!" he said in amazement.

"Yes."

He paused a moment in reverence. Then we resumed walking, and as we passed by the Sushi Garage, he asked, "Would you like to go for saki?"

"I can't stand saki," I said, still associating the place with Alphonso.

"Me neither," he agreed with a smirk.

"You know, I really don't have time to hang out tonight. I have to submit a collection of stories by tomorrow."

"Can't we spend a small portion of time together?" His eyes squinted ferociously at me, as though he were looking at the glinting snows of Mount Fuji.

"Well, maybe just a small portion of time then." I was about to suggest that we could sit on the dark benches of the housing project across the street from my house when he looked up and said, "We can go up to your roof, no?"

That was really a location for a second or even a third date, but the red wine from the restaurant had gotten to my head, and we had to go somewhere: "Let's go."

"How about we get a beer first?" He was a sly one.

"I can't drink any more tonight." I needed to think clearly for the writing.

"No, no." He pretended to misunderstand. "My treat."

"Okay, just one can of beer." I knew I could handle that much.

He dashed into the Arab deli on the southwest corner, raced to the reach-in fridges that lined the right side of the place, and returned to the counter where I was waiting. There I discovered that he had pulled another slick move, selecting two of those oil drums of Fosters Lager.

We headed toward my house. Halfway across the street, though, just as the light was changing, he unexpectedly shouted, "Excuse!"

Turning around, he dashed back into the deli. I tried to join him, but the ongoing traffic divided us. In another minute he was outside, smiling, jaywalking his way back to me.

"What was that about?" I asked.

He shook a box of bright red TicTacs. Slick Willy was planning on swapping spit. Well, just maybe we would. Once at my apartment, we climbed up the stairs until we reached the roof door. We opened up the rusty bolt and stepped onto the tar-blackness. Carefully we steered around skylights, rusty pipes, and filthy brick chimneys. Sako grabbed my hand and took the liberty of climbing onto an adjacent rooftop, where we took a seat on a low brick wall and stared at the distant mountain peaks of skyscrapers and nearby valleys of tenement rooftops.

He opened both our beers and handed me one. I only took a sip and instantly felt woozy. Although the conversation was a bit halting, we drank our beer and contemplated the gorgeous lightscape of the city's skyline. Sako's slippery hands quickly got twined into my hair like bats. Before I knew it, Sako was massaging my arms and neck. I was bigger and stronger than Sako and didn't feel threatened by him as I did with Alphonso. He also seemed sane, so I let him get away with a lot more. When I leaned against a chimney stack, he chivalrously placed his jacket around my shoulders so I wouldn't get all cinder-filthy.

I didn't know if it was one of the secrets of the Orient, but the guy really got into the Zen of massage. I felt like a small car being tuned up, getting my oil replaced and my wheels rebalanced. His magical hands reached into the muscles along my ribs and upper chest, where he seemed to clean the bones and put them back. When he rubbed my breasts, it was so casual and nonerogenous that I wasn't even aware he stole second base.

Primo gave a fair rubdown, but he didn't come close to this dear little man. And just when I thought he was done, Sako unlaced my kickers and went to work on my feet. This turned out to be the most electric and exultant part of the workout.

I think he actually had a secret form of communication with each part of my foot: the sole, the instep, the heel, the arch, and each toe. Every member of the foot family wanted a different sensation, and only he knew that feeling—he became one with it. The mounting ecstasy compelled a minor out-of-foot experience. Finally, urgently, I reached over with both hands and grabbed his tight little buns, pulling him up against me. Soon, when his lips clipped over mine, his TicTac-tasty tongue tingled in my palate. I found myself kissing him without effort. I don't know quite how it happened, but at some point we floated down the airshaft and into my apartment. Only Numb broke the spell by leaping up on Sako with his body outstretched. The dog was almost as tall as him. I pulled the pooch off and stuck him in the bathroom. Unlike Alphonso, he didn't even have to ask. If Caroline was in her room, I didn't hear her.

We slipped into the bedroom and resumed our lip wrestle. Sako wasn't a great kisser, but what he lacked in tongue-flickability, he made up for in sheer tongue-mopping. The man outlicked Numb. His pointy red swab voyaged its way down the cresting waves of my neck, navigating through the straits of my breasts, whirlpooling forever along the flat of my stomach. His hands pulled down my pants, attempting to explore my Cape of Good Hope, but it wasn't that easy, I held on to my panty elastic like a life preserver. I could feel his open mouth exhale over the sheer fabric of my panties, into my parted crotch. Finally he bypassed my bastion of neglect, sliding his lips down my legs, pausing on his real port of entry. His catlike tongue swam along the twists of my right ankle and lashed out and down my

Achilles' heel. There he stopped for a moment, breathing heavily. With a jolt, I bolted up. He was sucking my toes. I never imagined they were so sensitive.

Over the next few minutes, his tongue pumiced the callous of my heels, pedicured my hoof-like nails, and cleaned the jam between my toes. Then, his sweet mouth opened and he deep-jawed me. Looking down, I felt as though I were being swallowed by a python: he had about half of my size-eight foot down his expanding throat. I could also see he was rubbing himself over his pants.

He truly brought some exotic dishes to the erotic table. His mouth worked its way up; this time he tore my panties off like they were fastened by Velcro strips. But I didn't mind. His carnal credentials were in order. His tenacious little tongue went right to work, starting on the bristled periphery before going in for the kill. When his pants and boxers dropped off, and I could see his ruddy thing throbbing out like a large baby's pacifier, I called foul.

"What's the matter, Mary?" he asked innocently.

"Protection."

Out came a pack of condoms—Rough Riders—and I realized that that was what this Far Eastern Lothario had hastily purchased along with the TicTacs. He slipped a glove on, and then I did what I always swore I'd never do (but occasionally did)—had sex on the first goddamned date.

Unfortunately, that's when things started quickly becoming undone. He kamikazed almost as soon as he entered, screaming like Godzilla as he did so. Next he bounced up and down on the bed like some pint-size Tarzan. Spotting the half-finished bottle of Jack Daniels sticking out of one of Primo's banana boxes, he snatched it, unscrewed the top, and took a monster gulp. Then naked, as though doing some victory dance, he threw on the radio, and started bobbing and drinking to the music, his rhubarb flipping up and down under its spiky tuft of pubic hair. A few moments later, he was tuckered out.

"May I see your shoes?" he asked after a brief rest.

I pointed to my closet, and wondered how I was going to get rid of him and back to my writing. I watched him squatting over my dozen or so shoes, looking deeply into them, touching the leather uppers, sniffing the Vibram lowers, checking out the manufacturer labels like a boy fussing over baseball cards. Finally, he sighed over my two pairs of campy high heels.

"I don't mean to be rude, but—" I said, wanting him the hell out.

He didn't even notice me as I started panicking about his intrusion in my closet space. When I opened the bathroom door, Numb darted out and into the bedlam of the bedroom. I had gargled and showered as I wondered how I was going to flush this man, when to my surprise, I heard him scream, "Help me, Mary!"

I raced in to see him standing on the bed, terrified, holding one of my pumps in one hand and the bottle of Jack in the other. Numb, who had sniffed him, was now upon him, licking his sushi roll.

"Oh my!" He folded down from his freshly opened umbrella of drunkenness. I grabbed Numb by the collar and held him.

"Bad dog," I said to the both of them. "You can take the bottle, but I have to write."

"Yes, yes." He rose and started pulling on his pants and shirt. I waited patiently with the dog by the front door.

"I hope this was not too sudden," he said, probably quoting a line from the script of *Pretty in Pink.*

"Not at all, you were great." Which must have been a line from *Some Kind of Wonderful.*

"Thank you, thank you," he said, pulling on his shoes. I opened the front door. Before he could tie them, he staggered out, still holding my old pump and bottle. I grabbed the shoe and gave him his jacket as he passed into the unpainted, unswept hallway.

"Good night," I said, after I closed the door behind him.

I dashed to the computer, turned it on, and began hammering out my much-delayed story. After a few pages, though, I found my thoughts drifting and my eyelids drooping. I considered buying a cup of coffee but elected instead to take a short nap. The day of work, band practice, and then the sexual escapade had flattened me out. I needed a juiced-up brain to crank out work of any grade.

I awoke eight hours later, feeling refreshed but panicky. Aside from the fact that I was supposed to hop up and pull an eight-hour shift at Kinko's, I had to finish and hand off my collection to Tattoo Man, and be wide awake for our big performance at Mercury Lounge tonight—it was all too much.

My first act of the day was to call work and politely explain that I was sick and would not be able to come in. I felt guilty about it, and Scotty, the model of innocence for my Bartleby story, gingerly insinuated his despair with comments like "Jeff isn't going to take this well."

"Don't worry about Jeff."

He added that he was short-handed, and to my surprise, Scotty asked me the symptoms of my infirmities. He wasn't as innocent as he seemed.

"Runny nose, sore throat, fever—the usual." I said without even making an effort at sounding sick.

He concluded with, "If you have a sudden relapse of health, please come in."

I assured him I would and hung up. I washed, coffeed, and plopped back down in front of Mister Computer. I decided to narrate the story through the eyes of his female supervisor, Kristin.

She is a young punk who is transferred to manage a new Kinko's. She hires Bart on the first day of work. He quickly excels, proving himself to be the best worker, laboring hard and efficiently over the years, refusing promotions, never loafing, never missing a day of work, never even asserting a personality—just staying on as a clerk as others more temperamental and less productive pass through. Bart has found his niche; this is the pinnacle for him. He can Xerox faster and more politely than any other employee, juggling several Xeroxing jobs at once. Over the years, though, the machines get increasingly sophisticated. The punk manager loses her fashion statements as she gets older and watches as the latest trends and vogues come and go across the canvas of the younger generations. She fondly remembers her own years of flamboyance and abandonment. After twenty years or so, technology finally advances so that all copy machines are fully automated. All patrons have to do is set down their originals, verbally make their specifications, and slip their credit card—which everyone has—into the automated contraptions. Bart, the last customer service employee in the place, only has to oversee the process and occasionally explain it to those who fail the intelligence test of being able to perform the obvious.

On that first day of total automation, Bart just sits back, with little to do. However, over the next few weeks, the state-of-the-art equipment mysteriously starts breaking down. He has to do the copies by hand. His manager, Kristin, brings in experts to repair the problem. But a few days later, to her horror, she finds that all the machines are down again. After weeks of the machines repeatedly malfunctioning and needing to be repaired, Kristin installs a hidden video camera. To her dismay, she discovers that her lone employee is the culprit.

"Bart," she confronts him, "why have you been sabotaging the equipment?"

"Actually, I repaired them," he explains blandly.

"How's that?"

"They are designed to help us, not replace us."

"They are helping us. Freeing us to do bigger and better things."

"What happens when there's nothing bigger and better?" he asks.

"I assure you there are greater purposes in life than Xeroxing. In any case, you have to promise me you won't tamper with the machines again."

"I prefer not to," Bart responded.

She threatens to fire him, but he continues his rage against the machines. Kristin, who has known Bart over thirty years of working together, tries to protect him and conceal his Luddite compulsion from her district manager. But her boss, who has grown concerned over this recurrent problem, has hidden his own video camera, and he soon discovers what is going on. He not only fires the clerk but has him arrested for squandering thousands of dollars of the company's money on costly repairs. Bart is taken to the correctional facility downtown to await arraignment. When Kristin goes to visit him, she finds that he has died sleeping in his cell.

"Sleeping with copiers and Kinko employees of years gone by," she concludes sadly. This alludes to the last line of the Melville story.

"Bart the Xeroxer" was the last story in *The Book of Jobs*. The order of the stories was "Big Mac," about the McDonald's cashier in Harlem; "The Melting of an Empire," the Baskin Robbins suicide; "The Biggest Gap," the love story between two vapid Gap employees; "Kmart to Chaos," about Kay, the unfortunate sales associate; and "The Coffee Wars," about the zealous manager of a new coffee franchise who personally combats the managers of neighboring coffee franchises. On the screen the collection came to 182 pages. According to the word count, it squeaked in at just over fifty-two thousand words.

By noon, I was barely able to read another word; the mental fuel was draining from my eyes. I strained the entire mess through the meat grinder of spell-check. That took another hour and a half. Foolishly, I attempted to reread the entire monstrosity one last time just to give it a final syntactical check. Sleep felled me somewhere around sixty pages into it.

Within minutes of my slumber, the phone tortured me, ringing me from rest. It was Howard.

"Are your stories ready?"

"Is it five already?" I said, trying to sound wide awake, and stumbled into my commander chair in front of my cyber-universe.

"It's three o'clock, and I have to drop off the manuscripts in forty-five minutes. I'll swing by your house."

"Did you walk Fedora?" I asked as I went to the top of the document and punched the formatting functions.

"Walked him hours ago. Why?" he replied.

"What's it like owning a Weimaraner?" I set the running heads of the manuscript.

"They're sensitive, smart, soulful dogs," he alliterated.

"They have those tired-looking eyes." I put in the font and letter sizes, then centered page numbers. "They look sickly."

"Don't let William Wegman hear you say that," he cautioned.

"Who's that?" I asked, knowing perfectly well who he was.

"He's the artist that uses his Weimaraners in all his photographs, and he goes to the local dogrun sometimes." I checked to make sure all the opening pages of the different stories were four lines below the title.

"Okay," I muttered as I pushed the print key.

"See you in forty-five minutes," he stated.

"An hour," I pleaded. "I need at least an hour to get myself pretty." It would take at least that long for my printer to finish the hundred and eighty-two pages.

"In exactly one hour I'll ring your bell." He spoke like a warden declaring when he would throw the switch. As the printer methodically printed, I threw on a slip, brushed my teeth, and gargled. Out of nervousness, while watching as the pages spat out of the machine, I applied makeup.

In half an hour, only ninety-four pages were done. It was still printing. At forty-five minutes, it was up to one hundred and thirty-eight pages! I started pacing. The lovable mongrel, sensing I was tense and not wanting to incur some of my misaimed anxiety, slipped out of the room. I prayed that incredibly Tattooed Man would be incredibly late.

Five minutes before he was supposed to arrive, the doorbell rang. I intercommed down, coyly asking who it was.

"Me," he shouted back, "and I have to be at the office in twenty minutes. Bring it right down."

I checked the printer; it was up to page one hundred and sixty-two. Those last twenty pages were going to take at least another twenty minutes. I stood over the prehistoric printer, begging it to move faster, freaking out with every new page.

About five minutes later, the doorbell buzzed again. I pushed the intercom, and told him I was running a little late.

"I'm sorry, Mary, but I just can't wait any longer."

"I'm on my way down." The printer was only on page one hundred and seventy. It seemed to be slowing down. I dashed downstairs in bare feet with just my slip on. He stood in the doorway, sporting a brown knapsack, looking at his watch.

"Where's the tome?" he asked. "Where are your clothes?"

"Owwww!" I said, having stepped on something cold and pointy.

"What's the matter?"

When I leaned forward to look at my foot, he asked, "Is it your back?"

"Yes," I replied, adding that while playing tennis at East River Park, my back had gone out. With my other foot I stepped on something soft and wet.

"You should have said so," he replied sympathetically. "I give great back massages."

As he followed me up the stairs, I limped like a penguin pretending to have a back injury. As I led him into the living room, I could hear the printer whirring in the next room. Willing to do anything to bide my time, I lay down on the sofa and hoped he was half the masseur slick Sako had been.

"Not there!" he yelled. "Get on the floor."

"But it's more comfortable here," I said from the couch.

"Just trust me."

I spread out a towel and lay down on the living room floor. Numb came over and sniffed me mockingly. Tattoo Man took off his shoes like a Tibetan monk and came over. His hands gently moved down the Himalayan ridges of my shoulders.

"Exactly where is the pain?"

"Lower center."

With a mystical quality he ran his hands lightly along my vertebrae.

"Lower," I instructed.

Through the silken fabric, his fingers felt cold and clammy. When they finally landed on my buttocks, I yelled, "Up!"

He moved the heel of his mucilaginous palm up along my slip in a sort of gentle twisting motion.

"That feels good," I said as he did it.

"No," he stopped. "This isn't working."

"It's working great," I replied. "The pain is going away."

"Sit up a moment." I sat up. Without even asking, he took the strings of my slip and was about to bring them down over my shoulders.

"What are you doing?" I grabbed them just before he could bare my breasts to all the roaches in my apartment.

"Trust me."

I could still hear the printer laughing at me from the next

room. It came down to a single question: Was I going to let him see my tits in exchange for getting my stories in a ridiculous contest? I would have said no if it was really a matter of choice. *I had to submit.* Besides, Tattoo Man was not a lech. I knew he was interested in me, but I sensed his altruism, and if he was hiding some incidental horniness, good for him. I grabbed a towel from the bathroom, laid it on the floor, pulled down my slip, baring my breasts, and quickly lay facedown on a towel. He rubbed his hands together, presumably heating them up.

He massaged my lower back, which didn't feel so bad. Yet with each hand press I couldn't stop thinking how pathetic I was, compromising myself for this tawdry collection of stories. Slowly I started boiling, until I finally decided, enough!

Jumping up, I pulled my slip back up over my shoulders.

"Great," I said miraculously. Even though the slow-mo printer was still *p-r-i-n-t-i-n-g,* I didn't care any longer. When I checked, I discovered that it was spewing out blank pages. The book had finished printing at least ten minutes ago. I probably didn't even need to take off my slip. In self-disgust, I shoved the pages into a large envelope and brought it out to Howard.

"Thanks so much for fixing my back," I said to him robotically.

"I can stay longer," he volunteered kindly.

"You have an appointment, and I have to run to my gynecologist."

"I understand." He pulled his shoes on and took the manuscript. Before walking out the door, he turned and politely said, "You've got a great body."

I assured him that I knew, thanked him, closed the door, and collapsed into a short but troubled sleep. After an hour, Sue called and asked where the hell was I.

"Aren't we meeting at seven?" I asked groggily.

"I said we're all supposed to be at my house at six-thirty. We're supposed to load in before the first band plays at seven-thirty."

I told her I was on my way.

She asked me what I was planning on wearing. Clothes, I replied.

"What clothes?"

Without going into detail, I assured her they would be sexy, but not tasteless.

"I'd prefer if they were tasteless," she said and explained that she had hired a woman named Pearl who had a van and was supposed to move our instruments to the club. She had arrived earlier and, seeing no one else was there, had driven off to dinner but was coming back at seven-thirty. I washed up, took doggie out, grabbed a spring roll at the Vietnamese dive, and dashed over to Sue's place on Twelfth between First and Second Avenues. To my delight and astonishment, I arrived just as Marilyn was walking up with Norma in tow. I rang Sue's bell.

"Don't go up," Marilyn warned as Sue rang back.

"Why not?"

"'Cause the place is a mess," Norma said.

"That's not why, it's 'cause we'll never get out in time." Marilyn sounded like the voice of experience. Norma, who didn't look well, concurred with a nod.

"Will one of you bitches please get your fat asses up here and help me with this shit?" Sue snarled down to us over the intercom.

Marilyn stood next to our instruments, and Norma seemed permanently immobilized, so I headed up the three flights. Sue was waiting in the hallway with her guitar on a small aluminum fold-up hand truck, and a knapsack over her shoulder. She was saying good-bye to her child, who was standing in the crack of the door wearing his cute, little PJs.

"Now take care of Auntie Jane. She's not feeling well tonight."

"Yes, Mommy," said the adorable Primo love-child. Sue hugged and kissed him.

"What's the matter with Auntie Jane?" I inquired as Sue closed the door.

"She's passed out in front of the TV," Sue said and asked, "Is Pearl out front?"

"Not as far as I saw."

"She's probably gobbling down dinner."

"Where are the amps?" I asked.

"We're using Rent Control's amps. They're the first band in the lineup."

"That's good."

"Good, hell, I have to pay them."

Sue instructed me to grab the bottom of the light hand truck, and together we carried her instrument and supplies down the stairs. Out front the other two were waiting.

"Where's Pearl?" Marilyn asked, staring east down Twelfth Street. People were exiting the theater across the street.

"She came on time," Sue said, contrasting her with the rest of us. "She'll be back soon."

We waited for ten minutes before Sue announced, "Hell with this, let's grab a cab."

We tried hailing for another ten minutes before Sue snapped, "We're going to miss our time slot. Let's get down there on foot."

Our muddled crew silently headed down Twelfth Street, constantly looking behind for a possible taxi. After five tired minutes of lugging our instruments like a hip group of Kosovar refugees, we caught a cab and headed down Avenue A to Houston; the Mercury Lounge. Sue paid the fare, and we struggled out.

Independently we all knew Bobby Sox, the bouncer standing in front of the place. He turned to me and said, "I didn't know you were with them."

"Neither did I."

We moved past the tight, narrow bar, where the chubby-armed manager, Gary, commented that we were supposed to load in at six. We all apologized. The lead singer of the Deltoids, the band before us, gave us a fuck-you expression as we struggled past during their last song, getting everything down the stairs. Two members of Rent Control were still hanging around. Sue slipped them twenty bucks for use of their amps.

When the other girls took off their overcoats, I was shocked to see how skimpy and revealing their outfits were. Sue wore stockings and garters. Norma had a tight green tank top over a sheer push-up bra. To my mild embarrassment, I was the most conservatively dressed with my simple sleeveless black turtleneck and relatively tight blue jeans.

"What did you think this was, a Gap ad?" Sue shot out.

In the audience we spotted a few people we knew. I didn't know about my bandmates, but I made a point of not inviting anyone. Hell, I still hadn't told anyone I was even in the band. As we were setting up and plugging in, with Sue screaming instructions to us above the prickliness of miscellaneous chatter, I heard, "Holy shit, is that you, Bellanova?"

In the drunken dimness I could make out the shimmering dirty blond hair of Emily, with her mismatched gang. At first I tried not to notice, but she kept screaming at me, "That was my college roommate!"

"Hi, Em," I called out to her.

"You didn't tell me you were in this band!" She muscled her way to the front of the cramped stage.

"Can we talk about it later?" I screamed back, not good at hiding my performance anxiety.

"You know I'm playing at Brownie's in four days," she advertised.

"Yeah, I know."

"You're coming, right?"

"Yeah, I'll bring Zoë."

She backed her way into the squirming crowd. We took our

positions and tested our instruments. The sound man made some adjustments. One of the amps was all treble and no bass. Two of the guitar cables worked intermittently and had to be replaced. Sue tested her vocals in the PA, then gave her nod. "Colder Than a Witch's Tit" roared out of her lungs and our fingers. She was putting that anger to good use. All of them really cranked it up. I never saw Norma so alive. Marilyn too. Even though it was not my style, I tried to keep up with them. "Fuck You 'Cause You Can't" was next on our jukebox. One by one the songs punched out of the large amps, and remarkably, the music didn't suck. Some of the more provocative songs earned a "Do it, honey" and other complimentary catcalls. With each song we all took our little spills, missing occasional beats, strings, and words, but each mistake was one at a time, so that the others covered. Finally at the end of the last song, exhausted and covered with sweat, we heard some claps, stomps, hoots, and even a "Show your tits!" We packed up our instruments as the next band, Sloppy Seconds, started up.

"You guys are hot!" their lead singer, Hooch, said. Too bad he looked like an manatee covered with hair. On our way out Bobby Sox asked, "Hey, where's Zoë?"

"She couldn't make it," I said with a smile.

"I didn't even know you were in a band."

"It's just a lark," I replied and said good night. I knew that Zoë'd feel betrayed if she found out about this from anyone but me. I had to tell her soon.

Sue screamed at me to join the rest of them squeezing into a cab. Marilyn said we should all go somewhere for drinks, but Norma said she was already drunk, and Sue had to get back to her kid. As our cab approached Fourth and First, I told the driver to pull over and offered Sue two bucks.

"It's okay, you already paid," she explained, adding that we had got 10 percent of the door, which came to a total of twenty bucks, or five dollars per girl.

Rehearsal was tomorrow at ten, she concluded. I went upstairs, grabbed Numb, and tiredly walked the dog, then headed back upstairs, where I stripped and lay in bed. I felt half exhausted and half crazed about the two half-baked offerings of the day: a rushed submission to a literary contest and my first public concert without nearly enough practice or talent. I felt good.

I dreamed I was rising from great oceanic depths, through many atmospheres of pressure. My body floated up through the greenish waters toward the faint light. When I bolted up in a panic, I realized I was late. As soon as I showed up at Kinko's for work, Jeff marched over to me and asked why I had taken yesterday off. Scott couldn't get a replacement.

"I felt nauseous," I explained, and deciding to be clever, I suggestively twisted the blame to him. "You didn't have any stomach problems after eating at that Italian place?"

"No, but whatever it was must not have been too bad."

"Why is that?"

"Well," he replied with a frigid smile. "From what I hear, you performed pretty well with Sako and even better at the Mercury Lounge last night." I guess I couldn't blame Sako for toe-sucking and telling, but how did he find out about the performance?

"You're not just a liar," he went on, "but you have the nerve to blame me for a bogus food poisoning after I was kind enough to treat you to dinner."

"I'm sorry," I said sincerely.

"You think it's all funny and you can just apologize your way out of things like some child, but you can't."

"Look, you're right. I'm really sorry."

He walked away from me, giving me a good old-fashioned shunning. What worried me most was that if he knew about all my secret adventures, Zoë must have heard, and I knew she'd be pissed I hadn't told her. During my lunch break I gave her a call. She wasn't in. I left a message, and over time more messages—all without a response.

That afternoon, the neglect ended. Jeff returned as a sadistic prison guard. He timed my one bathroom break and noticed that some of my accessories, particularly a tiny smiley-face button on my apron, were not part of the official Kinko's uniform. Next, he rewrote my schedule for the upcoming week, giving me night shifts that he knew would fuck up my life.

I went home and burned a tray of frozen Tater Tots that I was making for dinner. Then I grabbed my pile of filthy clothes, took them to the laundry, and dumped them into a machine. While waiting for the wash, I found a paper and read an article about some guy who spent years working at a Fotomat out on the Island. While developing people's film, whenever he came across a picture of a nude woman, he would make an extra copy of it for himself. Eventually he discovered an added source of income: he would send his nude snapshots to a skin magazine that paid fifty bucks per photo. When one husband discovered his wife *au naturel* in a magazine, he called the police. They were able to catch the clerk. I tore the article out of the paper. Even though *The Book of Jobs* was already under submission, this story would be a perfect addition. I already had the title—"The Fotomat Junkie."

As I pulled my wet clothes out of the laundry machine, I discovered that I had accidentally destroyed the only cashmere in my wardrobe, a Bendel's three-quarter-sleeve boatneck sweater that had cost me over three hundred bucks. I glumly waited for the dryer, folded everything else, and brought it home. Then I took Numb out for the first time in eight hours. He whiffed every contour of earth without pissing once, filling me with anxiety that he would pee as soon as I left him alone.

That night at rehearsal, Sue produced a list of all the errors each of us had made during our performance.

"This is all routine," she scolded. "We all play the same notes and sing the same songs over and over and over!"

To her credit, she first reviewed the few lines she dropped

and thoroughly castigated herself in the process. Then she took turns yelling at each of us. When it was my turn, she had me play as she sang one of her Fuck songs.

"Now, why couldn't you do that last night?" she asked.

"I don't know, Sue, but I can't deal with this right now!"

"Oh, you can't?"

"No, I'm afraid I can't," I proclaimed, and tossing the bass in the case and grabbing my jacket, I stormed out into the hallway.

As I waited for the elevator, she approached from behind. I decided that if she said a word, I would quit right there. Surprisingly, she put her hands on my shoulder and began rubbing my upper back. "I'm sorry. Go ahead home. Take it easy. If you're having a hard time, all you got to do is tell me."

When the elevator door opened, she said, "You played fine last night."

The next day at work, Jeff hovered over me, watching for mistakes. He deliberately embarrassed me in front of a really cute guy—"She's bungling it up again!"

All the while, he kept up his grudge with a smile, refusing to forgive, even after I apologized a few more times for taking the crucial day off. Over the next few days, he didn't let up. Jeff seemed to prefer humiliating me to firing me. I waited for his mood to blow over, but his storm system was stalled over me. Meanwhile Zoë refused to return my calls; I assumed she was doubly pissed at me. To make matters worse, Howard was not in the dogrun. I figured that it was his nonconfrontational way of saying that I had lost the contest.

The withdrawal of social life became an opportunity to write. This was the one real benefit to hacking out the collection of stories. After years of malingering, it put me back into the literary groove.

I was ready to undertake my great proletariat novel. Throughout the years of living in this city, while working in offices or waiting for trains, I would catch sight of them at the opening flaps and closing hatches of the day. Small, hard-edged women, usually immigrants, who held the million little thankless jobs that glued this city together: waitresses, cashiers, seamstresses, day-care workers. Before my mother went back to school and got her teaching credentials, shortly after my father left her, she was one of these menial laborers. Without ever intending to, I had collected endless observations about them.

During my hitch at a corporate law firm, I talked at length to a battery of females—young, old, Latin, Russian, African American, Asian. I loosely plotted a novel on this group of evening cleaning ladies. Some had children to support, others were sole providers. Some lived alone. Few used moisturizers. Instead of a line of beauty products, Clinique was a place they'd take their feverish children to in the middle of the night.

The next day I cut my hair shorter and in a more practical style than ever before.

It wasn't until four days later, at eight in the morning, just as I was heading to Kinko's, that Zoë finally called me. In a cold, decimated voice, she apologized that she hadn't returned my messages, but she had been out of town. She further explained that during the past week, after a steady run of knock-down, drag-outs, Jeff had finally accused her of sleeping with another and slapped her—that had occurred the day I played the Mercury Lounge. Poor Zoë was back in Singlesville.

"That fucker!" I said. He was a typical woman beater.

"I kind of initiated the hitting," she conceded.

"That's no excuse."

"I should have expected this. You warned me," she said, instantly choking back tears.

"I'm sorry for storming out after that dinner with Sako." It was the last time I had seen her.

"He wanted me to break off my friendship with you," she revealed.

"I can't believe this!"

"He kept saying he did you this big favor getting you a job, and you made a joke of him."

"Did he tell you anything about my missing work a few days ago?"

"I haven't spoken to him in a while." She didn't know about my being in a band.

"I've got some news to tell you," I began in my slow stammer.

"I got to run off to work now. Are we meeting tonight?" she asked, sensing my long delivery.

"Tonight?" There was no rehearsal tonight, so it was possible.

"Emily's playing at Brownies." I had completely forgotten about it.

I had to run to get abused by her ex at Kinko's, so we agreed to meet and talk later.

The bottom line was Jeff was pissed at Zoë and was using me as his whipping girl. I had to bail out of this awful job. This was a damn shame, because I was just making strides. Every time I had the freedom to just sit down and write, fate interrupted me like a needy, whiny child. The last time I had a good writing day, Gregor left me for Gwyneth Paltrow.

When I arrived six minutes late for work, Jeff waded right in with the remark, "It's coming out of your paycheck." He said this in front of three coworkers and about a half dozen customers.

"You know, you're a nasty little prick," I decided to tell him, in case he didn't know.

"And you're an ungrateful bitch! I got you this job, and you backstabbed me. You think just because I slept with that slut friend of yours, you get to do whatever you want around here!"

"This guy is a woman beater!" I announced to the gang of customers and fellow employees.

One of the female customers said, "That sucks." Another walked out.

"She screwed some guy in my apartment! In my bed!" he

screamed. "And I'm sure you encouraged it." He stormed off, but still hadn't fired me. He was content just to keep me there, suspended in his abuse.

I grabbed my jacket, along with several reams of blank paper that I could use for writing, and headed home. I called Zoë at work and explained what had just transpired. She swore that she'd never cheated on him. He walked in on her at the bar on Third and A while she was talking to Bobby Sox, the doorman at the Mercury Lounge. In front of everyone Jeff became livid, accusing her of all sorts of things.

"Were you guys kissing or something?" I asked her.

"We kissed once about six months ago. I had too much to drink, big deal." Instantly, in a tone of fright signifying the appearance of a supervisor, Zoë concluded, "Got to go. Later!"

That day it didn't really rain; the sky just sort of dripped, as if the gray ceiling of clouds had a thousand little leaks. I took Numb to the run, and tried to smoke and coffee my worries away, but they lingered. I went back home and tried to write some more of my fledgling novel, but the magic was gone. Anxiety was seated in its place. One needed to be in a good head to write. Dead-eyed, I watched TV in a paralyzing panic that kept me from getting a job.

For the unemployed, daytime TV viewer, the real teaser to watching all those freaky talk-show hosts or unofficial courts run by "people's" judges, or hammy soap actors is that they all seem so amateurish: you can't help feeling that with a little moxie you too could moderate a sex fight, or arbitrate a dispute between idiots, or act through a script filled with unlikely cliff-hangers.

That night around eight o'clock, feeling telebotomized, I stumbled out to Brownies, where I paid, got my wrist stamped, and anesthetized myself with a drink. Zoë showed up about half an hour later. We both tried to pretend that everything was A-okay.

Emily's band, Crapped Out Cowgirls, was first in the lineup.

Zoë bought me a couple of beers while Emily droned a kazoo to their first number, "You Don't Need a Trailer to Be Trailer Trash." Thank God she only did that for one song. The differences between my band and Emily's band were Apes and Orangutans—they were rockabilly, while we were punk. Musician for musician, we were about the same. In the end, despite the redundancy of melody and rhythm, Sue's songs were a notch better than Crapped Out's. And as far as appearance, although we had to wear tight, tacky, slinky outfits, at least we didn't have to coordinate cowboy hats and boots like they did. One of the girls in her group played a fiddle, which was nice.

Their set lasted about an hour. As they packed up, the next band, Three Mile Island, set up. The place was a snowglobe of East Village flakes; they were mainly self-deluded "youths" whose actual youth had melted away long ago. Zoë bought us a couple more drinks, and though I could see her assessing the males in the mist, she was on a guy moratorium. Amid the swirl and mix, I told her that I'd been fired from Kinko's.

"You should apply for unemployment insurance," she said automatically.

"I wasn't even there a month." I replied and asked her if she knew of any additional temp jobs where she worked.

"I wish I did," she said politely. "I hate my own."

Three Mile Island's music had the toxic effects of a radiation leak. They were so loud that the only way we could continue any kind of discussion was by screaming at the top of our lungs into each other's ears, supplemented with broad gestures. Out of the corner of my eye I spotted the young peroxide-haired community servant; presumably her Tompkins Square sentence had been served. I watched as she talked to some older man who bought her a drink. I couldn't help but wonder how she was able to distinguish vocational from recreational sex—when to charge and when not to charge.

"Hey!" Someone yelled after one nuclear song. It was Emily.

Her band had packed all their equipment downstairs, and she was now available for hanging out.

"Hey yourself," Zoë yelled back.

"I can't believe this one was holding out on me," she retorted, third-personing me.

"What are you talking about?" Zoë shot back. I held my breath and realized that I still hadn't told her about my bandification.

"She's in a band," Emily gushed.

"WHAT!!" Zoë exploded, rolling sound waves around her. I looked and acted defunct.

"She is in the Crazy and the Beautiful," Emily transposed the title. "And they played at Mercury Lounge a few days ago."

"You didn't!" Zoë blasted.

"How dare you!" Emily added, "You called me up grilling me about Sue Wott, and the whole time you were playing with her."

"How do I know that name?" Zoë asked suspiciously.

"She's the crazy Chinese chick," Emily replied.

"She's Cambodian," I corrected.

"Oh no, wait a second." Zoë added one plus one. "Don't tell me this is Primo's famous prima donna."

"Yeah." I came clean. "I meant to tell you."

"Are you fucking nuts?" Zoë asked soberly.

"This is embarrassing." At that moment the music seemed too loud and the place too dark. I headed for the door.

"You're showcasing with my band and Purple Hooded Yogurt Squirter at CBGBs, do you realize that?" Emily asked gleefully.

"Your band is a lot better than us," I insincerely deflected.

"I know we are," she replied immodestly. "Want to see why?" She pointed across the room. Sitting at a table, or rather passed out with her head on a table, was a tall limp string bean of a woman. I pushed my way through the crowded darkness until I made out large heady blotches of black and blond. Norma was conked out, facedown. Emily explained to Zoë that the zonked one was the drummer in my band.

"She's only that way because when she's awake, she gives her all to the drums," I elaborated.

"Are you going to claim her?" Zoë inquired.

"I know this sounds rather heartless, but I'd rather leave her and respect her than wheelbarrow her home and hate her forever."

"You're just going to leave her there?" Emily asked, twisting my conscience like a Twizzler. I sighed and turned to see Sue standing right behind me.

"What are you doing here?" I asked her in shock.

"I came with Norma." She pointed to the collapsed drummer. "What are you doing here?" Sue asked, stepping into the little coven, which included Zoë and Emily.

"Emily's a friend of mine. She played tonight." Sue shook her hand.

"I've heard a lot about you," Zoë said eagerly, taking her hand as well.

"What did you hear?" asked the slightly paranoid one. I darted a look over to Zoë.

"Nothing." She picked up my concern. "Just that you were Primo's ex and all."

"Primo?" Her silent alarm went off. "What does he have to do with anything?"

Although Zoë instantly realized that she had accidentally placed my foot down on a land mine, she had the good sense to freeze. It was Emily who triggered the bomb by stating, "Mary was Primo's last girlfriend."

"What?!" Only with the subtle hint of Sue exploding like a terrorist bomb did Emily realize she messed up big-time.

"What the fuck is this!" Sue followed up.

"What?" I asked.

Emily and Zoë both started backing up, either realizing they had done enough damage or not wanting to get wounded by Sue Wott's shrapnel blast.

"You did this deliberately." She put lock in key. "You're some kind of sick fuck who deliberately did this to find out about me!"

"Primo died." I laid it out for her. "He had a heart attack in my apartment a few weeks ago."

"So what the hell do you want from me?"

"He loved you. He loved you more than any of his other girl-friends."

"So you joined my band?" It did sound insane.

"I went to the audition just to talk to you. Remember? I kept trying to talk to you, and you just kept blowing me off."

"You didn't have an appointment," she remembered with widened eyes, as if she were looking at a ghost.

"All I wanted was to tell you he died and talk to you! But you're so goddamned arrogant and egotistical that you shoved a bass in my hand and roped me into the audition, so I played it and was hired."

"If you had something to say, you could have just said it."

"I guess I was curious about why he loved you so fucking much, but—"

"Ah-ha!"

"But I was really only there for your kid," I added, and paused, unable to explain that when I was a child it was a while before I learned about my father's death.

"My kid is none of your fucking business, so stay the fuck away from me!" she yelled back. Dashing over to Norma, Sue grabbed her limp drummer around the waist and dragged her out of Brownies.

I stood there awhile before Emily came over to apologize. Zoë did likewise, but it was all my fault. I apologized for not telling them. The last band, Three Mile Island, was finishing up. The van was double-parked out front, and Emily had to help pack up and move the remainder of her band's instruments into it.

"Are you okay?" Zoë asked me tenderly, seeing that I was emotionally dismembered.

"I'm sorry," was all I could say to her.

"Let's get out of here." She led me out by the hand.

Since Zoë's TV set had more inches than mine, we went to her place. As we headed to the Korean greengrocer, she asked, "Why didn't you tell me you were in a band?"

"The truth is," I explained, "I felt embarrassed. I feel too old, and I've lived in this neighborhood far too long to have any hopes like this."

"Amazing." Zoë smiled back. "I go out night after night praying to find Mr. Right, but hard old Mary Bellanova can't have any hopes."

We bought a fat-free pint of Ben & Jerry's Vanilla Fudge and split it watching a montage of her blockbuster video library: the last sinking half an hour of *Titanic,* the first destructive twenty minutes of *Independence Day,* and the opening forty-five minutes of girl-cliquey *Heathers.* That was when I said I had to watch one movie from beginning to end. She picked *sex, lies, and videotape,* but after the opening scene in which one sister cheats on the other with her husband, Zoë was out like a light. I felt sleepy, but decided that I didn't want to wake up there. I headed home at four in the morning, only to find poor Numb frantic. He had to go, but he also knew that I was exhausted so as soon as I took him downstairs, he relieved himself on the pavement. I finally got to bed just as the sun was returning late from its own wild drunken night.

chapter 17

Every day is dyed its own hair color. The next day a depressing blue was cast. While lying in bed that morning, lamenting the loss of my job and band, I was yanked up by an annoyingly polite series of knocks upon my door. After two months the brand-new roommate wanted out. Caroline's rice was cooked.

"Dorn and I found a place together in Park Slope," she cheered.

Aside from learning that Dorn was gay, she was also going to find out that most people are lovable at a distance, up close it's a whole 'nother story.

"Even though I was supposed to give you a month's notice, I'm moving out today, but I'll still pay you."

The idea of living alone for the remainder of the month was nice, but the bleakness prevailed.

"Are you okay? You look really depressed." She seemed concerned, which was similar to kindness.

"I just lost my job," I replied tiredly.

"Someone told me they're hiring people over at the Strand."

The Strand was not just a bookstore, but a local workfare program for unemployed white slackers. They'd sit hidden in the narrow aisles on crates of books, until some bitter, rectal manager behind the inner desk yelled, "Books to go down."

Needless to say, I couldn't sink that low. I thanked her for her crappy advice. It was time to get back to my permanent career of temping, but not today.

The blues spread over the strands of the week and darkened as I accepted my fate and waited for my savings to run out.

Perhaps as a supreme act of self-denial, I started writing again. If I could control working-class people and moderate fictitious suffering, everything seemed okay. As coffee cups littered my house and turned into ashtrays, I turned all the women in my novel into divorcees, widows, or never-marrieds. Like my own mother, though, they were all single parents.

Details breathed out of my fingers. Plots sprouted subplots. The major characters engendered minor characters. For the first time in what seemed like forever, I felt the joy of writing and stopped feeling unemployed.

Compared to playing in a band, writing was lonely business. Numb curled around my feet, and whenever I stopped typing, he'd look up at me lovingly and yawn. That week, I also had a remarkably guiltless conversation with my mother about nothing in particular, since I refused to divulge any details that she might use against me. Sako called and asked if we could meet again. Even in John Hughes's world of teenage love, no one sucked a foot or danced around in naked ecstasy. I had to think about it. Scotty called to give his condolences about my getting fired.

"I'm sorry that Jeff is such a mega-idiot, but he's really going through hell about his breakup with Zoë," he concluded.

Norma called me and said when she finally sobered up, she had heard about what had happened at Brownies—about my being ousted—and she was sorry. No longer beautiful or crazy. I was now ugly and sane. She told me Sue had canceled the show at CBGBs and two other dates she hadn't even told anyone about.

"You don't think there's any chance of her forgiving me, do you?" I asked, knowing the answer.

"She doesn't even allow us to mention you," Norma said. "She is starting auditions for a new bass player tomorrow, and this time she swears that anyone who even knows Primo will be tossed down the stairs."

After she hung up, I thought, Primo could be selfish and petty, but he wasn't malevolent. Whatever harm he did to Sue, he did out of weakness and sloth. Like a mutt you picked up at the pound without knowing its history, Primo was a rescue boyfriend. Any woman who was hurt by him only had herself to blame. And that slipped right into Sue Wott's greatest frailty—her reluctance to accept blame.

Toward the end of the week, when I felt supremely entitled to some good news, Howard finally broke his silence and called me. "Can you meet me in ten minutes? I've got something to tell you."

Eight minutes later at the dogrun while I waited, I figured he was going to tell me my stories had been rejected. After all, if I had been accepted, he would have told me on the phone. When he showed up, he let his dog loose and walked up to me with sad dog eyes.

"Don't apologize," I rushed right in. "I took a stab. No big loss. Art is about rejection."

"Did anyone notify you?"

"No."

"Well, no one told me you've been rejected either," he said.

"My book hasn't been rejected?"

"Not to my knowledge. All I know is, the editor called to ask where the manuscript came from and why I hadn't done the reader's report. I told him that it was in the stack of works he gave me, and I overlooked it. Then he gave the manuscript to another reader. About a week ago I heard that it got a good report."

"Why didn't you tell me a week ago?" I asked, always dying for any positive tidbits.

"I didn't want to get your hopes up."

"So why are you telling me now?"

"Because you're asking," he explained. "But this isn't the reason I called you here."

"Oh."

"Do you remember some time ago when you told me about that friend of yours, Joey Lucas?"

"No."

"Remember you said you didn't know anything about him and I mentioned running a superficial background check?"

"Frankly, no," I replied honestly. I'm sure it all happened, but my memory was heading right down the toilet.

"I told you I had a friend who was a private investigator."

"Oh, yeah." The light flicked on in my brain.

"Do you know how old your neighbor is?"

"Around fifty. Why?"

"And he was born in Hoboken, right?"

"I think so."

"Do you know if Joey is his given name or if he had a name change?"

"WHY?" I demanded.

Howard handed me a page from a small spiral notepad with three names scrawled on it:

Joseph Lucachevski, 1025 Washington Ave., born 9/11/45,
    died 7/20/77
Joey Lukas, 123 Clinton St., born 2/7/28,
Joe Lugars, 218 Eighth St., born 11/29/58.

"Holy shit," I uttered.

I wasn't a hundred percent sure if he was born in Hoboken or what year he was born, but 1025 Washington Street was the address where I had spent the first ten years of my life. He lived right above us. It would have been too much of a coincidence if there was another Joey Lucas or ethnic name that it had been derived from. According to the record in my hand, Joey had died twenty-two years ago. So who the hell was this man who over the last few years had become one of my closest friends and most trusted confidants?

"There must be some mistake," I uttered, nodding my head.

"You want to go on a date?" Howard asked, as I wondered who had intercepted me on the Internet—that cyber-funhouse of false identities and pedophiles.

"There's a good movie at the Angelika," he added, vividly underscoring male insensitivity.

"Fine," I said thoughtlessly. He imparted time and place coordinates, and I walked disjointedly home, where I felt my mental floor collapse under me.

I called Joe's number and carefully listened to his greeting: "This is me, leave a message." A long beep signified a full tape of unheard messages, and I hung up before leaving one. There had to be some simple explanation for this. Howard and I met for a pizza at Two Boots and headed to the Angelika Film Center.

We were early as we walked down Mercer Street, so, passing a used bookstore we slipped in to waste some time before the film began. Howard looked under Literary Criticism, as I veered through Fiction, hoping to distract myself from Joey's false identity. While browsing a small shelf entitled Erotica, I spotted a collection of six pornographic paperbacks, all with lime green covers, published by Journey Men Press. They had funny titles: *Billy Club Cops, A Finger in the Dyke* . . . Before my brain completely registered it, I let out a howl: *Cuming Attractions,* by Primitivo Schultz.

"Oh, fuck!" I wailed. The notion that Primo's offensive drivel had actually made it into print, and I couldn't even get a story in a decent literary magazine, filled me with a great and sudden rage. I snatched it from the shelf and opened the pages.

"What's the matter?" Howard called out.

It was his book all right. Before I could even think about it, I tore the paperback down its aged spine.

"What the hell's going on?" the clerk called out. Howard came right over.

"Nothing, I'm sorry," I said, suddenly realizing what I had done, trying to link the two parts together.

The clerk came over and, yanking the two torn halves out of my hands, he charged, "This book was part of a set! We had the entire collection, do you realize that?"

"It's disgusting porno," I replied, sounding like some puritan.

"Look, we have a First Amendment, lady."

"No, I didn't mean that. It's just that this book is so badly written—"

"Hey, I don't give a fuck what you think!" The clerk was obviously enraged.

"How much does it cost?" Howard asked meekly, before the situation could spiral out of control.

"Twenty-five dollars," he shot back, quoting the price from nothing other than some internal system of outrage. I had eighteen dollars, Howard added seven others.

"I'll pay you back," I assured him. He shrugged.

"And don't come back!" the clerk shouted as we were leaving.

We walked silently to the corner. Howard softly asked, "Who is Polly?"

I looked over and saw that he was reading the dedication page of the novel.

"Another nitwit like me," I said, feeling like a total idiot.

"Do you want the book?"

"No, thanks," I said and asked, "Would you mind if we skipped the film?"

"No," he replied and slipped the torn paperback into his pocket.

"I feel like such an idiot," I said, after a few minutes of silence. "I really have an awful temper."

"You were probably pissed about the whole Joey thing."

"That doesn't excuse what I did," I said. "Primo didn't do anything wrong. And nothing is worse than destroying a book."

"He could have told you he wrote it."

"He told me he was a writer. And I found the fucking manuscript. Hell, I read it. It was awful. There weren't enough sex scenes and . . . I just assumed it was rejected."

The evening ended with us both walking our dogs. When I returned to my apartment, Sako was smearing another message on my message tape, begging me for a second date.

I picked up and thanked him for the experimental evening of sensual pleasures, but I simply couldn't risk it again.

"Why?" he asked, "If I acted a bit disorderly—"

"Actually, you gave me a bad case of athlete's foot," I lied. He apologized, recommending I use Dr. Scholl's powder, and hung up.

I went to bed and tried to sleep, but Joey's identity had worked its way back into my head. I finally decided to try something that Zoë told me she had once done in discovering a boyfriend was cheating on her. I called Joey, and when his machine picked up, I plugged in a series of unsystematic permutations in an effort to crack his three-digit code. The first several times, it was to no avail; I was automatically hung up on. It wasn't until the fourth attempt that I got a strange beep and the sudden swish of the tape rewinding. Finally the swishing ceased, and it began to replay, "Hey, Rudy, did you or did you not say Aqueduct at ten? I'm waiting for you, you fucking gumba."—*beep*—"Goddamn it, Staf, I hear you dislocated Jimbo's arm. I fucking tole you, if he can't work, he can't pay you." —*beep*— "Hey, Mister Stafiglianno, I was hoping if you didn't mind, maybe I could pay you just two hundred this week and the rest next week."—*beep*. The messages unraveled.

I hung up and called him back: "You cocksucking coward, if you ever call me or see me again, I'll fucking kill you!" I slammed the phone down and started weeping. I didn't care that he was some kind of strong-arm. Rudolph Stafiglianno, who I always thought was dead, was my father.

Half a revolution of the earth later, around noon the next day, the phone rang, waking me up. Howard was telling my machine that they had selected a book for the contest.

"Which one?" I picked up.

"*Stark,* the one about the priest. The author sent in an alternate ending in which the cleric gets caught in a scandal and is ostracized by the parish."

The new ending sounded like the conclusion of the movie *Priest,* but if the publisher didn't see the film, that was his problem. I still couldn't believe that Primo had gotten a novel published, and I hadn't.

"But hey," Howard said. "I have some good news. You were in the finals, and I think I can get you an agent."

"That would be great," I said, still facedown on my pillow.

"Do you have anything else you're working on?"

"Yeah, I'm about a quarter through a novel about a group of cleaning ladies."

"Who pull a caper in their office?" He anticipated the ending for me.

"No."

"Any sex scenes with their boss?"

"No."

"Do they shoot their boss?"

"Tell you what," I compromised, "if I have them screw the boss, I'll be sure to have them shoot the guy."

He gave me a Midtown address and phone number. "Tell him I recommended you."

"I appreciate it," I said glumly.

"Are you walking your dog?"

"Later. I have to run now." Aside from the joblessness, I had to find a roommate. The echo from the empty room sounded like a forlorn future. In the bathroom, a baby cockroach crawled up to me and stopped. By not killing it, I figured I had done something good. I didn't need to do anything else that day. I rustled through my pockets and my purse but found no cigarettes, no chewing gum, no TicTacs. I turned the TV on, picked up the telephone, and called Zoë at work.

"What's up?" she asked in that edgy, flighty tone that told me she was being loosely supervised.

"Yesterday, while in a Mercer Street bookstore, I found a copy of *Cuming Attractions,* a porn novel by Primo that was published."

"So what? He told me he wrote," she said tiredly.

"I just went nuts. I ripped the book to shreds. I didn't even know I was doing it."

"Are you kidding?" she murmured.

"Why would I be kidding?"

"You've been at this long enough. Don't you think it's time to scatter him both figuratively and literally?" She hung up; the prison matron must have passed her cell. I didn't even have time to tell her the most painful news about Joey.

She was right. It was high time to dispose of the ashes and finally forget about the liar, the cheat, and the fraud who slept with me for six months and one day died.

Looking through my phone book, I located Helga Elfman's business card and dialed. A perky receptionist answered, "Barbarosian Gallery."

"Ms. Elfman, please."

"Whom should I say is calling?"

"Primo's girlfriend," I replied, half enjoying the trashy sound of it.

"Even dead, that man has a girlfriend," Helga said by way of a greeting.

"I'm sorry for calling you in the middle of the day like this, but you asked me to inform you of the scattering."

"When and where, quick?" No mincing words with her. From silence equals death to time equals money.

"Tonight," I decided right then and there. "In Tompkins Square Park."

"Tonight might be a problem," she replied.

"Well, problem or not, I'm done. I'll wait until seven. No later. I want to get rid of all the shitty men in my life tonight."

"Where exactly should I meet you?" She sounded as though she were holding pen to appointment book.

"Do you know the Horseshoe Bar?" I asked.

"I'll try," she said and hung up.

I called the other quasi-ex-girlfriend, Lydia. She didn't pick up, so I put the information on her machine. I thought about calling Norma but didn't want to get her in trouble with Sue. Last, I called Zoë back at work and announced that tonight was the fateful night of the long-overdue scattering.

"I'm so glad," she said and hung up. I called several of Primo's male friends, leaving messages on their machines about that night's service. Then I realized that by being on the telephone while the TV was on, I was being rude to the picture box, so I watched it uninterrupted.

It was five o'clock when *Oprah* was done. Both I and the dog were stir-crazy. Another day was shot out of the sky without sunlight or forward motion. I left a message on my outgoing machine: "In case anyone should call, Primo's ash toss will be at seven-fifteen tonight at the dogrun in Tompkins Square Park."

I dressed, grabbed the dog, located the Primo box, and headed out to the park. While I passed through the housing complex between First Avenue and A, I felt my pockets for a cigarette and found an envelope of blue, diamond-shaped pills instead. I remembered that I had found them in Primo's banana box some time ago. As I came out on Fifth Street, I went to the corner pharmacy across the street for smokes. I purchased a pack from the pharmacist himself.

"Excuse me," I asked him, a bespectacled man in his sixties. "You couldn't tell me what these are?" I handed him the packet.

He took one and held it up in the light. "You really have to go to a laboratory to find out something like that. But by just looking at the shape, size, and color—" He paused, went to a shelf in the back, and muttered, "Yep, just as I thought." He returned into view. "I don't know the strength, but these are Viagra."

"Viagra!" I could hardly believe it. At first I laughed. The fucker was taking Viagra. Even with them, the sex was crappy. Buying my first cup of coffee of the day at the Koreans', I headed north to Tompkins Square, where I lit a cigarette, swilled down my coffee, and watched the dogs run. It was only about five-thirty, but the day looked combed-over and double-chinned, prematurely old. I had an hour and a half to kill before meeting my fellow mourners.

"Hey," I heard. Looking up with a start, I half expected to see the demon dad standing over me. It was Howard.

"How you doing?" I asked and stubbed my ciggy.

"You look philosophically preoccupied."

"I'm scattering Primo's ashes at seven."

"Good." He leaned forward. "Is that the only problem?"

"Hell, if my problems were beads, I would have the longest necklace in the neighborhood," I quipped, but it was now only one problem, and I felt too ashamed to talk about my undead father. I hated the fact that this man, my utterly despicable co-creator, had spread through my life like a cancer. Tattoo Man stood alongside me, silently sensing that I was in a pensive mood. I lit another cigarette and tried not to think that one out of every seven Americans will come down with cancer.

"If you need money, I can loan you some," Howard offered, kind as usual.

"I'm just worried about work in general." He sat down next to me on the bench and endured my anxious smoky belches. I felt like crying. I kept trying to imagine what it must have been like for my mother nearly thirty years ago. It made my problems seem so minuscule. The idea of my mother going out clubbing at night, swinging from temp job to temp job, and boyfriend to boyfriend was unthinkable. The societal notion of happiness that she bought into as a young woman was so convoluted—a husband and child before thirty—that she unwittingly ended up sacrificing true happiness in the process. The difficulty of raising me with a cheating, lying, abandoning deadbeat of a husband was unthinkable.

Here I was living in the hedonistic East Village and I wasn't happy either. I didn't even have a kid to show for my frustrations. A green, shit-eating fly landed on my arm, compelling me to jump forward.

"Sorry," Tattoo Man said, he was stroking my back.

"It's okay," I replied.

"You know, this isn't easy for me to say," he began. "I've been hoping to tell you that I like you." His voice took on an achy, itchy tone.

"You were, huh?" I lit up another smoke and remembered that I also needed a new roommate.

"I really like you." He caught himself. "And I know this sounds odd, but I really want to get to know you better."

I sucked hard on my cigarette and tried to repress a yelp. An unwanted "get to know you better" still lost out to a flush of hatred for an undesirable father.

"Have you ever cheated on a girlfriend?" I asked him boldly.
"Never."

"Have you ever freeloaded off one?"

"Absolutely not. In fact, just the opposite," he added.

"Have you ever taken Viagra?"

"Not knowingly." He laughed.

"Have you ever hit a girlfriend, or dumped her with a love child, or lied about your age, or pretended to be someone else, or . . . or dumped your dog on her?"

"No, to all the above," he said.

I actually didn't mind about the dog—that had turned out to be the only nice thing. Perhaps sensing that pain was festering just under my epiderm, he gave me a sympathetic little smile and put his hand gently on mine.

"I have no job, no skill, no money, nothing to offer. You can do a lot better, even with all those ridiculous self-hating tattoos."

"I don't think so," he replied after a chuckle. "You're witty and intelligent, you're kind in a cruel way and beautiful, and any man who is with you would be very, very lucky."

"What exactly do you want?" I asked him with narrowed eyes.

"Well," he replied and let loose a nervous sigh. "For starters." He leaned forward, opening his mouth as though I were going to pull his molar. I opened mine a crack, which was enough for him to slip his tongue in. I let him kiss me.

As we kissed, his hands collaterally moved up along the large of my back, around my shoulders, and to the sides of my breasts.

"Want to go to my place?" he asked simply.

I just felt empty. I wanted to withdraw from life, move to Montana, and take on a new identity. But that wasn't an option. I wasn't tired, but I couldn't stay awake.

"I live right over there." He pointed just north of the park.

I never agreed. I just didn't have the energy to resist. He collected me, leashed both our dogs, and walked me out of the park. We headed up to Tenth Street between A and B. It was a lopsided old brownstone with a long, polished, tonguelike banister that took us up several flights. Each floor had two apartments. He must have moved here in the early eighties, because that was the last time you could get a half-floor apartment adjacent to the park without paying a small fortune. He opened a door on the third floor. I barely had time to survey the place. He switched on the light. It seemed to make me move in slow motion and accelerate him. He unbuttoned my blouse, unhooked my bra, and began sucking my nipples.

Although I was attracted to him, I felt emotionally and physically anesthetized. But I desperately wanted to feel more as he unclasped my belt, unbuttoned the jeans, and slipped his hand into my torn panties.

In another second he was naked, and we were two forms on his mattress. He put a rubber on, slipping himself inside of me slowly at first, then moving quickly. Humping, banging, bumping away. Not looking at my face, not kissing me, hiding his face in my neck. Finally he jerked forward, wresting some kind of demon out and expelling it deep inside of me.

He rolled over moist and zonked, trying to catch his breath. At last I had an opportunity to check out the room. It was a civilized East Village apartment; white walls, high ceilings, rough wood floors. Three large windows revealed a wonderful view of the park. The overcast sky was smooth, the color of skim milk. In a metal frame above his desk he had a large photograph of the well-known misogynist Friedrich Nietzsche. Upon another wall was that tired *New Yorker* poster that shows New York City next to the rest of the culturally dwarfed country. Although it was meant as a joke, it wasn't. Everyone who lives here thinks the city is such hot shit. New York just sucks you in with all its coolness. But the Empire City has no clothes. It was buzz, spin, and hype without any substance.

"Want something to drink?" he asked, helping himself to a glass of water. I said no. "How about a shower?"

That sounded good, but when I rose, I saw his VCR—it was 7:23.

"Oh, shit!" I exclaimed. "Primo's ash toss! I'm supposed to meet everyone at seven at the Horseshoe."

Both of us frantically pulled on our clothing. As I was leashing Numb to bring him along, Howard suggested, "Leave the dog here. It will be easier."

Numb and Fedora were happily licking each other's privates, so I accepted his offer. I grabbed Primo's ashes, and together we dashed out and down Avenue B, along the park over to the Horseshoe. Looking pale, Zoë was sitting alone in the dark.

"Where were you?" she yelled as soon as she saw me.

"It was my fault," deflected Howard kindly. Then he went over to order drinks at the bar.

"That *Hell*-ga person just left," Zoë said, staring nervously at Howard, who was talking to the bartender. "Oh, God, you guys weren't having sex, were you?"

"None of your goddamned business," I said, trying to fix my hair and check all my hastily buttoned buttons.

Zoë looked at me with a disgusted nod of the head and smirk that seemed to say, You can do a whole lot better.

"Is anyone else supposed to arrive?" Howard asked, putting three full beer mugs down before us.

"Yeah, Lydia probably," I replied.

"To Primo," Howard toasted, raising his mug. Both Zoë and I raised and clicked our glasses meekly. I gulped mine down, thirsty from the recent activity. Zoë and Howard barely touched theirs. Realizing that it was the first time the two had seen each other since the mugging, I said to Howard, "Someone would like to apologize to you."

"Unless Lydia confirmed it," Zoë said, ignoring my remark, "I don't think she's coming."

"Don't you want to say something?" I asked her.

"I have nothing to apologize for," she replied blandly.

"It's okay," Howard said. Zoë looked away with an obvious disdain.

"What is your problem?" I asked her.

"Nothing," she groaned. She sipped from her glass. I waited patiently for an answer.

"I'm sorry if I just don't take a shine to all your friends, Mary," she said obnoxiously. I began to think that this was her revenge for my animosity toward Jeff.

"No," Howard replied looking into dead space. "That's not it."

"Why don't you just shut the fuck up?" she lashed out. "You're not even supposed to be here. You weren't Primo's friend."

"What are you talking about?" I asked her.

"That's it! I've had it with you," he yelled back at her, uncharacteristically. "I've tried to be nice to you, but you're just too terrified, aren't you? Well, I didn't do anything. It's not my fault, so get over it!"

"Get over what?" I asked. Neither of them responded.

"What are you terrified of?" I asked Zoë. She started crying, jumped to her feet, and ran out the door.

"What the hell?" I asked Howard, utterly confused.

"Mary," he began, "I used to go to the dogrun every day, and I'd see Primo, and I didn't want to be the one to tell you this, but he'd be with different women."

"You mean cheating on me—I know," I clarified.

"Yeah, well, that was when I first met your friend. I thought her name was Josie."

I gasped. Zoë had slept with Primo! True to his record, behind my back, he had screwed my best friend.

"Oh, shit." I rose. Howard got up as well.

"I didn't want to tell you, but she was obviously taking out her guilt on me, and—"

"I need to be alone," I said softly. He followed me out the door.

"I FUCKING NEED TO BE ALONE!" I screamed, freezing him in his tracks. I dashed into the park.

I collapsed on a bench adjacent to the dogrun, lay down on the long wooden slats, and looked up at the darkening sky through the swaying branches. Several lost and homeless locals were fluttering about. I held the bag of Primo in my hand. It made complete sense. Primo was a girlfriend fucker from way back. Zoë was a sexually insecure maniac. She was only what a man made of her. I could effortlessly imagine the two of them together, a psychological yin and yang.

"God, isn't the moon beautiful?" said a dry male voice. I assumed it was Howard, so I just kept staring at the sky.

Between cracks and fissures in the clouds, I saw the half-moon. It resembled a sideways guillotine blade, just waiting to fall. I felt tears tickle their way down my cheeks.

"Every night it gets a new chance to come up just right. And every morning, no matter how imperfect it is, it's just washed away." This charmer was no Howard. He was smooth and talented, but not talented enough.

"When you're young, you have all these chances, and with time you blow them, one after the other."

Thirty was a matter of months away—an obelisk to opportunities blown.

"Finally life becomes a very specific thing—and that's what we are. Ultimately, looking back, I'm beginning to believe that we need to always be fucked up. We need to always have some reason to hate ourselves, something to make us feel eternally incomplete."

"Why? How come?" I asked, with a very personal despair. I still didn't look at him.

"Because that's what it all comes down to. A struggle for forgiveness in an unforgiving world."

I didn't buy this, but didn't feel the energy to dispute him. I figured he must have called my machine and heard I was going to be here.

"When your mother and I met, it all happened so quick. We were in love—simple as that. I would bring her gifts every time we got together: flowers, earrings, chocolate—ask her. I wasn't making any real money, I wasn't doing what I do now. I did nickel-and-dime jobs. I drove a bread truck, but I did love her. I'd give her anything I could. She kept saying she wanted a kid, so I gave her one, but I wasn't ready. I don't know if anyone is ever ready. I never wanted to be a bad person. I really loved her."

"She didn't say much about you. She said you slept around, stole from her, dumped her, moved out West, and then she heard you died."

"I did a long stretch in jail, and when I got out, as payment for keeping my mouth shut, I got set up in a comfortable position." He paused. "I never stole from your mother. I borrowed on a Tuesday and intended to give back on a Thursday. There just wasn't enough money."

"Give me a break." I sat up.

"When I lost your mother, I lost the great love in my life. But you were my little girl."

"So why didn't you come and visit?"

"I was young. I thought I had forever. But after prison, years gone by, I found a new sweetheart and got married. More years went by. Another divorce. Several layers formed over that old life."

Every word that came out of his mouth was horseshit, and yet I also knew he was my father. I began crying. As I rose and took a couple steps away, he grabbed me.

"Let go!" I yelled, pushing him hard.

"You're my daughter, please!" he begged, still clinging to me, grabbing my shirt.

I swung the heavy bag at him, hitting him on his perfectly coiffed crown. He didn't let me go or stop me. On his knees he held my pants by the belt. I whacked him again with everything I had, and then did it again. He dropped flat to the ground and didn't move.

I stood perfectly still.

"Lady, you bes' get outta here, you gonna get in big trouble!" some Latin man said, awaking me.

I tried to stop the bleeding until a female cop came puttering up on a motor scooter. She saw all the blood splattered on me and Joey moaning on the ground. She quickly took his pulse, called something in on her radio, and asked me what had happened.

"I hit him." I pointed to the box holding the jarred ashes of Primo.

The cop told me to turn around and grab the gate. She patted me down for weapons and handcuffed my wrists together. A crowd slowly formed, drawn by the revolving red light on top of her motorized tricycle. Soon sirens grew in the distance, and an EMS ambulance arrived, as well as another cop car. With a second cop as witness, she asked me again what had happened.

"He was stalking me," I said, which was half true.

"Did he attack you?"

"Yes," I replied.

"What the hell is this?" she asked, looking at the torn bag containing the boxed remains of Primo.

"My ex-boyfriend, I was about to scatter him."

"How did he die?" the other cop asked, holding up the small dented cardboard box. I told her I didn't know, but I didn't kill him.

Joey—or Rudy, as was my father's name—had a fractured skull when they loaded him into the back of the ambulance and drove off. I was taken to the Ninth Precinct and, over the course of the hour, fingerprinted, photographed, and questioned by two different detectives. I told both of them that I thought he was about to attack me.

"What was your relationship to the victim?" asked a fresh, new cop.

"He is my father, but I hadn't seen him in over twenty years."

I was placed in a small detention cell with another woman who was arrested for dealing on Ninth Street. After a couple of hours, around three in the morning, we were handcuffed together and transported downtown.

I called my mother from jail and gave her the good news: Rudy, her ex-husband of decades gone by, had impostored himself back into my life under the guise of poor, dead Joey Lucas. Upon discovering this, I had clobbered him with Primo's remains. It turned out Primo was good for something. The district attorney was filing charges against me for assault. Trial, jail, the whole ordeal was on the horizon.

"Wow," she replied softly, employing her signature minimalist style. Now she had something new to make me feel crappy about.

I was taken down to Center Street, where I was given a trial date and desk ticket. Then I had my keys and cash—five dollars—returned to me and was released on my own recognizance.

The first thing I did when I got back to the neighborhood was return to Howard's house. When I rang the doorbell, he rang me up.

"Are you okay?" he asked. "I've been calling you all night."

"Yeah, I just needed to be alone."

"Want to go for breakfast, talk about things?"

"Not really," I said, slightly pissed that he was so forthcoming when I didn't need him to be, and not there when I did. Once Numb and I got home, I fast-forwarded through messages from Howard apologizing for telling me about Zoë, and then asking me when I was going to pick up my dog.

After the crappy night of incarceration, I lay in bed and stared at the ceiling. At noon, I flipped on the TV to watch the news. To my horror, some pushy female reporter had discovered the catchy detail of Primo's ashes being used as a weapon. She tracked down Primo's slightly senile mother, June. I watched as June was asked what she thought about her son's ashes being used for an assault.

"What are you talking about?" she inquired, slouching tiredly in her wheelchair, parked in the doorway of her Flatbush home.

"Your son's ashes were used to bludgeon a man."

"Oh, well, that'll happen," she replied, almost bored.

"Does this anger you?" the reporter pressed, slightly miffed by her philosophical attitude.

"The Malio Funeral Home gave me the wrong ashes, and I gave them Lucretia," she recounted with partial accuracy.

"Do you know why the ashes were used as a murder weapon?"

"Oh, my God, no!" she exclaimed, understanding the message for the first time.

"Do you know Mary Bellanova?"

"I never heard of her in all my wildest days."

By five o'clock other stations were broadcasting the item. One came up with a sidebar story: "It was learned that Mary Bellanova, the East Village resident who attacked her father with her boyfriend's cremated ashes, had first perpetrated a vicious practical joke. When a funeral director accidentally gave her the wrong remains, a Syosset widow asked for her husband's ashes back. What she got was quite different."

The camera focused on the offended party: "That girl gave my son a jar of doggie doo and claimed it was my Edgar."

I immediately called Long Island information and found the insulted widow's number, then I called her at home.

"This is Mary Bellanova," I began. "I'd like to apologize for what I did."

"You have some nerve, young lady!"

"I just want you to know it wasn't a practical joke."

"Oh, really?"

"I spread your husband's ashes at the dogrun in Tompkins Square Park, believing they were my boyfriend's remains. That's what I returned to you, soil from the dogrun."

"Why in God's name didn't you just tell me that?"

"I wanted to tell you, but Primo's mother told me to go back and get the ashes. She was afraid you wouldn't return his ashes unless you got your husband's remains."

"How infantile," she remarked.

"I agree, but that's the whole story, and I just wanted you to know. I'm sorry it happened, but I felt like it was my fault and just did what I was told."

I could hear the Syosset widow sigh sadly, then say, "Edgar always wanted to be cast over a wide-open space."

"Well, I don't want to sound cavalier, but one could do a lot worse," I said sincerely and explained that Tompkins Square was the biggest dogrun in the city. I detailed that it was larger than the Madison Square and Washington Square runs. It was even bigger than the run behind the Natural History Museum and the one in Riverside Park.

"Edgar always liked dogs," she said.

"They're so much better than people," I replied. "They can't love you enough, and they forgive you no matter how badly you neglect them or treat them."

"I guess if I want to be with him, I'll just have to have my ashes scattered there," she concluded peacefully.

About an hour later, Zoë called and left a message. She quickly broke into tears, going on about how sorry she was about my arrest. She explained that I was her best friend in the whole world. She offered to take care of Numb in the event that I had to serve time. Although I didn't intend to, I picked up the phone and told her that Numb would be happier with Howard and Fedora.

"Is there anything at all I can do?" she pleaded, hungry for forgiveness. I told her I wanted to know *everything.* She told me how Primo smooth-talked her every time she called for me. How he said that he always wanted her more than me. One weekend while I was away at my mother's out on the Island, the two met at a club. They talked, danced, got drunk, went to my place, and screwed. She blubbered through tears whenever she got into the dirty parts.

"I thought you didn't find him attractive," I said, puzzled. "I mean, you had your opportunity."

"What can I say?" she gasped through tears. "He showed me all this attention, and I couldn't get away from him. And . . . and I guess the fact that you went for him showed me that he had some worth."

"So it was just a one-time thing?" I asked hopefully.

No such luck—Zoë said they would meet two, three times a week, usually at her place, sometimes in my apartment. It went on for months. They must have had great sex, because she wept painfully.

"Mary, there's something else, and this is the most difficult of all." She paused. I couldn't even imagine. "I was with him when he died."

"What?"

"We were doing it when . . ." Her voice trailed.

"What!"

"I was the one who killed him," she burst out crying. "I tried everything to bring him back. I did CPR and mouth-to-mouth. And when I realized he was gone, I cleaned him up and left. I didn't want you to know what had happened."

I hung up the phone. Fuck her—I didn't want to know she even existed. I wasn't sure what power Primo had or what neurosis compelled Zoë to commit such an act of betrayal, but it was unforgivable.

So Primo had something in common with John Garfield, Errol Flynn, and Nelson Rockefeller: all allegedly died happily. Sometime later, I saw the death certificate. It was right there in black in white: "Evidence of Viagra abuse." In the East Village, that soiled and unkempt fountain of youth, there was no such thing as growing old gracefully.

In the course of the night, my phone machine gathered up a bouquet of messages from people I hadn't bumped into or spoken with in years. Howard called again upon hearing of my arrest. This time he was even more remorseful and contrite. He asked if there was *anything* he could do. I didn't pick up.

The last odd call that night was from Sue Wott.

"I saw in the news what happened to you, and I just want you to know I'm sorry," she said reluctantly.

Since I felt I had done her an injustice, I picked up. "Thanks for calling."

"Are you okay?" she asked.

"More or less," I replied and added, "I just learned that Primo cheated on me with my best friend."

"I could've told you that before I even met you," she remarked.

"There should be a name for it—best-friend-sexual or something. He must have been stimulated by betrayal, like the notion he was getting away with something. Like doing something behind his mommy's back."

"I don't think half the girls he slept with even knew he was with someone else," she said, which oddly lessened his guilt.

"I really didn't join your band because of Primo," I slipped in.

"Then why did you!" she barked back.

"You know, I confess that I went to the audition because I was curious, but I sure as hell didn't go to rehearsal after rehearsal and take all your crap for that cocksucker."

"So why did you?" she asked again, this time calmly.

"I guess because it gave me hope. It gave me a belief that I was doing something in this awful neighborhood that might lead to something bigger. I enjoyed the whole process."

"Well, it doesn't matter anymore," she finally said after a long pause.

"Why not?"

"I just got a seventy-two-hour notice of eviction taped to my door."

"The judge didn't decide in your favor?" I remembered that her case was coming up.

"No, I knew he wouldn't," she said. "It wouldn't bother me so much, but I hate to put the kid through this, and it means I lose the free alcoholic baby-sitter."

"What is she doing?"

"Jane's moving back in with her family in Fort Lee." Sue paused and added under her voice, "Forty-three years old, and moving back in with her family."

"You know, I have a spare room," I heard myself saying.

"You?" Even she couldn't believe I said it.

"Yeah, my roommate just moved out."

"Is that an offer?" Finding apartments in this city, even shares, was a minor miracle.

"I don't know," I replied. "I don't have a job right now. I can't even pay my half, and I guess I might be going to jail."

"Well," she said hopefully, "if you get off on probation, I can get you a job."

"What kind of job?"

"It pays well," she said without telling me. For a glinting instant I expected her to say stripping or at least phone sex. "It's designing websites."

"Wow," I replied, "but I don't know anything about it."

"I can teach you. It's not that hard if you have half a head, and you can work your own hours."

"Well, I don't want to get my hopes up, because I still might be going to jail."

"If you do go to jail," she said, "I'll hold your place until you get back." She giggled at this, and so did I. Then she added, "You know, I'm probably not the easiest person to get along with."

"That's okay, I am," I responded jokingly.

"What time do you get up in the morning?" she asked.

"Nine if I'm working, eleven if I'm not."

"I don't get up until noon," she replied. "We won't have any problems." She agreed to come over tomorrow and give the place a look. I spent the evening trying to battle anxiety by watching television, but it was so dumb that I had to turn the volume off. I was amused by how many shows made brief use of New York exteriors only to have their real action filmed on Los Angeles soundstages. My tired eyes couldn't endure the radiation emanating from the screen, so I began turning down the brightness. Only cop shows actually made an effort to shoot entire scenes on the streets of New York. But this made me feel like a hypocrite because I hated being detoured due to film shoots. I wanted them to shoot in New York City, but without bothering me.

By one in the morning, I turned the TV almost black. The cumulative depression of the entire day manifested itself into a free fall. As though my phone understood me, it rang. For the first time in eons, I picked it up without screening.

"Mary, are you okay?" It was Howard.

"This hasn't been my very best day."

"You remember what I said?"

"Remind me," I responded, not disguising my impatience.

"I wish I were with you," he submitted and backed into silence.

"Well, why aren't you here, then?" I asked. Ten minutes later he was. We didn't really do anything but hug and kiss, yet he was good at it. Eventually we fell asleep.

Howard and I went for breakfast, and then he started his

long walk uptown to fetch a fresh batch of manuscripts that needed copyediting.

"Gardening books," he shivered.

A half hour later, Sue Wott came over with her little boy and inspected the empty room.

"This is twice the size of the place we have now," she said cheerfully to the child as though it was their choice to move.

"This place stinks," he said candidly, as kids tend to, then he followed the dog into my room.

Turning to me, Sue said, "Now I just got to get people to help me move."

I didn't volunteer anymore, but she wasn't afraid to ask, "You couldn't help me, could you? I'm packing up all day, so I should be ready around five."

"I don't move well," I hinted politely. "Can't you ask Norma?"

"Oh, Norma will be there, but Marilyn is out of town." She lowered her voice so the kid couldn't hear her. "And they're going to put my stuff out on the sidewalk tomorrow morning." A pause elapsed. The child returned with the dog.

"Sure," I said, but I had to ask a final question that was lodged in my head like an arrow. When her kid chased Numb back into my room, I asked, "After Primo left you with a kid, you said you didn't blame him. Why not?"

"Because that was all my idea. Hell, he said up front he didn't want one, couldn't support or handle one. Actually, he did do me one big favor. He had me sell his paintings under my name because he knew an art collector who would pay more for them, and he gave me half the money."

"Just half."

"Primo never gave all of anything. But he gave enough. The cash paid for the birthing expenses." She looked up and smiled. "All that was years after we broke up. Hell, we even made the kid after we broke up."

"You mean, you got pregnant by him after he cheated on you with all those people?"

"There are two reasons for that, which are really the same. He's the only guy I ever loved, and he's the only guy I ever slept with."

I stared at her in disbelief. What could I say? She thanked me for my help and told me she would see me at her place that evening. To make my job easier, I called Zoë at work. I figured I could convert some of her guilt into backbreaking labor. She agreed to meet us at Sue's place, Howard was unreachable, but the call-waiting beeped as the phone rang. It was Helga.

"I saw what happened in the news. I'm sorry I couldn't stick around." She had come and gone before the planned Primo-scattering.

"You couldn't help me, could you?" I asked.

"Need an alibi?"

"No, actually, a van."

"A van?"

"Yeah, at five o'clock tonight."

"What in the world for?"

"Sue Wott," I said. "She's being evicted."

"Good, I hope the bitch suffers."

"She has, but you shouldn't blame her for Primo being an asshole. She was cheated on just like you and me and everyone else, and she's got a kid who doesn't deserve it."

"Look, there are two types of people, those who can forgive and those who can't. I wish I could forgive, but it's just not in me," she said.

"How can you forgive Primo and not her?"

"Because Primo was just being Primo."

"And she was just being herself."

Unable to argue further, Helga wished me a good life.

It turned out that the girl named Pearl with the van was moving Sue tonight.

Soon Ma called to say that we had a two-o'clock meeting with a good, yet economical trial attorney—in the past year his record had been six and two. I tried to keep busy to fend off the anxiety, but it didn't do much good.

By one, I had started getting ready to leave when I got a phone call from the detective handling my case. In a tightly wound statement he said, "Thank you for your help in the recent investigation. We're sorry if we caused you any discomfort. No charges will be filed against you in this case."

"Why not?" I asked, slightly suspicious, before breaking into utter relief.

"Do you prefer if they were?" he asked, perhaps joking.

"No, fine. Thanks. Bye." I hung up.

I called Ma and gave her the good news.

"You're kidding," she said. She had just finished dressing and was about to drive to the LIRR station.

"I just got the call," I responded.

"But I called all those lawyers and made arrangements for a loan and everything." She went quiet, and then I heard a sound that I don't remember ever hearing; I heard my mother crying.

"Mom, it's okay," I said softly.

"I know," she replied. "I just . . . the whole thing. I was so worried about you. I mean, I would've given anything to get you out of this, and . . ."

"I know."

"And your father was such a fucker, and for him to return to our lives like this—" Tears started coming to my eyes, and the more I tried to restrain myself, the more they fell.

"Thanks for all the help," I sputtered. "You know how I feel about you, Ma."

"It damned well better be love," she blasted.

"Or you'll come right over and beat the crap out of me."

We both laughed, and I promised I'd come home over that weekend to get into one of our good old-fashioned fights.

It was a warm and sunny afternoon, and I felt this immense sense of gratitude just being able to sit in the park with the dog and a cup of coffee. Even though thirty was on the horizon, the idea of not having to spend time in jail made me feel like I could relive my twenties all over again.

By the time I finally brought Numb back home, there was a message on my machine. It was from the man formerly known as Joey: "Mary, they asked me to sign a complaint against you. Of course I couldn't. I told them I attacked you and you defended yourself. I knew they wouldn't press charges against me 'cause I'm the one that just came out of the hospital with bandages around my skull. Look, the reason I didn't tell you who I was is 'cause I didn't think things would turn out the way they did. I didn't even expect you to respond to my e-mail, let alone turn out to be you. Then, after meeting you, the reason I kept calling you was because I fell for you. I loved knowing you. . . . I love you. But I guess if love means anything, it means respecting the wishes of the other person, even if that means leaving them alone. I grew up in a world where a guy got to keep anything he could get away with. It takes some of us longer to grow a conscience than others. Anyway, this is to let you know that losing you, losing a family, is the biggest fuck-up in my life, and if you ever need anything, money or support or advice—you got it. You have a father who doesn't just love you, but is tremendously proud of you. See, I never thought I could make something better than me—but you're it."

I couldn't have typical parents like everyone else.

By the time I recomposed myself, I knew that eventually, after a few weeks tops, I'd have to call the son of a bitch. I'd have to curse him out and then reconcile, because that's all life is, a series of battles and treaties.

It was a quarter after five by the time I arrived at Sue Wott's.

"I guess I can't yell at you," she said, as I huffed and puffed up to her apartment, "but in the future, if you come this late for practice, you're not going to be as lucky." That was her nasty way of inviting me back in the band.

Zoë, Norma, Sue, and myself all carried her crap down the stairs and packed it into the back of the van. As we took turns going up and down the stairs, carrying bigger items together, I thought to myself that all together, we could've made one hell of a *Jerry Springer* episode. Primo was a stage in our lives that we had all passed through, specifically when we were feeling our worst or just too young to know better.

Sue's roommate sat on her sofa, sipping from a bottle of chardonnay and quietly watched as we moved Sue out. Even though she was being evicted tomorrow, the inebriated cohabitant didn't pack a stitch, as though intent on sinking with her repossessed ship. She was ripe for a Primo type.

The four of us worked well together, bringing everything down into the van, then shuttling it over and carrying it up into my apartment—all done in under three hours. Afterward we went out for sushi nearby. That evening, Sue was a genuine pleasure to be with. Each of us, for different reasons, felt a general sense of relief. Zoë was witty, and Norma was wide awake. We had a great time and spent hours sitting, chatting, drinking, and laughing.

Amazingly, Primo's name never even came up.

East Village cats and dogs (like Numb) are up for adoption at:

Social Tees
125 East 4th Street
New York, New York
212-614-9653
(ask for Robert)

Like this is the only one...

More from the young, the hip,
and the up-and-coming.
Brought to you by MTV Books.

POCKET
BOOKS

As many as 1 in 3 Americans
have HIV and don't know it.

TAKE CONTROL.
KNOW YOUR STATUS.
GET TESTED.

To learn more about HIV testing,
or get a free guide to HIV and
other sexually transmitted diseases.

www.knowhivaids.org
1-866-344-KNOW

The Alphabetical Hookup List

A new series

A–J
K–Q
R–Z

Three sizzling titles
Available from
PHOEBE McPHEE
and MTV Books

www.mtv.com

www.alloy.com